MURDER MAKES MISTAKES

ALSO BY GEORGE BELLAIRS

Littlejohn on Leave
The Four Unfaithful Servants
Death of a Busybody
The Dead Shall be Raised
Death Stops the Frolic
The Murder of a Quack
He'd Rather be Dead
Calamity at Harwood
Death in the Night Watches
The Crime at Halfpenny Bridge
The Case of the Scared Rabbits
Death on the Last Train
The Case of the Seven Whistlers
The Case of the Famished Parson
Outrage on Gallows Hill
The Case of the Demented Spiv
Death Brings in the New Year
Dead March for Penelope Blow
Death in Dark Glasses
Crime in Lepers' Hollow
A Knife for Harry Dodd
Half-Mast for the Deemster
The Cursing Stones Murder
Death in Room Five
Death Treads Softly
Death Drops the Pilot
Death in High Provence
Death Sends for the Doctor
Corpse at the Carnival
Murder Makes Mistakes
Bones in the Wilderness
Toll the Bell for Murder
Corpses in Enderby
Death in the Fearful Night
Death in Despair
Death of a Tin God
The Body in the Dumb River
Death Before Breakfast
The Tormentors
Death in the Wasteland
Surfeit of Suspects
Death of a Shadow
Death Spins the Wheel
Intruder in the Dark
Strangers Among the Dead
Death in Desolation
Single Ticket to Death
Fatal Alibi
Murder Gone Mad
Tycoon's Deathbed
The Night They Killed Joss Varran
Pomeroy, Deceased
Murder Adrift
Devious Murder
Fear Round About
Close All Roads to Sospel
The Downhill Ride of Leeman
Popple An Old Man Dies

MURDER MAKES MISTAKES

AN INSPECTOR LITTLEJOHN MYSTERY

GEORGE BELLAIRS

OPEN ROAD
INTEGRATED MEDIA
NEW YORK

All rights reserved, including without limitation the right to reproduce this book or any portion thereof in any form or by any means, whether electronic or mechanical, now known or hereinafter invented, without the express written permission of the publisher.

This is a work of fiction. Names, characters, places, events, and incidents either are the product of the author's imagination or are used fictitiously. Any resemblance to actual persons, living or dead, businesses, companies, events, or locales is entirely coincidental.

Copyright © 1958 by George Bellairs

ISBN: 978-1-5040-9254-8

This edition published in 2024 by Open Road Integrated Media, Inc.
180 Maiden Lane
New York, NY 10038
www.openroadmedia.com

MURDER MAKES MISTAKES

1
THE DEATH OF UNCLE RICHARD

Last week-end she stewed some rhubarb and I'm sure she put the tops in as well. They're poisonous, you know. She didn't eat any herself. I was very ill after it..."

Littlejohn politely scribbled a few words on a sheet of paper and looked up at the woman sitting on the other side of his desk. Someone from quite another world; a world of half a century ago. An old brown fur coat, a black hat decorated with battered roses, an imitation crocodile-skin handbag, an umbrella... and black boots.

A little, oval-faced, elderly woman, with bright, busy eyes which reminded you of a mouse. His colleagues called her Littlejohn's favourite client. She came regularly to tell him that her step-sister, with whom she lived, was trying to poison her to get her money.

"If I were you, I would think of setting-up house on my own. You'll have a bit of peace then, Miss Hankey."

The woman cackled.

"I can't afford. I've nearly gone through my little bit of money. Agnes is going to have a shock if she succeeds in making away with me."

Miss Hankey had called four times before at quarterly intervals, asked for Littlejohn, and told him the same tale. He wondered how long it would be before they quietly removed her to a home for the persecuted and he never saw her again. It often happened that way. Scotland Yard had a regular clientele of them. Poor souls who were either going to be murdered or who fancied they were murderers themselves.

It was April. What they call a 'soft' day in Ireland, and the breeze blowing through the open window was gentle and warm. The noise of traffic and the hooting of river craft wafted in. Holiday-makers and trippers had already begun to appear on the Embankment, the trees of which were three weeks ahead of their seasonal schedule. The invasion for the week-end's soccer cup-tie at Wembley had started and men in mufflers and rosettes of the contending colours were plainly to be seen among the passers-by on the pavements below.

"Would it be possible for you to call at our house one day? Not officially, of course. I could say you were a distant relative from overseas..."

Telephone.

"Please excuse me."

Littlejohn tried to keep the relief from his voice.

"Mrs. Cromwell to speak to you, sir."

Cromwell was away on a few days' leave. His Uncle Richard, who lived somewhere in Cheshire, had died and the sergeant was one of his executors.

"Hello!"

"Is that Superintendent Littlejohn?"

"Yes. Who's speaking?"

"Dorothy Cromwell..."

He didn't recognize her voice. Usually gay and carefree, in spite of the responsibilities of a husband, three little girls, and a flat in Shepherd Market, she now sounded utterly crushed and lifeless.

"I'm so glad you're in. It's my husband..."
She seemed as though she didn't know where to begin.
"What is it, Dorothy?"
"He's been shot."

Life seemed to stand still for a moment, like a cinema film breaking down. Miss Hankey, sitting opposite and trying to make out what was being said, the sunny morning, the familiar things in the room, the noises of the streets below. Everything seemed to vanish, except the great twist of fear, like a cold hand gripping him inside.

"...The Cheshire County police have just phoned. It seems it happened last night and they've only just found out who he is. He's dangerously ill in hospital. I... I..."

"I'll come right over. I'll be there in ten minutes. Keep your chin up, Dorothy."

He was only half aware of disposing of Miss Hankey to a subordinate and of ordering an official car. Mrs. Cromwell met him at the door. She gave him an imploring look, as though begging him to do something, and then burst into tears.

Inside the flat, all was neat and tidy. A suit-case packed, a hat on the table, and a coat hanging ready across the arm of a chair.

"What happened, Dorothy?"

She dried her eyes and straightened her rich auburn hair in an instinctive gesture.

"Uncle Richard lived at Rushton Inferior and it seems somebody shot Bob in the dark last night in the street. He must have lain there a long time."

She could hardly control her voice and sobbed at the thought what had happened.

"He must have taken a walk after supper and he'd changed into his old sports coat and left all his papers in his other jacket. When he was found they rushed him off to the infirmary and he was only identified when Uncle Richard's widow missed him this morning. The bullet hit him in the head and they later moved him to Manchester Royal Infirmary for an operation."

"You've packed ready for off?"

"I'm getting the noon train from Euston."

"I'll come with you. I'll telephone the Yard and tell them, and ask my wife to pack and send a bag of things to the station."

It was like a dream. His wife, Letty, meeting him at Euston with the suit-case, the journey north, the strain and lack of news, the long silences between himself and Cromwell's wife, who had usually had so much to say to each other, the endless drab journey by taxi to the great hospital. The long corridors, the atmosphere of sickness, anxiety, isolation from the world.

"Neuro-surgical ward. I'll take you there."

A kindly little nurse with bright lipstick, and wavy blonde hair under a coy cap, led the way. More long corridors, open here and there to the fresh air and the refreshing patches of lawn visible. Nurses and sisters coming and going like worker bees. Students, their stethoscopes round their necks, trying to look like doctors, technicians, consultants, orderlies wheeling beds and trolleys. The hospital cats strolling about or sunning themselves... Finally, the department of brain surgery. The nurse halted in front of the operating theatre itself and went to find the sister.

Littlejohn writhed with impatience. The calm fortitude of Mrs. Cromwell made him feel a bit ashamed of his own feelings, but he couldn't help it. On and off, Cromwell and he had been close colleagues for fifteen years and he had taught the sergeant all he knew. He was more like a brother than a subordinate. And to be shot in the night, irresponsibly, by someone who could have borne him no grudge, and in cold blood...

"They think he'll be all right. The bullet missed the vital spots and the surgeon has removed it. He's been two hours in the theatre."

The sister hurried off again, leaving them standing helplessly waiting for more news. Someone led the way to a small room and brought them tea. It was still like living in a dream. Everyone was very kind. No silly sentiment; just practical sympathy and confidence.

A buxom elderly nurse took the dirty cups away on a tray.

"He'll be all right... The best brain surgeons in the country are looking after him."

She mentioned two great names with pride and intimated that the specialists in question could do just as they liked with her brain without causing her the least anxiety.

Littlejohn and Mrs. Cromwell exchanged brief words and phrases, hardly realizing they were speaking, their eyes and ears concentrated on the closed swing doors which divided them from the skilled, healing work of surgery. The sister reappeared, just to tell them it would soon be over.

"Smoke if you like. It's all right here."

Littlejohn took out his case and lit their cigarettes. It seemed futile, but it was something to do.

Then the sound of something important stirring, a trolley being wheeled away, the doors of the theatre flapping to. The two in the waiting-room stood still, holding their breath. Two surgeons arrived, clad in white, removing their rubber gloves. A tall elderly man with a kindly clever face and his companion, younger, heavier, with a homely efficient manner and a smile which gave you confidence as soon as you saw him.

The elder of the two did the talking.

"No reason why he shouldn't recover. It will take a long time. After all, brain injuries are that way. He'll need great care, but we'll look well after him."

He gently patted Mrs. Cromwell's arm.

"Be brave. It will be all right."

He turned to Littlejohn.

"Superintendent Littlejohn? I've heard of you."

They shook hands.

"This is a bad business. Nobody seems to know quite how it happened. But he's very lucky It was done with a small weapon, I'd say, judging from the bullet..."

He dropped a small wad of cotton-wool in Littlejohn's hand. It contained a piece of lead little larger than a fair-sized pill.

The younger surgeon turned over the bullet with his forefinger.

"The revolver must almost have been a toy. A pop-gun. I extracted more bullets than I can count during the war, but I've never seen one so small. Almost made for a lady's handbag..."

"I'd better take this with me, sir. I don't suppose my friend has spoken since this happened?"

"No. He was unconscious when they found him and, until the situation was relieved by operation, was likely to remain so."

"It will be some time before he's able to speak?"

"We shall have to see. A few days, at least. He's had a bad shock and in these cases one can't take risks. We'll let you know. He's in bed now. You can take a peep at him, if you wish."

Cromwell was asleep, his head swathed in a turban of bandages. He looked like a corpse, pale, drawn, hardly breathing. Littlejohn remembered when last he had seen him at the Yard, smiling and ruddy, talking about his Uncle Richard, who had married a girl more than thirty years his junior and had suffered from duodenal ulcers ever after. In fact, he'd died from them. And someone had shot Cromwell in cold blood, almost murdered him. It was bad enough when the victim was a stranger. Now, Littlejohn felt like finding the criminal and shooting him himself.

The younger surgeon was back, dressed in his outdoor clothes.

"I'd like just another word with you, Superintendent."

They went to the waiting-room again.

"I wanted to ask you if by any chance your colleague has suffered from coronary thrombosis, or anything such..."

Littlejohn almost laughed.

"Why, no. He was the healthiest man alive before this happened. He took great care of himself."

The Superintendent recollected Cromwell's many little fads about his health. Morning exercises, yoga, patent foods like *Strengtho*, little tablets and medicines which he carried about with him. In the past he'd teased him about it. Now, it didn't seem funny at all.

"Why do you ask, sir?"

"I don't know whether or not they've told you, but Mr. Cromwell was wearing an old sports coat when he was shot. It seems he'd left his ordinary jacket in his bedroom where he was staying. There was nothing in the pockets of his coat except a pipe, pouch and matches, and this..."

The surgeon produced a plain envelope and from it shook two small white tablets into the palm of his hand.

"In searching the coat for evidence of identity, the police found these and asked us if we knew what they were. Our pharmacist recognized them as tablets of dicoumarin. It's what's known as an anti-coagulant drug and is used in cases such as thrombosis where we thin the blood to destroy clots. In the hands of the unwary, it is very dangerous. Too much of it will cause extensive bleeding internally, or even through the skin... That's why I asked."

"I'm certain he never needed a drug of that kind."

"It rather made us anxious. You see, operation under such conditions may be very risky."

"I can't think how or why he got the tablets. I'll try to find out."

Outside the great doors of the Royal Infirmary the sun was shining, life was going on as usual, the flowers in the gardens opposite formed masses of glorious colour. Ambulances shuttled to and fro, doctors and nurses crossed the courtyard and mixed with the throngs of passers-by, students came and went to the nearby university, members of the committee of management emerged talking and laughing and made off on their ways.

Mrs. Cromwell was going to stay in a nearby hotel and, having made the necessary arrangements for the Cromwell children to be cared for by good neighbours, Mrs. Littlejohn was travelling by a later train and coming to keep her company. Littlejohn himself had work to do at Rushton Inferior. He had a bone to pick with someone unknown.

The village of Rushton Inferior was four miles from the nearest station, which, into the bargain, provided no taxis. As the next bus was an hour and a half away, Littlejohn managed to pick up a lift from a plumber, who complained all the way about how long the wealthy people of the neighbourhood took to pay his bills.

"A year's nothin'... Some of 'em take a couple of years to pay a quid or two. Scandalous... Enough to make a chap turn communist."

For some reason, Rushton Inferior was the metropolis of three small communities, and the parish church was there too. Rushton Inferior, plain Rushton, and then Rushton Superior. The plumber told Littlejohn that he'd find a pub and a temperance hotel at Inferior.

"Take my advice, you'll put-up at the temperance. The pub's too noisy. Wot with young bloods drivin' there in fast cars and revvin' 'em up, it's like bedlam at the *Brown Cow* till after midnight. The temperance used to be a pub, too, but the justices thought one was enough for the village. It was called the *Weatherby Arms;* now it's the *Weatherby Temperance.* You can get a drink with your meals, but they 'ave to bring it in, if you get wot I mean. Landlady's a nice woman. A cheerful widow. Mrs. Groves..."

The plumber dropped Littlejohn in the centre of the village and made off to his home in Superior. It was six in the evening and all was quiet. Dinner time. Already a string of cars was festooned in front of the *Brown Cow.*

Littlejohn looked around. The place was trim and neat and seemed to revolve round its old-fashioned church. A large graveyard, a tall square tower, a lych-gate, and the vicarage and tithe-barn behind. Great yew-trees hung over the church wall across the gravel sidewalk. Opposite the lych-gate, a large house, standing back in a garden full of daffodils and wallflowers. Then a string of small shops, with tasteful windows, apparently constructed from a converted row of cottages. Wool, Fruit, Butcher, Grocer, a café, which sold bread and cakes, and then the *Brown Cow*. On the same side as the church, and to the left of it, the post-office and newsagent's, a shop selling antiques and bric-à-brac ancient and modern. To the right of the church, a chemist's, another café, and then the *Weatherby Temperance Hotel*, bearing a gilded sign to that effect and sporting the motoring clubs' accolades. A tall, square, trim Georgian place, with a small lawn in front and a car-park behind. At an angle across the road from it, another red brick Regency house, apparently converted into flats, for the door was peppered with letter-slits, each bearing a small brass plate above it.

Mrs. Groves tallied with the plumber's description and she blushed slightly when Littlejohn mentioned by whom she had been recommended. Whether she was one of the "bad payers" or whether she fancied the plumber as a possible successor to the late Groves, the Superintendent never knew. He was received like a brother and when he signed the register there was an even greater commotion. The affair at Rushton Inferior last night had reached the evening papers, Cromwell's identity had been given, and it was stated that Littlejohn, of Scotland Yard, was on the case.

"You can have the best room, sir," said Mrs. Groves, and led him to a huge bedchamber facing the road, on the first floor. It contained a four-poster bed which looked like a galleon in full sail.

The whole place was free and easy. Judging from the knots of people standing about drinking sherry and gin, in spite of the sign over the door, there were about a score of inmates, a dozen of whom seemed regulars. They wandered in and out of the kitchens behind, asking the cook what was 'on' for dinner and passing remarks about it and giving advice.

The whole place had been rejuvenated by fancy Regency wallpapers and in some of the rooms each wall bore a different pattern. Candlewick bedspreads, arty curtains, floors covered in springy rubber-backed carpets, the blues, pinks and yellows of which were already fading from the sun.

The mood of the whole place seemed to emanate from Mrs. Groves, who was almost infantile in her jollity. Large, fat, and with a clear pink complexion and blue eyes, she reminded you of a big china doll, except that her white hair had been a bit overdone with blue rinse.

"We've heard all about you, Superintendent. How is your sergeant, poor man?"

"The doctors hope he will recover, although it is going to be a long job."

"We're so relieved."

She always spoke collectively for everybody there, as though the place were somehow run on co-operative lines. She might have been fifty, or a little more, judging from appearances, but she was one of those ageless types who enjoy a long maturity and then suffer a tragic rapid decay at the end of it.

Littlejohn was a bit doubtful about the plumber's advice. The place lacked the impersonal atmosphere of the traditional licensed hotel. Here, inspired by Mrs. Groves, they were one big happy family. Littlejohn had too much work to do and didn't want a perpetual Christmas party... however... One could only try it. In fact, one of the lodgers might easily be the one who shot Cromwell!

He ate his dinner undisturbed and it was an excellent one. Looking around him from the table-for-one at which he was sitting, the Superintendent could make out those who had merely called for a meal and those who were living-in. Some sat at table with a lack of familiarity and examined the menu as though they'd never seen such a thing before. Others were on easy terms with the two waitresses and behaved as though they owned the place. Half-way through the meal a young couple with two children arrived, somewhat dishevelled from the day's outing they had been taking, and, judging from the faces of the boarders when the children raised shrill cries for food, the little family were lodgers as well.

Mrs. Groves tripped about here and there, greeting people as though each was the one person in all the world she was most glad to see there. She introduced Littlejohn to a tall dark young man in heavy spectacles and with a slight stammer, who sat on the next table. A man called Valentine, an engineer in charge of a new gasometer in course of construction in a town four miles away. Then she sat down and ate a meal large enough for three.

After dinner, Littlejohn quietly left and took a walk down the main road. More cars than ever in front of the cafés and the village pub. It was quiet enough out of doors and the air was full of the scent of wallflowers. Cherry and almond trees, heavily laden with blossom, hung over the garden walls and fences. An old countryman was mowing the grass verge in front of a substantial-looking villa in a neat garden almost opposite the *Weatherby*.

"Could you tell me, please, where I can find the police-station?"

The old man removed his pipe.

"You another of 'em?"

"Another of whom?"

"Place 'as bin crawlin' with police an' newspaper men all day. Chap was shot 'ere last night. County police 'ave been all over the village the whole day, interviewin', measurin'-up, terrifyin' every-body. There an't been doin' any good with Ted Bloor. Got a bit above hisself, 'as Ted. You'd think 'e was the on'y policeman left in the world, the high-an'-mighty ways he's taken on."

"Is Bloor the constable?"

"Aye. Police-house is jest along the road there. As a rule, you'll find 'im about, eyein' the cars to see if they're proper lit-up or else if anybody's tryin' to drive 'em drunk. But with shootin' on 'is 'ands, cars is too small fry for Ted at present. 'E'll come back to 'em, be sure o' that, when all the fuss is over."

Littlejohn thanked him and left him, much to the old man's regret, for he preferred earning three bob an hour gossiping, instead of shoving a mower here, there and everywhere.

Ted Bloor was sitting alone in the police-house writing laboriously on sheets of foolscap when Littlejohn disturbed him. He'd sent his wife to the pictures at Wiston Purlieu in spite of the fact that she'd seen the film the summer before at the seaside. "I want to be on my own, mother. I want to concentrate on my report," he'd told her when her sister had turned-up to quiz him about the *big* case on which he was engaged.

Bloor was a middle-aged countryman with a heavy red face, bushy eyebrows, a small sandy moustache, and wondering blue eyes, which wondered more than ever when the Superintendent arrived. When he'd opened the door—a difficult feat because the police-house was new and all the wood unseasoned and swelling in its sockets—he'd almost fallen flat to discover who was calling on him.

"Come in, sir. Have you been to Chester?"

"Not yet, Bloor. I'm not on the case officially. I came north to see my colleague, Cromwell."

"'Ow is he? I'm sorry this has 'appened. Disgraceful, I call it."

He looked heart-broken that such a crime should have happened on his own beat.

"I think he'll be all right. It was touch and go, though. I can't understand it, Bloor. Cromwell was a stranger here. Who would want to do such a thing?"

"I'm as much in the dark as you are, sir, but I'll find out who did it, if it's the last thing I ever do."

Bloor raised his hand as though swearing a solemn oath.

"This is just a courtesy call to let you know I'm here. I'm staying at the *Weatherby*."

Bloor nodded to show that he approved of the place.

"If there's anything I can do, let me know, Bloor."

"Oh, but, if the Chief Constable knows you're 'ere, sir, he'll put you in charge. I can assure you of that."

Bloor hoped so. He'd taken a liking to Littlejohn right away.

"When was Mr. Richard Cromwell buried?"

"Cromwell...? Oh, I see. His name was Richard Twigg, sir. I understand he was brother to Mr. Cromwell's mother. He was laid to rest in the churchyard the day before yesterday."

"He'd been ill for some time?"

"Not long. He'd had ulcers for a long while. It was his hobby, sir. Always talkin' about them. Then, as far as I can gather, one of them burst and killed 'im. They say 'e bled to death almost before the doctor arrived."

"Who was the doctor?"

"Clinton, of Wiston Purlieu... He doctors most people in the village."

"Would you care to show me just where the shooting occurred?"

"With pleasure, sir."

Bloor put on his flat cap and held open the door. This was going to be good, he thought to himself. On the job with Scotland Yard. He couldn't get out and in full view of the village fast enough. On the way he told Littlejohn how the case was going.

Nobody knew when the shot was fired. Nobody seemed to have heard it. With all the cars about, it might have been mistaken for a back-fire. A passer-by, arriving home late from a masonic meeting in Wiston Purlieu, three miles away, had found Cromwell unconscious on the ground. He couldn't have been there long, otherwise he'd have died. Of that Bloor was sure. It was moonlight, so whoever fired the shot could see his quarry. Cromwell had been taken to the Wiston Cottage Hospital right away and was so badly injured that it needed a special brain surgeon to operate. So they sent him to Manchester Royal, where there were famous men to do the job. That was all.

"Where did Mr. Twigg live?"

"Just through the village on the way to Rushton Superior. A largish house on the left. You can't miss it, sir."

"Has Mrs. Twigg inquired about Sergeant Cromwell's condition?"

"When she was told about the shootin', sir, she passed out, and she's been in bed ever since."

They were on the scene of the crime. It had occurred almost opposite the *Weatherby*, fifty yards along on the other side, right in front of a square of land turned into allotments.

"The county experts have combed the place all day. They've questioned everybody. I've been busy, I can tell you, sir. Nobody saw or heard anythin'."

Darkness was falling and the village street had grown suddenly very quiet. Lights had gone on in houses and cottages, and blinds and curtains were drawn. Now and then, a car passed, but most of the traffic seemed immobilized for the time in the string of red rear-lights in front of the pub and a café, which was still open and through the windows of which people could be seen crowded round tables drinking wine and eating the omelettes for which the place had a local reputation. Then a bus arrived and poured out about a dozen people who'd been to the pictures at Wiston Purlieu. Among them were Mrs. Bloor and her sister.

Two large heavy women who engaged in breathless conversation until they drew abreast of Bloor. One of them half halted and looked hard at the bobby.

"I thought you were wantin' a night in on your own," she said, tossed her head, and drew her sister past the two men as though to avoid being contaminated by her untruthful spouse.

"The missus," said Bloor, sighed, and then, as if to change the subject, "There should be a comet in the sky to-night, accordin' to the wireless..." But there was no interest in his voice.

As usual, his missus had spoiled it all!

2
THE SINISTER MANSERVANT

Littlejohn looked at his watch with the aid of a match, with which he then lit his pipe. Nine o'clock. The church bells had started to ring at eight and were still at it. It must have been a practice, a learners' night. There seemed to be two experienced ringers, with the rest nowhere. Halting for breath or instruction, dotting and carrying, too early or too late, and then cantering to catch up with the rest. Across the dimly lighted window of the ringing-chamber, shadows flitted pulling ropes.

Littlejohn was anxious to see Uncle Richard's widow, Widow Twigg, as he had begun to call her in his own mind. He wondered if there had been some jiggery-pokery about Uncle Richard's death. The dicoumarin, perhaps. And had Cromwell come across it and somehow fallen foul of Widow Twigg, her lover, or maybe an accomplice? The story went that the attempt on Cromwell's life had bowled her completely over and she'd been ill in bed ever since.

The Superintendent followed the road from Rushton Inferior to Rushton Superior. At one time, judging from the shadows of old trees hanging and rustling overhead, it had been a pleasant avenue between the two villages. Now, it was ribbon-built with substantial villas set back in long gardens. The peace was frequently disturbed, too, by pubcrawlers rushing past in high-speed, sometimes unsteadily-handled cars. It was a sporting local custom to drive from *The Cock* at Rushton to the *Brown Cow* at Inferior, and thence to the *Bull and Bush* in Superior. This circular tour, on a road like a car-racing track, could be continued until closing-time or until the driver was incapable of negotiating Gibbet Corner, tore through the hedge, and ended up in Kirkley Ditch.

Littlejohn had no right whatever to call on Mrs. Twigg. So far, he'd no authority to investigate Cromwell's case at all. That would probably come in the morning when they heard he was there; until then, he was on his own. All the same, he pursued his course almost instinctively, quite sure he wouldn't rest for the night until he'd broken the ice of the inquiry.

He didn't even know where Uncle Richard had lived and he hadn't remembered to ask Bloor. There wasn't a soul about except odd ones who passed at sixty miles an hour, but a man was just leaving a house higher up the road and in front of which a car was standing. Littlejohn hurried and caught him just as he was starting his engine.

"Would you kindly tell me where Mrs. Twigg lives?"

The stranger looked at Littlejohn peevishly through the open window of the car. He was formally dressed, bowler hat and leather driving-gloves, a round, fresh face, snub nose, and spiteful eyes behind black-rimmed glasses too large for his features.

"If you're here on business, she's not well enough to see visitors. This is the house, but it's no use your calling. I'm the doctor and I've just seen her..."

"There will be servants at home, sir?"

"Cank and his wife. Not much use your seeing them."

"Cank?"

"Yes, Cank. He and his wife keep house for Mrs. Twigg. And

now I must be going, if you'll allow me. I've some more calls to make."

He let in the clutch and moved away without another word.

Littlejohn turned to the main gates. *Ballarat.* He might have guessed. Uncle Richard, according to Cromwell, had been the black sheep of the family who'd run away to Australia, made a fortune, and returned to marry a good-looking blonde of half his age. He'd called his house presumably after the spot in which he'd made his lucky strike.

A long avenue of flowering cherries and almonds, all in full bloom, the scent of wallflowers again, a wide lawn surrounded by flowering shrubs. The house itself was square and modern, built in brick with broad bow windows. A light shone in an upper room and two old gig-lamps, one on each side of the heavy front door, lit up a few square yards of the terrace with their bright electric bulbs. Littlejohn rang the door-bell.

A man appeared almost right away. A little hatchet-faced fellow, who might have been a retired jockey. Lightly built, bow-legged, sandy eyebrows, thin silky grey hair, bald in front, a large straight nose and little mean eyes. He wore an open-necked shirt, flannel trousers and a sports jacket, and carried a lighted cigarette.

"Yes?"

An awkward customer!

"Are you Mr. Cank?"

"Yes. What is it?"

"I understand Mrs. Twigg is ill... too ill to see anybody..."

"That's right."

"I'd like a word with you, then. Superintendent Littlejohn, of Scotland Yard."

Cank flinched slightly and then pulled himself together.

"Well, Mrs. Twigg's not available, as I said. The county chaps were 'ere to-day, askin' a lot of questions. We told 'em all we knew, which was precious little. He just went out for a walk. We thought he'd come back and gone up to bed. Next thing we know, he's in the local hospital and being sent off to Manchester. That's all there is to it."

The manservant had all the insolence of the owner of the house himself.

"I've not said what I've called for yet, Cank. But I'd better come in. Here's my card..."

Cank licked his lips.

"It's late."

"I won't take long. I want to see my colleague's room, if I may. I suppose it's been left as it was when he went out."

"The bed's been made and the place tidied. Nobody said it hadn't to be touched."

"Perhaps you'll take me up, then."

"If you insist, I suppose I'll 'ave to, but it's not the time of day for police visitin', and the mistress ill in bed, too."

"I won't disturb her."

A door at the end of the corridor opened and a woman emerged. She was as big as Cank was small. A large dead-pan face, a mop of unruly grey hair, a huge floppy bosom, and enormous arms and swollen legs. She panted as she walked.

"What is it at this time of night?"

"It's the police. An unearthly hour to be callin', I must say. He wants to see Mr. Cromwell's room. I'll take 'im up. He says 'e won't be long. You'd better get back to the telly. No use two of us having our evenin's pleasure spoiled."

"It is an unearthly hour to be sure, as you was sayin'. Well, don't be long. You're missin' a good show."

She wobbled back to the television set, which had been playing revue music punctuated by a comedian's wise-cracks and the regular laughing of an invited audience.

"This way."

Past the heavy mahogany hat-stand and a lot of modern brass hanging on the walls and balanced on shelves. A ship's bell, some brass riding-lights, and a large brass pestle and mortar. The wide staircase was carpeted in thick pile. They turned at the landing and went to the back of the house. Cank opened a bedroom door, switched on a light, and indicated by a wave of his hand that this was it.

"Cank!"

A feeble voice called from the room in front, the one with the lighted window.

"I'll be back," said Cank, suggesting he'd made a mental inventory of the contents of Cromwell's room, so Littlejohn needn't try any tricks in his absence. He took his time on the way to his mistress, as though he resented being shouted for.

A pleasant room with another heavy flowered carpet underfoot and chintz curtains at the windows. Expensive modern walnut furniture. Littlejohn looked around him and bit hard on the empty pipe between his teeth. It reminded him so much of the trips he and Cromwell frequently made together on cases. Cromwell had set it out in his normal methodical way. On the bedside table, the little leather photograph-case he carried wherever he went had been erected, as usual. On one side a portrait of his pretty wife, smiling, her auburn hair a bit ruffled in the wind; on the other, the snap-shot he'd taken himself at Worthing, showing his three little girls in bathing costumes, smiling at their father as he snapped them.

On a hook behind the door, Cromwell's chest-expanders without which he never began the day. Peeping from under the bed, the old suitcase he took everywhere, crammed with everything he imagined would be needed in the course of an inquiry. He'd even left his spectacles, a bird-book, and the binoculars he used for his hobby of bird-watching. On the night-table, a detective story in paper backs, with the place marked by a letter addressed in immature handwriting from his eldest daughter, who wrote to Cromwell every day wherever he went.

"That's the missus. It's disturbed 'er, you callin'. But she says

I'm to tell you anythin' you want to know. She's sorry she's not fit to receive you, and would you like a glass of sherry?"

"No thank you, Cank. Your mistress seems more hospitable and good-mannered than you are yourself... I'm glad of that."

"I didn't mean to be rude, but it's late, sir."

"I won't keep you, then. Did Mr. Cromwell seem quite himself when he left for his walk last night?"

"Yes. Quite cheerful. He'd had a good dinner and a long talk with the lawyer."

"Who is the lawyer?"

"Mr. Stokes, of Wiston Purlieu."

"Had Mr. Twigg been in good health until his last attack of stomach trouble?"

"Yes. It came a bit sudden, like. He was gone before we knew where we was."

"He wasn't troubled with his heart, at all?"

"Oh, no. When he felt like it, he'd mow the lawn or go for a five-mile walk. He wore very well."

"Is Mrs. Twigg a usually healthy lady?"

"Yes. Never ails much."

"And you and your wife?"

Cank looked irritated and bewildered. He couldn't fathom what Littlejohn was getting at.

"Yes. Why? Missus has bronchitis now and then and her legs swell if she's on her feet a lot. But beyond that, we're both very fit, touch wood. My stomach bothers me a bit now and then—indigestion. Nothin' to worry about."

"I'll just take a look at Mr. Cromwell's things and then I'll leave you. I suppose his clothes are in the wardrobe."

"Yes. That one. Not much. He didn't bring a lot, seein' as he was on'y 'ere for a day or two."

The dark suit Cromwell had used for the funeral, a couple of shirts, black tie, collars... The usual paraphernalia of a short visit. Littlejohn felt in the pockets of the jacket. Wallet, keys, odds and ends, like pencils and bits of paper, some more letters from home, his warrant-card from the police... He'd apparently only intended to take a short stroll the night before and had put on his old coat and flannels and simply dropped his smoking tackle in the pocket. That, and the envelope containing the two dicoumarin tablets were all they'd found on him.

"His notebook's missing."

"Well, I've not taken it. I've not been near his things."

Cank looked indignant, assumed a hurt expression, and sniffed.

Cromwell carried it everywhere and Littlejohn knew he'd brought it to Rushton. When the sergeant had called in Littlejohn's room to say good-bye, he'd had it with him. He'd taken a final look at the page on which he'd scribbled, with his usual care, the times of trains and the date and hour he'd be back on duty.

Littlejohn pulled out the old suitcase, opened it, and turned the contents over. A few more books, a tin of *Strengtho,* a beverage in which Cromwell pinned great faith, a pamphlet on yoga, reserves of tobacco and matches... But no notebook.

"Did you see Sergeant Cromwell using his notebook? A black shiny back and an elastic band to keep it closed."

"No. Why should I?"

"You may have seen him consulting it or writing in it."

Littlejohn was just going to ask Cank something about his past history, when he remembered that probably the county police, armed with proper authority, had already covered the ground. He decided to go.

"That will be all for the present, then, Cank. I'll call again at a convenient time. I hope I'll be able to see Mrs. Twigg then, as well."

"That all depends on the doctor. She's in a pretty bad way."

"What is the matter?"

"Complete nervous exhaus'ion. Not to be wondered at. First

'er 'usband; then Mr. Cromwell. She's not been married all that long, you know. Nicely settled and then this 'appens."

"How long were Mr. and Mrs. Twigg married?"

"About three years..."

Littlejohn realized that he knew nothing at all about the late Uncle Twigg, and the very man who could give him a full colourful account was completely *hors de combat*. Cromwell had rarely mentioned his uncle and then only casually. He'd been quite surprised when the old man's will had revealed him as an executor along with a lawyer. Perhaps Twigg had thought Cromwell, as a detective, would be a safe bet, in spite of the fact that he belonged to a rather estranged branch of the family.

It was striking eleven when Littlejohn got back to his hotel. The bellringing had long ceased, the *Brown Cow* was closed, and most of the lights in the village were out. Mrs. Groves was sitting in her little room, half office, half private quarters, when he entered. She emerged to meet him.

"You've had quite a busy evening, Superintendent."

"I've been up to *Ballarat* to try and see Mrs. Twigg. I wanted to be sure that all my colleague's affairs were right and, of course, try to get as much information as I could about what happened last night before he was shot. Did *you* hear anything?"

"Come in my room where we can talk. I've just made myself coffee and you can have a cup. That is, unless you prefer some sherry or benedictine."

She was still smiling and chuckling in her half infantile way. She seemed pleased with herself all the time, happy at her work, happy with her lodgers, eager to share in all that went on.

"Coffee will do nicely, thank you, Mrs. Groves."

The room was small and cosy. A roll-top desk which seemed to contain all the business side of the hotel; the rest a sitting-room. Again, papers of two different patterns on the walls, modern curtains, contemporary furniture. Deep lounge chairs, a long settee, a bookcase, several little tables, all in natural oak.

Over the fire place, a portrait of the late Groves, in the gown and chain of office as mayor of a distant town. Two or three pictures of still life which Littlejohn couldn't quite christen.

"That's my late husband as mayor of Cobley. Ten years ago... I lost him the following year."

She still smiled as though it had been a pleasure.

"And those pictures were done by a young artist who stayed here two years ago. He was said to have a great future, but when in London, he put his head in the gas-oven. He took life very seriously. Do you take brown sugar in your coffee? Black or white?"

"Black coffee and brown sugar, please, will suit me fine."

They sat down with a little table made of strong copper wire and three-ply between them. It reminded Littlejohn of a large mouse-trap.

"This little table was given to me by a young man who stayed here last summer. He made and sold them and, I believe, is doing quite well."

Littlejohn wondered what he would be expected to leave behind when *he* left.

Mrs. Groves opened a corner cupboard and took out two large tins. She opened them and offered the Superintendent a choice of fruit cake or chocolate biscuits. He declined and asked permission to smoke his pipe.

"Of course. You don't mind if I eat a little. My digestion isn't very good and the doctor says I ought to eat every two hours. A little and often..."

She chuckled again, cut a large wedge of cake, and started to chew it ravenously.

"I often have to get up in the night for a meal. My stomach works too fast and when there is an excess of gastric juices, it needs something to absorb them... But you don't want to hear about my troubles. You were asking about last night. I didn't hear the shot. Nobody seems to have done. But the commotion afterwards woke several of us. The ambulance and people running about."

"What time would that be?"

"Just after midnight. Mr. Moore, who lives just past the post-office, found him. He was on his way from a masonic lodge at Wiston and was walking home from the centre of the village where some friend had dropped him from his car. Two or three of us got up and went to the door, but, by then, the ambulance had arrived and they were taking him away."

"Were all your boarders indoors at the time?"

Her eyes opened wide.

"You surely don't think...?"

"No. I wondered if they might have seen anyone about the village when it happened."

"No. They were all indoors. I never go to bed until the last is in, unless they warn me they'll be out late, and then I give them the key sometimes. Miss Marriott, in the room above yours, will be late to-night. She's gone out with one of her boy friends. One never knows which one it is, she's so many."

Another wedge of cake. Mrs. Groves ate with gusto, reluctant to lose even a crumb or a raisin.

"More coffee?"

"Thank you. Did you know the late Mr. Twigg?"

"Yes. Quite well. He often took a walk past here and was always ready for a friendly word. A nice gentleman."

"What age?"

"I'd say nearly seventy. His wife is much younger. Around forty perhaps."

"Were you here when they settled in the village?"

"Oh, yes. I remember Mr. Twigg arriving himself. About six years ago. He was a wealthy bachelor, then. Fresh from Australia, where I believe he made a fortune. He was a generous giver to the parish causes. Three years ago, he went on a cruise to Madeira and met his wife. They were married almost at the end of the cruise and he brought her here."

"Do you like her?"

Again the smile, but a little frosty this time.

"I must confess we don't know what to make of her here. Her background is a mystery and she seems fond of the admiration of men. Oh, don't misunderstand me. As far as we know, there's nothing wrong. But a young woman married to an old man is bound, if she's that type, to seek admiration from younger men, too. She couldn't have married him for love... Now, could she?"

"She may have done. One never knows the way of the feminine heart, Mrs. Groves, does one?"

She was struggling to open the chocolate-biscuit box and paused to give him a coy smile.

"Go on with you, Superintendent! Don't tell me she wasn't after his money. That's probably why she went on the cruise. To find what she could."

"You don't seem very fond of Mrs. Twigg."

"I'm not. No use saying I am. She doesn't mix here. She's said to come from London. What she does down there when she goes to see her Ma, as she calls her, I don't know. I wonder if she has a Ma at all. Mr. Twigg used to let her go when she wanted. After all, she didn't seem to look after him much. They'd got the Canks there cooking and doing the housework."

"Who is Cank and where does he come from?"

"Cank is a very unpleasant man. Believe it or not, he used to be the village postman, or one of them. He was doing one of the rounds when I first came to live here eight years ago. Sam, our main postman, is a permanent man, and is due for a pension when he retires. The place has grown and it became too much for one, so they took on a temporary help. That was Cank. He'd been something at a racing stable...groom, or ostler, or something, I don't know the terms...and had given it up. I guess he'd been fired. He began to look for work and the post office signed him on. Not long after, he started to agitate to be put on the pensionable staff. He got quite offensive and gave poor Sam an awful time. Finally, he left in a rage. Mr. Twigg had just arrived in the village and, somehow, Cank persuaded him to take him and his wife on as indoor servants. He's a kind of house-boy doing the garden, driving the car and the like, and his wife does the cooking and other chores."

"Nobody knows what he really did before he came to Rushton?"

"No. A very sinister character, I call him. I don't know how Mr. Twigg put up with him, although he and Mrs. Twigg seem to get on very well. He drives her down to the village, even though she could walk here in the time it takes to get out the car. She sits in front with him, too. He's familiar and offensive when he's that way inclined."

"Didn't Twigg drive the car?'

"Now and then. Mrs. Twigg can drive, too. But it probably suits her to have Cank with her, carrying the parcels, opening the door, putting the rug over her knees. She's that sort. No lady, if you ask me."

She ate a final biscuit and put away the tins regretfully.

"Mr. and Mrs. Twigg got on all right?"

"As far as I know, yes. Of course, one never knows what goes on behind the closed doors and drawn curtains of homes. I'll bet if we could see through the walls of half the houses of this village we'd have a surprise. Don't you think so?"

She rolled her eyes at him. He smiled back, but he wasn't thinking of Mrs. Groves or even of what she was saying. He was thinking of Cromwell in bed, still unconscious probably, in the Infirmary, and of his wife and Mrs. Cromwell, one consoling the other, in an hotel in Manchester.

"Do you think Mr. Cromwell discovered something about them and she shot him?"

Littlejohn jumped.

"I beg your pardon."

"I thought you weren't listening."

She repeated the question.

"I really don't know, Mrs. Groves. I simply can't imagine anybody wanting to take a shot at Cromwell. The thing seems so stupid, so unreasonable. I think I'd better just telephone the hospital before I turn-in. May I use the phone?"

"Of course. It's under the stairs. We haven't got them in the rooms yet. I'm hoping to soon. Shall I get the number?"

"I'll manage, thanks."

It was a coin-box affair and Littlejohn was soon through to Manchester.

The patient is as well as may be expected. He is asleep and quiet.

Perhaps he'd better tell Mrs. Cromwell and his wife. He asked for their hotel.

"Please bring Mrs. Littlejohn down to the desk. I don't want any noise in the bedrooms."

It took quite a time.

"Yes, it's me... How are things with you? And Mrs. Cromwell...? Good. I just rang up the hospital. No real news yet... Yes, I'm quite comfortable here. A nice place... How about you?"

Somehow he didn't feel as free and easy with his wife as he usually was. There was none of the impersonality of a normal hotel about the *Weatherby*. You always felt someone or other was watching and listening.

After the call, he strolled to the front door and looked up and down the village street. A few lights on here and there, the sound of a river somewhere, running under a bridge, the noise of a car or two in the distance. The moon was shining across the spot where Cromwell had been shot. From where he stood, Littlejohn felt that he himself could knock a bottle from the fence with his own revolver. Whoever fired the toy pistol must have been very much nearer.

Over the way, there was a light in the bedroom of the villa in the large garden, the scents of which reached Littlejohn across the road. He wondered who lived there and what was going on at this late hour. It was the nearest place to where Cromwell had been fired upon. Had they heard or seen anything?

Indoors he asked Mrs. Groves about the house opposite. She had cleared the table and was now sucking sweets.

"The Beetons. Middle-aged people. She's a bit of an invalid. Sometimes she has bad turns. When one takes her, the lights will be on half the night. Her husband is a shipper and goes abroad quite a lot. It must be awkward, him having to leave her. One of the women from the village comes then, an ex-nurse, which is convenient."

"Well, I think I'll retire. Good night."

"Good night, Superintendent. Sleep well. Breakfast in bed?"

"No thanks. Nine o'clock will suit me."

He slept badly. Perhaps it was the strong coffee. At any rate, it wasn't the church clock, the striking of which was suspended between eleven and seven in the night, after a complaint from the tenants of the flats opposite the church.

He heard Miss Marriott arrive back in a car at about two o'clock. There was a whispered conversation and the silence of parting kisses, and then the car left noisily. Miss Marriott began the rhythmic process of retiring. He even heard her kick off her shoes, wash, and clean her teeth, open the window wider, and then bounce into bed. All in a mere five minutes...

The lights were on in the house opposite when he fell asleep at last, just as a stable-clock somewhere in the village struck three.

3
A SICK VISIT

Littlejohn awoke at seven as the church clock, beginning its day, struck the hour. His sleep seemed to have been very short, but he felt none the worse for it. He lay on his back, listening to the sounds of the house and the village outside.

Cars were already on the move taking the early birds to business. A dairyman tramped here and there, putting down his bottles and rattling the empties. Sam, the postman, was on his rounds, knocking on doors as he slipped in the letters and shouting about the road as he met his friends.

Inside, there were sounds of running water everywhere. Baths, washbowls, someone slopping water about in the hall below. Miss Marriott in the room above began to get up. Littlejohn heard the springs of the bed creak, a bump on the floor, taps turned on. Then Miss Marriott descending at high speed, as though late for her bus.

He rose, put on his dressing-gown, and explored the landing. The bathroom was occupied by someone whistling and splashing. He returned, lit his pipe, and drew back the curtains. The road was deserted. A cloudless blue sky with the sun shining on the houses across the way. Bloor appeared, on parade, officially examining the village after the long night. He wore a puzzled expression and his lips moved as though he were talking to himself.

The curtains had been drawn back from the upper window of the villa opposite. *Rushton House.* Littlejohn could just read the name chiselled in the stone of the gatepost. The sun illuminated the portion of the upstairs room in the vicinity of the window. The Superintendent, from where he was standing, could see a man stowing the last of his packing in an open suitcase lying on a chair. It was an opulent-looking case of pigskin and the man placed various objects in it with meticulous care, patting them down, carefully putting them in place.

A medium-built, middle-aged man, with a paunch and a bald head. Probably Mr. Beeton himself getting ready for one of his shipping trips. He came and went, disappeared and returned to within the sunlit bit of stage which Littlejohn was watching unseen. He was dressed in a neat blue suit with a white collar and shirt which stood out plainly against the dark clothing. He performed his task with an abstracted air, as though thinking of other things. A taxi drew up outside; Beeton peeped at it through the window, spoke to someone unseen, and then closed the bag, snapped the catches, and locked them with a key which he took from his pocket.

Then a woman came in view. Also middle-aged, with white hair gathered in a net. She was tall, too, slim, and wore a dressing-gown wide open at the throat, showing a white expanse of withered bosom. The man embraced her, picked up his bag and, in a few minutes, opened the front door and got in the taxi, which drove away in the direction of Wiston Purlieu. The woman watched him until the car was out of sight, then turned, took a deep breath, and drew the curtains, perhaps to continue her sleep.

Littlejohn felt almost ashamed of eavesdropping on a little harmless domestic scene of parting.

The children and their parents descended from the floor above. The Bachelors. Mr. Bachelor sounded to be scolding the family in general and they seemed to be differing in views about spending the day.

"I had enough yesterday. We're not going to the river. Every time we go near the water, one or the other of you falls in."

Valentine followed on their heels, hurrying on his way to his gasworks. Then, another young woman, called Miss Broderick, who was secretary of a zoo a few miles away. The smell of coffee and bacon began to rise from below and cups rattled on the tables of the dining-room.

Littlejohn was in the bath when the telephone bell rang and Mrs. Groves tapped on the door and, in her best infantile, chuckling voice, told him he was wanted.

"It's the county police... I didn't know you were awake or I'd have sent you up a cup of tea."

He asked her to tell them to ring in a quarter of an hour, and dead on the minute, the phone bell rang again.

"Inspector Tandy, of Wiston Purlieu..."

Littlejohn was ready and waiting for him. Mrs. Groves met him on his way to the box.

"Don't be long... Would you like eggs and bacon, sausage and bacon, a kipper, or sweetbreads and bacon...?"

He listened patiently to it all, ordered bacon and eggs, and then took his call.

Tandy was a dry-voiced north-countryman, who greeted Littlejohn with soft-pedalled enthusiasm. He sounded as if he wanted to roar approval, but was holding himself in until he knew with whom he was dealing.

"We spent all yesterday on the case, sir, and got nowhere. Your arrival's a real windfall. The Chief Constable was going to send a C.I.D. man from headquarters, but as the victim's a Scotland Yard man and you're from the same place, he's inclined, if everybody, including yourself, is agreeable, to ask you to take charge."

Mrs. Groves's pink face appeared outside the box and she pantomimed that his breakfast was ready.

"Are you coming here this morning, Tandy?"
"Yes, sir. As soon as you like."
"Let's meet in an hour, then."
"Right, sir. I'm looking forward to meeting you."
"And I to meeting you..."

Two more calls, greatly to Mrs. Groves's exasperation. She even brought out a plate of bacon and eggs and showed it to him through the glass to indicate it was spoiling.

Better news from the hospital.

The patient has spent a good night and is doing as well as may be expected. He has recovered consciousness, but is now sleeping again. A visit? Later this afternoon, when the surgeons have seen him.

Mrs. Littlejohn sounded more cheerful over the telephone, too. Mrs. Cromwell had spent a good night and the news from the hospital had cheered them both up. Littlejohn arranged to call for them on his way to the Infirmary in the afternoon.

"I've cooked you a fresh plateful..."

Mrs. Groves laid enough bacon and eggs for three in front of the Superintendent.

"Was that your wife?"

She asked it in a voice flavoured with astringency, as though people under Mrs. Groves's wing had no right to be involved with other women.

Dead on the hour, Inspector Tandy arrived. He was followed by a subordinate whom he introduced as Sergeant Buck. P.C. Bloor, who had met them in the village, hung about in the rear.

Tandy and partner wore bowler hats and raincoats. They were evidently impressed and a bit overawed by the presence of a famous Scotland Yard man. The party adjourned to a small lounge and Littlejohn made the mistake of asking Mrs. Groves if they could have something to drink.

"Tea? Coffee? Cocoa? I've no licence, you know. The *police* opposed it at the last sessions. Why, I don't know. I've seen the cook giving Bloor malted milk at the back door. Perhaps he'd like some of that..."

The visitors looked anxious and Bloor turned fiery red even to the backs of his hands.

"Coffee, please."

Sergeant Buck was disgusted, threw his bowler hat on a vacant chair, and looked ready to sit on it in temper.

Tandy was a medium-built man, well set-up, dressed in a brown suit and a dark-red tie. He was going bald and the flesh of his solemn face hung in folds down his cheeks. His nose was large, and his brown eyes carried an ironical twinkle which saved his features from being commonplace. Buck looked like his bodyguard; a huge man with big hands and feet, homely face and homely ways like those of a good-class 'pug,' and a light tenor voice, which, emerging from such a large mouth and big features came as a perpetual surprise.

The drinks arrived and Mrs. Groves herself served the coffee, with a sharp look at everybody except Littlejohn, who, now being her favourite lodger, was smiled upon.

"Let me know if you want any more."

Tandy took out a large notebook and consulted it.

"As far as the case is concerned, this book might just as well be blank. I took a lot of notes, but on reading through them last night, sir, they conveyed nothing whatever to me."

"S'right," said Buck, who was devoted to his inspector and prepared to swear that black was white on his behalf.

"Nobody saw the shot fired, nobody heard it. Mrs. Twigg, who was bowled over by her husband's death, went to bed as soon as Sergeant Cromwell went out for his walk. That's quite a good alibi, because Cank and his wife were in the house at the time and confirm that she was indoors. Cank left the hall and stairs lights on for when the sergeant returned, and found them still on when he got up. That's what made him look in Mr. Cromwell's room and find the bed hadn't been slept in."

"Do you trust the Canks, Tandy?"

The Inspector rubbed his jaw and started to fill his pipe.

"No, I don't, really. They're not a pleasant couple, at all. But if they're not telling the truth, all three of them, the Canks and Mrs. Twigg are in league."

"S'right," added Buck.

Bloor nodded sagely. He blew on his coffee and took a solemn gulp. He only wished those of the village who ragged him about his job could see him now. In conference, that was it.

"So, you see, sir, it's difficult to think why anybody wanted to shoot the sergeant. He's not known in the village and couldn't, by any stretch of imagination, be said to be a menace to anybody. It was either accidental, or, shall we say, he came upon somebody doing something improper and was shot simply because he turned up unexpectedly."

Buck, who had a mouthful of coffee, merely nodded confirmation this time.

Littlejohn lit his pipe.

"Or else, Tandy, the Canks gave a false alibi for Mrs. Twigg and she did it."

"But, why?"

"Why?" fluted Buck and Bloor gave him a scorching look. He was sick of the echo already.

"It may be that Mrs. Twigg was tired of the old man and speeded his departure. And perhaps Cromwell came across something which aroused his suspicions."

"What might have aroused them, sir?"

"These..."

Littlejohn took the envelope from his pocket and shook out the two tablets in his palm.

"With the exception of his pipe and pouch, this envelope and its contents were the only things found in Cromwell's jacket. The tablets are, I understand, dicoumarin...a drug which, taken in excess, causes severe thinning of the blood and fatal internal bleeding. Mr. Twigg died of internal haemorrhage from a ruptured stomach ulcer, according to all accounts."

Dead silence as the three local policeman pondered in awful admiration the first shots of the man from Scotland Yard.

"Where do we go from here, then, sir? We've got to have proof. Does it mean a post-mortem after exhuming the body?"

"We can hardly do that, yet, Tandy, although the sooner the better from the point of the autopsy. I would think a case of death like this, from an anti-coagulant drug, might become more and more obscure with the passing of time. However, the first thing is to trace the dicoumarin tablets. There must be hundreds of them in circulation, now. It's the prevailing treatment for coronary thrombosis."

Buck turned pale. His Uncle Joe had dropped dead from it a month ago. In bounding health one minute; dead the next. Buck didn't like to think of it. Everybody said how much he resembled his late Uncle Joe in every way.

Tandy who had been making notes chewed the end of his pencil.

"What do we do?"

"Try to find out who's suffering from coronary thrombosis in the neighbourhood and see if there's any tie-up with Mrs. Twigg. That might mean talking to the local doctors. Are they very approachable or are they likely to be sticky on account of medical etiquette?"

"They're all very co-operative except Clinton, of Wiston Purlieu. He's an awkward cuss and will probably show us the door."

Buck whinnied behind his large palm. Tandy turned on him irritably.

"What's the cackle about, Buck?"

Buck pulled himself together with a jerk.

"I was jest thinkin' about Dr. Clinton, sir. If I may say so, and as we're all officers together, I think we might even get wot we want from him, sir. We can do a deal. He was caught comin' from a cocktail party blind drunk, and not only that, when P.C. Ratcliffe tried to do him a good turn by pointin' out that he'd better not even enter his car—which was waitin' in the road—otherwise he'd be booked, the doctor lost his temper and *hit* Ratcliffe. A passer-by who knew the doctor, interfered and took him 'ome in his own car. But Ratcliffe booked 'im drunk and disorderly. What a charge against a doctor who fancies himself as much as Clinton! He'll be the laughing stock of the three Rushtons and Wiston Purlieu for months... Haw, haw, haw..."

"Well?"

A stony silence.

"I thought we might do a deal, sir. No charge if he gives the necessary co-h'operation."

"Buck, you wicked fellow! All the same, *you* can try it. And don't say it has official blessing, because I wash my hands of you."

Buck rolled about to show he understood and was repressing his mirth.

"Please get on with that right away, then, and let me have a list as soon as you can, Tandy."

"Right away, sir."

"It's likely to be quite a job, sir. There seems to be plenty of coronary thrombosis in these parts. What with rushing around, motoring, business worries, people bothering themselves about trying to be somebody they're not... All the causes of blood-pressure and hyper-tension."

"You're quite a medical man, Tandy."

"I read a bit, sir. Is there anything else we've got to do, sir?"

"I believe Mrs. Twigg came from London and frequently goes there to visit her Ma. I'd like to know a little more about Ma. Have any of you heard of her?"

Bloor, hitherto silent, cleared his throat and gave tongue.

"She's always talkin' about her Ma, but nobody's ever seen her.

She didn't come to the funeral. And she's never visited the Twiggs as far as anybody knows."

"All the more reason for looking her up if we can only find her address. That's going to be a bit difficult. We can't very well call on Mrs. Twigg and ask for it."

Bloor put up his large palm to show he was about to speak again.

"Perhaps I can 'elp there, too, sir. If you'll excuse me, I'll go and take a peek in the church registers of marriages. You see, Mr. Twigg married his wife in the local parish church. Caused a bit of a sensation and a lot of talk. She insisted on a wreath and veil, which was said to be highly inappropriate... At least, the ladies said so. I can perhaps catch the vicar in the church. When he put up the banns, he'd have to have the address of the bride-to-be, wouldn't he?"

"You excel yourself, Bloor."

"Don't mention it, sir."

"Off with you, then."

Bloor put on his hat and hurried away. Mrs. Groves thrust in her head.

"Any more coffee?"

"No, thanks, Mrs. Groves."

"Are you being in for lunch?"

"Yes; if it's convenient."

"What would you like?"

"Whatever's going."

"I'll see you later, then."

The coy smile again and she vanished.

"Will that be all, for the present, sir?"

"I think so, Tandy. Keep your eyes and ears open just in case there was anyone about the village when the shot was fired. And then, there's the matter of patients from the doctors. Do your best."

The local men left, promising to return and report at the same time next day. Littlejohn strolled out into the street and made his way to Mrs. Twigg's again.

Ballarat seemed deserted. The old gardener was mowing the front lawn and halted to ask Littlejohn what he wanted. A garrulous old man, ready to talk for as long as he could find a listener.

"They're in. Missus is still in bed. Bowled over, she was, when the old chap died on 'er. Which was funny. Never showed much love for 'im when he was in the land o' the livin'. Married 'im for 'is money. Wonder if he left it to 'er. We'll soon know. His will'll be in the local paper come Saturday, I wouldn't be surprised."

"He was well-liked locally?"

"None better. Pop'lar chap. Always a smile and a bob for a pint to any as needed it. Free with his money. You ought to look at the wreaths on 'is grave in the churchyard. Never seen so many since old Maloney died at the *Bull an' Bush.*"

Littlejohn let old Maloney pass.

"What about Cank? Do they like him in the village?"

"Cank!"

The old 'un spat on the lawn.

"Like as not he's peekin' at us through the curtains at this very minute. Not that I care. To 'ell with Cank! If he was 'ere I'd tell 'im so. When the old man was alive, he was kep' in 'is place. Since he died, Cank's got above 'isself. I allus said 'e would. He's got a hold over Mrs. Twigg, believe it or not. She's like a bird with a snake with Cank. He's got 'er proper in his power. Wot the 'ell do I care? Eh? Wot the 'ell? I does me work and I gets me pay. Let 'em do as they like."

The curtains were still drawn in the front bedroom and the sun was shining on the house. A very nice, comfortable little place for a wanderer to come home to. Uncle Richard had thought so and it was quite likely he would have been there still, if someone hadn't polished him off.

Littlejohn half rebuked himself for wilful thinking. Perhaps he'd died from natural causes. There was no proof otherwise and he couldn't judge until he'd seen Mrs. Twigg in person.

Even as he was thinking, he saw two fingers appear round the drawn curtains of the upper room, and he knew they were being watched. He was giving the old man half-a-crown and the old man's jaws were working ready to spit on it before he pocketed it, when Cank appeared at the front door.

"We don't pay you for talking. Get on with your work, Turner."

"You go to 'ell."

The old man gave Littlejohn a what-did-I-tell-you look and kicked the motor-mower into action again. Cank walked to meet Littlejohn.

"She's not up yet."

"I think she is. She's up in the bedroom, isn't she? She's just been peeping round the curtain at me. Did she tell you to come and see what was happening?"

"I don't know what you're talking about."

In the daylight, Cank looked even more villainous than on the night before. He hadn't had a shave and the light glistened on his grey stubble. His linen was soiled and his finger-nails dirty.

"You know very well what I'm talking about, Cank. And now let me tell you something. I'm now in charge of the case concerning the shooting of my colleague. Shooting a policeman's a very serious matter. It may not seem so to you, but we think so in the force."

"I didn't do it, did I? Why keep botherin' me?"

"He was staying here and he left here just before it happened. I've tried to get a proper account of what he did and his movements up to the time of the shooting. I've asked you and you've just been awkward. Furthermore, I think Mrs. Twigg could very well see me now, but is either keeping to her room and making excuses, or else you, for some reason, don't wish me to see her. Don't argue any more. Go to Mrs. Twigg right away, say I must speak with her and I believe her well enough to see me. It will be better for all of us to get it over. Now, do as I tell you."

"I don't know what Dr. Clinton'll say about all this."

"I'll be responsible."

"I don't approve of it."

"I don't care what you approve or disapprove. You are a servant here. Go and do as you're told and no more insolence."

Cank didn't like it at all, but he couldn't stand arguing any more. He went indoors and was soon back.

"She'll see you. Up the stairs, and the first room on the front."

"Take me there."

Cank's yellow teeth gleamed like those of an angry animal.

"This way, then, if you can't find your own way."

He followed Cank up the now familiar stairs and the manservant made a gesture of tapping on the door of Mrs. Twigg's bedroom.

"Come in!"

The curtains were still drawn and the room, illuminated by the light filtering through the fabric, was dim and stuffy. Cank turned on the electric light.

"Don't put on the lights; draw the curtains, Cank."

Cank obeyed his mistress without a word and let in the sun.

Mrs. Twigg was sitting up in bed, a woollen bed-jacket covering the neck of her nightdress. She had evidently titivated herself to receive him. Her hair was fresh from the comb, and there were traces of powder on her cheeks and lipstick on her mouth.

Littlejohn had formed all kinds of mental pictures of Mrs. Twigg, said to have married an old man for his money. Young, frivolous, uneducated, peroxide on her hair, paint on her face... They had all passed through his mind. But none of them tied-up with the woman now waiting for him. Her hair was dark brown and so were her eyes. A rather chubby face, with well-made features, a generous almost too heavy mouth, a small nose, almost snub, and a good forehead. From what could be seen of her figure, it was well-formed and she had shapely white arms. A bit of a surprise!

"I'm sorry to disturb you, Mrs. Twigg. I hope you're better."

"It's kind of you to say so. I'm not very well, so without seeming bad-mannered, I'll ask you to be brief."

Her voice had a trace of Cockney accent, hardly noticeable.

Cank was still hanging about. Littlejohn turned to him.

"That will be all, thank you, Cank. If Mrs. Twigg needs you, I'll call."

Cank gave him a venomous look and his eyes travelled malevolently to Mrs. Twigg.

"Yes, Cank. You needn't wait."

He left, almost slamming the door behind him.

"A rather insolent fellow, Cank?"

"He tends a little that way, but he and his wife are indispensable. Help is so hard to get. One has to be careful. Since my husband's death he's become more masterful. When I get up, I'll have to change all that."

She spoke slowly and lethargically, in keeping with her general attitude of languor. She looked pale and there were dark shadows under her eyes.

"You haven't been well, lately? The doctor forbade me to see you last night. I'll try to be brief."

"The death of my husband was a bad blow. We were very fond of one another. Then, on top of it all, the attempt on Mr. Cromwell's life. It just got me down."

"It's about that I wanted to ask you. I can think of no reason why anyone should wish to harm Cromwell. Did he seem all right the last time you saw him?"

"Quite all right. He arrived the day before yesterday for the funeral. Then, as he was an executor, he spent a lot of time afterwards with the solicitor, Mr. Stokes. I gathered Mr. Stokes was taking out probate, and after he left, we had dinner. Mr.

Cromwell was quite himself. We talked about tidying-up my late husband's affairs—his papers and the like. Then, about half-past ten, I think it was, Mr. Cromwell said he'd go for a walk down the village. He put on his comfortable old jacket and went out. I had nothing to do, so I went to bed right away. He never returned and, when Cank reported next morning that his room was empty, I told him to telephone the police, who, in turn, got in touch with the hospital. He was there, badly wounded..."

"And, in your opinion, there was nothing on his mind, nothing he seemed puzzled or curious about?"

"No."

"Did you see him using his notebook at all; a rather large official-looking affair held together by a loop of black elastic?"

"No. I never saw it."

"It's missing. I know he had it with him."

"Do you think whoever shot him took it?"

"That must be the case. I can think of no other reason."

"I never saw the book."

"In short, you can't give me any line on why he might have been shot or who might have done it?"

"None at all."

Her large eyes were on his face all the time, questioning, trying to probe what he was thinking. Now, she closed them and laid back her head.

"You are feeling tired?"

"No. Please go on. We may as well get it over."

He felt no friendliness in his reception. To Mrs. Twigg he was a nuisance, perhaps a menace. There seemed a trace in her of fear lest he lay his finger on some awkward point.

"You were married three years?"

"Yes."

"Happily?"

She opened her eyes.

"Has anyone said anything to the contrary?"

"No. Just a natural question."

"We were very happy. That is my husband."

She pointed to a wedding portrait in a frame on the mantelpiece. For the first time Littlejohn saw Uncle Richard. He liked him. Tall, well-built, an elderly man who had worn well. His face was strong and lined and he wore a small moustache. A typical colonial. He looked a bit solemn with his bride on his arm. She wore, as Bloor had said, a white wedding-dress and a veil.

"He was the best man in the world. So kind, so considerate. Everybody's friend..."

She wasn't looking at Littlejohn any longer. Her eyes were fixed on a spot somewhere in the sky through the window. It was almost a melodramatic pose.

"Had he any relatives?"

"I don't know. He quarrelled with his own family, the Twiggs, I believe. They didn't come to our wedding and never called here. The only relative he cared about at all was Robert, that is Mr. Cromwell. It seems he was the son of Mr. Twigg's favourite sister, who was the only one of the family who kept in touch with him till she died. He'd met Robert casually a time or two, and when he made his will, nothing would do but that Robert should be executor along with the lawyer."

"You were employed when you met Mr. Twigg?"

"I was private secretary to a business man."

"May I ask whom?"

She looked hard at him, still trying to fathom his purpose.

"His name was Casadessus, a French importer in London. I've lost touch with him. I think he went back to France."

"I see. Thank you."

"Were you ever engaged before you met Mr. Twigg?"

"Really, Superintendent, your investigation's getting rather deep, isn't it? I don't see how an account of my past life can help. *I* didn't shoot Mr. Cromwell. I was in bed all the time. Cank will tell you."

"I quite agree. I was just interested in all the background to this case. Perhaps I went too far. Please excuse me."

She softened at that.

"It's nothing. You must excuse me, too. I'm irritable. It's my nerves. Yes. I was engaged before. He was in the RAF and died over Germany. That was all. One or two men asked me to marry them after that, but I couldn't settle. Then Richard—Mr. Twigg—came along. He was very kind and understanding. When he asked me to marry him, I agreed."

"His will... Were you sole beneficiary? I ask this because, you will agree, Cromwell was concerned as executor."

"My husband left everything to me unconditionally. There were a few legacies. Five hundred each to the executors and a few to village charities and the like."

"Nothing to Cank?"

She looked hard at him.

"No."

"May I ask you a personal question, please? Don't take it amiss, because it's for your own good."

"Ask it."

Her hands tightened over the bedclothes.

"Has Cank some hold over you, Mrs. Twigg?"

She forced a laugh.

"Whatever makes you think that? Certainly not."

"He's more insolent than normally and I got the impression that he didn't want me to see you."

"It's your imagination."

She closed her eyes wearily again.

"I'm tiring you, Mrs. Twigg. I must go. Thank you for seeing me and answering my questions."

"I only hope it will help you to catch whoever did that shocking thing to Mr. Cromwell. If you visit him, please give him my best wishes. He is better, isn't he?"

"A little. It's still touch and go. He's had to have a serious brain operation. It all depends on the next few days."

She turned pale and laid her head languidly on the pillow.

"Good morning, then, Superintendent."

"Good morning, Mrs. Twigg."

On his way back to the village, Littlejohn took the old gardener's advice and called in the churchyard to see Richard Twigg's grave. The faded wreaths and flowers were still there. The grave was covered. *His loving wife. Three friends. The Bowling Club with deep sympathy. The regulars at the* Brown Cow *with happy memories. The Dramatic Society in remembrance of an old patron and benefactor. The Old Age Pensioners of Rushton Inferior, to a good friend. Robert Cromwell and Family. Mr. and Mrs. Cank. Joe, Harry and Fred from the* Bull and Bush... The *Bull and Bush* again!

Quite a man, Uncle Richard. A decent fellow with many friends who probably owed much to him.

Littlejohn wondered how long he'd lie at rest there before they had to exhume him.

4
STRUTT STREET

Every morning the village of Rushton Inferior enjoyed a fête of shopping. The ladies of the neighbourhood arrived in new frocks, displayed the latest models, and drove up and down in expensive cars. There was an atmosphere of competition and tension as well as social grace. The shops were visited and orders placed. In days long gone, the tradesmen had circulated among the big houses of the countryside, obsequiously taking orders and craving custom. Now, they had the upper hand. They were short-staffed and independent and, thanks to years of war and rations, wealthy. Their prices were higher because they, and their customers as well, regarded themselves as a cut above the multiple shops frequented by the workers of Wiston Purlieu and Marborough; they allowed the extended credit which was often needed, added more to their final accounts for the favour, and—in the words of Mr. Sherlock, the grocer—'Bob's your uncle.'

Littlejohn threaded his way through the fashion parade and a wedding which was taking place at the church. There seemed to have been either a mistake or very severe mixing of social oil and water in the match, for the bride wore white and her family morning dress, whilst the groom and his retinue were in lounge suits and costumes. Over lunch, Mrs. Groves explained to Littlejohn that it was a love match between the daughter of a tycoon and the son of a well-known local communist. The meal was interrupted by Bloor, who arrived excitedly with some particulars about Mrs. Twigg extracted from the church registers. These had been examined by the limb of the law under the protesting eye of the vicar, who was busy preparing for the wedding.

Mrs. Twigg, née Emily Waldron, was the daughter of Mrs. Evelyn Laxey, retired actress, widow of Fred Laxey, dec'd., and of Sydney Waldron, dec'd., of flat 4., 163 Strutt Street, Edgware Road, London, W2.

Littlejohn thanked Bloor, who asked him not to mention it, made a note of the information, and asked the constable to telephone for the police-car placed at the Superintendent's service by the county constabulary. He then telephoned the Yard to advise them that he was returning to London by the train leaving Manchester just after four. He wished to visit Strutt Street himself.

The village was quiet when he left for the hospital. The plumber and the joiner were comparing lengthy notes as they leaned against the wall of the house opposite. As Littlejohn glanced at them and returned the greeting gravely signalled by Mr. Clissold, Member of the Amalgamated Society of Plumbers and Glaziers, who had given him a lift the day before, he raised his glance to the windows of the Beetons' house and met the eyes of the pale invalid who occupied the upper front room and who retreated at once, drawing the curtains as she did so.

He met his wife and Mrs. Cromwell at their hotel. He and Mrs. Littlejohn said little to each other, exchanging understanding glances. Mrs. Cromwell had lost her self-assurance under the strain and was pale, with dark circles under her eyes. To hide his embarrassment the Superintendent adopted a breezy, businesslike manner, quite alien to him, expressing assurances that all would be well with Cromwell and citing even worse cases than those of the sergeant from which the victims had fully recovered very quickly.

At the hospital, there was a repetition of the previous day's ordeal. The long corridors, the atmosphere of silent suffering, the detached and skilled air of doctors and nurses, the awed hesitancy of visitors. In the neuro-surgical ward, the sister met them cheerfully, but firmly. The patient was getting along as well as might be expected, had briefly recovered consciousness, could be seen, but for a few minutes only.

Littlejohn had often seen Cromwell in bed. When they were on exhausting cases together and the sergeant had, with his usual energy, done most of the menial and routine work, he had from time to time tiptoed to his bedside in the morning, found him fast asleep, and left him in peace. But he'd never seen his friend look so distressing before. He was asleep, his head swathed in a turban of dressings, stubble on his chin, and the sockets of his eyes so dark that he looked to have been assaulted. The sad eyes of the patient slowly opened as they looked at him, fixed themselves on his wife, and suddenly grew bright with what might have been tears. Then the glance fell upon Littlejohn and changed to surprise and serenity.

"Time to go..."

The sister led them away to the comfort of cups of tea and Littlejohn said good-bye and left the women together. Mrs. Cromwell didn't even ask him if he had any idea who had committed the crime.

It was late in the evening when Littlejohn reached the Edgware Road. The place was alive with people enjoying the fine weather. It was the end of another soft day, with the last of the sunshine lighting the drab streets. There were bunches of spring flowers in the windows of shops and flats and, in the last of the old trees in a forsaken garden, a thrush was singing amid the hubbub of the traffic.

Strutt Street was a characteristic thoroughfare running at

right-angles to the main highway. The part nearest to the Edgware Road had already been transformed into modern flats, offices and shops by speculative builders, but as it receded from the busier neighbourhood, the street became more and more quiet, Littlejohn could hear his own footsteps on the pavement, and the houses began to change in type. Old terraces of large Victorian styles, with here and there a gap torn by bombs, tidied-up, and left to harbour children, cats, and weeds. No. 163 was a tenement house, converted into about eight flats, poor-class and sordid, with names in ink on scrubby bits of paper, announcing tenants, stuck on doors and letter-boxes here and there.

There were one or two shops in the vicinity, too; poor affairs, selling everything, and an off-licence from which people were bringing their supper-beer in jugs and bottles. A little, thin anaemic-looking woman, yellow-faced and fagged with too much child-bearing and climbing up and down stairs, was sitting on the top step of No. 163, resting like someone at the end of her tether.

"Does Mrs. Laxey live here?"

"Not any longer."

The voice might have been answering one of many questions in which despair and weariness were involved.

"Where has she gone?"

"To Highgate Cemetery, to lie with her two husbands. She died four months ago."

Littlejohn paused for what to say next. But the woman was beginning to warm up.

"You another of 'em?"

"What do you mean?"

"Creditors. She seemed to go mad after her Emily married, and ran up a lot of debts. Emily used to call and pay the bills at one time, but since the old girl died, she's never been near."

"Her room's been let, I gather?"

"Of course, it has. The landlord hadn't been paid for weeks, so he took possession again. The furniture was sold to meet the arrears of rent, and precious little they got for it. What's it to you?"

"I'm a police officer."

"Well, well... So she was mixed up with the police, too, was she? I'm not a bit surprised. She was one who always kep' herself to herself and that sort's usually dark horses. She'd seen good times, though. She always looked a lady, right to the end. Fat and with the dropsy, she always looked as if she'd known better things. I will say that. It was said she'd been an actress and made money in her day. But most of 'em come to the same end, don't they? They spend it as it comes and then they want at the finish. Not that it's a sin to have a good time while you can. Look at me. I never had any money, but I'll end up just the same as poor Mrs. Laxey."

She slowly gathered herself up and turned to climb the stairs to her room.

"What 'ad Mrs. Laxey been up to? Is it askin' too much to want to know what an old neighbour had done wrong?"

"Nothing wrong. I'm interested in her and her daughter in connection with a case we're on. As far as I know, Mrs. Laxey had a clean record."

"I'm glad to 'ear it. Decent old girl. As for her daughter... She was always lucky. A good-looker, you see, and that's a passport to a lot o' things, especially when there's men about. She's had a few in her time. She didn't live with her mother for many a year, but visited 'er reg'lar. Some of the cars that 'ave brought her down this street would surprise you. She was lucky, as I said. Men took a fancy to 'er. But whether the money's earned on the street or the way she did, the easier way, it's all the same trade, isn't it? I did 'ear she married an old man with money in the end. Decent chap he seemed, too. Visited old Mrs. Laxey a time or two and I seen him when he did. Lucky agen, wasn't she? Although what her husband 'ud say if he knew about 'er past life I wouldn't like to guess. I bet the balloon would go up... Well... I must be up them stairs. They'll be the death of me, but I got an invalid 'usband and although I've six children they all got married and never pay a cent towards our keep. You'd think, wouldn't you, that when we've always done our best for them...? Thank you very much, sir."

"By the way, what did Mrs. Laxey die of?"

"Bad heart. Had two or three attacks. One of 'em'll carry 'er off, I sez to me 'usband who's bedridden. And I was right. She was found dead in bed by the woman in the next flat who used to pop in now and then to see she was all right."

"Was she under the doctor?"

"Oh, yes. Why not? It costs nothin'. Not that Dr. Tompion's much good. He's too busy to be good. In and out and a bottle of medicine an' a free death certificate when it's time to bury you."

"Does he live locally?"

"Just round the corner in Sidgwick Road. So long..."

She turned and started slowly to climb the weary stairs, Littlejohn's pound note still in her hand.

Sidgwick Road was little better than Strutt Street. Tenements, waste ground, houses converted into small factories and offices, property falling in decay. Outstanding among the rest, a detached house in a sour garden with a knotted tree overhanging the front door. A brass plate badly in need of cleaning. *H. D. Tompion, M.D., Surgeon.* Littlejohn rang the bell. A tired-looking woman clad in black opened it.

"Is the doctor in?"

"Yes. It's after surgery hours and he's resting. It's late."

She looked underfed and defeated and pursed her thin pallid lips in determination not to have the doctor disturbed.

"I won't keep him long. I'm from the police."

The woman looked scared, and hesitated.

"Won't it do to-morrow?"

"I'm afraid not. It's urgent."

"I'll tell him."

Littlejohn stood in the gloomy hall and waited. Old-fashioned furniture looking as worn-out as the woman who had left him. The air was heavy and stale and there was a muffled silence about the place as though the occupants only spoke in whispers and moved on tiptoe over soiled old carpets and shabby rugs.

A door opened and a man appeared. Littlejohn could not make him out until he reached the thin glow of the hall light. He was speaking to someone in the room as he emerged.

"Don't keep worrying, Amy. There's nothing wrong. I'm quite all right."

The anaemic woman must have been his sister. She had worn no wedding-ring and he addressed her with a mixture of familiarity and affection.

"What do you want at this hour? I've had a busy day."

The man reminded Littlejohn of Crippen. The same high bald forehead, shaggy moustache, gold lozenge-shaped spectacles, peering look. He was dressed in old-fashioned clothes, too. A high starched collar held together by a string tie. Red fleshy lips under the whiskers.

"I won't keep you. I'm interested in a deceased patient of yours..."

"Won't it do to-morrow? It's not all that urgent, is it?"

There was something furtive, almost sinister, about the man and, as he approached Littlejohn, the Superintendent realized that he was half drunk. He reeked of whisky. No wonder his sister had tried to keep him away.

"Oh, very well. Better come in the surgery."

He opened a door to the left and motioned Littlejohn to follow him. An annexe, a lean-to, adjoining the house. A long waiting-room with cane chairs set against the walls and then a consulting-room behind, with a washbowl and soiled towel, an examination couch, cases of instruments, and a large cheap desk with a shabby swivel chair. The atmosphere here was stale, too, with the added unpleasantness of unwashed humanity mingled with disinfectants and drugs.

The doctor took a cigarette from a packet and lit it without offering one to Littlejohn. His moustache was nicotine-stained and his small shrivelled fingers trembled as he held the match. He waved it in the air to extinguish it and threw it on the floor under his desk.

"Well? What is it? Not an inquest on Mrs. Mackay, I hope?"

"No. Mrs. Laxey, doctor."

"A perfectly normal case, which ran its course and ended in the only way... death. Nothing funny about it. Perfectly clear in me conscience about certifying it."

He sat on the corner of the desk to steady himself and looked at Littlejohn suspiciously over his glasses.

"She died of heart trouble, I believe."

"Yes."

"Coronary?"

"Yes. She'd had two attacks before the one which finished her. She might have been living to-day if she'd done as I told her. She refused to go to hospital and would persist in getting up and messing about in her rooms. She didn't give herself a chance. But why a police investigation? There's nothing wrong, is there?"

"Not really, sir. How did you treat her for her illness?"

Tompion was on his guard right away. He became strictly professional.

"What has that to do with you? I've always had a good reputation and I didn't sully it on this case. She was well looked-after medically, considering that she wouldn't co-operate."

"I'm not saying she wasn't. Did you use the new treatment for coronary thrombosis?"

"Of course I did. I might look an old-stager, but I keep abreast of current medical practice. I've found the new method very good if patients will co-operate. They ought to be in hospital, but as

Mrs. Laxey wouldn't go on any account, I had to do my best at home."

"Why wouldn't she go?"

"Don't ask me. She was a stupid old woman who said she wanted to die in her own bed."

"You used dicoumarin, doctor?"

"What do you know about dicoumarin?"

Littlejohn might have been preparing to set up in opposition over the way, or else seeking free advice on how to treat himself for illness.

"I only know it is an anti-coagulant and is dangerous when used to excess."

"Well?"

"Did you give the tablets yourself, sir, or did you leave a supply for Mrs. Laxey to take as directed?"

"I'm a busy man. I couldn't be running round there and up three flights of stairs every time she'd to take a tablet. I left a small supply with strict instructions as to how they were to be given."

"Who gave them to her?"

"Her daughter was here for about ten days. The old lady died while she was there."

"You knew Emily well?"

Tompion took off his glasses and polished them with a soiled handkerchief. In the dim light he looked like a waxwork model of a poisoner.

"Yes. Known her for years. Ever since her mother came to live here. Have you finished? I've had a busy day and..."

"Did you get back any dicoumarin tablets left after the old lady died?"

"No, I didn't and I was very put-out about it. One can't play about with drugs like that, and though there couldn't have been more than two or three tablets in the box, Mrs. Twigg said she'd thrown them in the fire. I couldn't do anything else but believe her. But I was damned annoyed."

"Did you, by any chance, doctor, tell Mrs. Twigg about the tablets you were giving her mother?"

"I told her they were poisonous, that's all."

"Did she know their name? I mean, knowing the name, she could have found out their nature and purpose in any up-to-date medical dictionary."

"I didn't tell her their name, I know that. But I do recollect that she asked what they were. Were they morphia, or some pain-killing drug? she asked me. I told her, no. They were what we called an anti-coagulant to destroy the clots in the blood and enable the damaged artery to heal. She was quite an intelligent young woman and understood what I was talking about."

"Did you give her a little lecture on the dangers of using too much of the drug?"

"Of course I did. I've known her a long time and it's easy to chat with her. I told her how it acted and how it had been discovered—by the observation of haemorrhagic disease caused in cattle which have eaten rotted sweet clover."

Tompion preened himself a little as he'd probably done when swanking to the charming Mrs. Twigg.

"You've known Mrs. Twigg a long time, you say, doctor. What do you think of her?"

"I like her. Mrs. Laxey had a struggle to bring the girl up after her second husband died. In any event the fellow was a no-good and a sponger. Emily worked hard and later supported her mother. She got a good job as secretary to a shipping chap called Casadessus. I've no doubt she got in disreputable company sometimes. In fact, I know she did. I've seen her driving about in flash cars with bright young men who meant no good to her. I'm sure she was her boss's mistress, too. But she seemed to settle down. Then, she developed debility and I told her the best thing for her was a sea voyage. She went on a cruise and Casadessus paid the bill. He must have rued the day for, on the cruise, she met the man she married."

"He died last week of haemorrhage. A ruptured stomach ulcer, they said. Could it have been dicoumarin?"

Tompion almost fell off the desk.

"What the hell do you mean? Of course it couldn't have been dicoumarin. Are you trying to involve me in something?"

"No. I'm just trying to find out what happened to the remainder of the prescription you gave to Mrs. Laxey."

"I'm sure Emily wouldn't kill anybody. She was too decent a girl. I've known her since she was a kid, and I've always liked her."

"I'm glad to hear it, doctor."

In the lobby of the house, the bell was pealing again. The woman called Amy appeared.

"It's P.C. Gadsby... There's been an accident in Strutt Street. Someone's fallen from a bedroom window. Will you go, Harold?"

"I suppose I'd better... I've had a busy day and now I look like having a busy night. Have *you* finished, officer?"

"Yes, sir. Thank you for seeing me."

"Don't thank me. I'm at everybody's beck and call, so one more or less doesn't matter, does it?"

He rushed off, seized his bag, and slammed the front door behind him without another word. They could hear his footsteps running past the annexe. A harassed practitioner in a very seedy quarter, disappointed, lonely, and doing his best.

Amy led Littlejohn to the door. She looked like a waxwork figure, too. Stiffly respectable, smelling slightly of gin and eau de cologne. Probably she and her brother consoled one another and mourned with each other in their cups.

"I hope you've not upset my brother. He's tired out. It's time he retired."

She opened the door as she spoke and, as she didn't face Littlejohn as she addressed him, she seemed to be talking to herself.

"Good night."

The streets were dark and the lamps were on. An ambulance passed, its bell ringing, and a crowd of women and children followed it eager for the spectacle of a body which had fallen from a third-floor back. A drunken man was singing in the street. "Oh, Genevieve, sweet Genevieve..." The Salvation Army were holding an open-air service three blocks away and their singing mixed with that of the drunkard. "Oh that will be, glory for me..."

A telephone-box shone like a lighthouse at the end of a street a hundred yards away. Littlejohn made for it, shut himself firmly in against the music of the road, and dialled 999. He asked for Scotland Yard.

Through the night the wheels of the law moved fast. Several people were roused from their beds. An exhumation order was issued. An old lady whose house in Rushton Inferior overlooked the graveyard, got up for a dose of bicarbonate of soda, saw dim lights moving among the graves, plunged back into bed, and covered her head with the clothes. Two pathologists from the county laboratory worked in the night. They found that Richard Twigg had died from extensive internal bleeding and that his stomach was free from ruptured ulcers.

By morning, all was as before behind the church in Rushton Inferior. The faded wreaths were back in their places on the grave of Uncle Richard, and Littlejohn, who had travelled back on the midnight train, was eating bacon and eggs.

"You naughty boy," Mrs. Groves was saying coyly, "where have you been all night?"

5
CANK GETS THE SACK

"Certainly, sir. I'll tell her right away."
Cank's politeness gave Littlejohn quite a shock. Instead of being frowned upon and treated with insolence, here he was with Cank tumbling over himself to oblige.

He found Mrs. Twigg up and dressed and she received him in what appeared to be the living-room, a light and airy place at the back of the house, and furnished in expensive antiques.

"I'm glad to see you better, Mrs. Twigg."

"Yes. I've improved distinctly to-day and feel more like myself again."

She looked it, too, whether with the help of art or not it was difficult to guess. She wore a summer frock without sleeves, which accentuated the shapely whiteness of her arms, and she was taller than Littlejohn imagined from seeing her in bed. The people in Strutt Street had been right. She was a good-looker, with just a trace of vulgarity in the swing of her hips as she crossed the room to welcome him. If it could be described as a welcome. Mrs. Twigg looked scared and was obviously wondering what had caused another police visit so soon.

"Cank is much more polite, Mrs. Twigg."

"I spoke to him about his manner. He said he'd been upset by Mr. Twigg's death and the apparent suspicions of the police."

"Who said we were suspicious?"

"Those were Cank's own words. *Are* you suspicious?"

In her anxiety she even forgot to offer Littlejohn a seat.

"I've one or two more questions to ask you, Mrs. Twigg, just to clear up some matters which have puzzled me."

"Sit down, then. Cigarette?"

He asked permission to smoke his pipe, and Mrs. Twigg took a cigarette for herself, and he gave her a light.

"Do you know what these are, Mrs. Twigg?"

He took the envelope of anti-coagulant tablets from his pocket, shook out the contents in his palm, and showed them to her.

If he had expected her to turn pale or fearful, no such thing happened. Instead, she flushed angrily and turned a glance of flaming reproach on him.

"Really, Superintendent, it wasn't fair of you to search among my personal possessions when you were here before. You came to ask me a few questions, not to turn the house upside down for clues."

It was Littlejohn's turn to be irritated. He wondered if this was clever bluff or the real thing.

"What do you mean, Mrs. Twigg?"

"The tablets in that envelope were in a drawer of that desk."

She crossed to an antique escritoire, opened the top, and then slid out one of those famous 'secret drawers' which everybody expects them to contain and everybody knows where to find.

"They were here. Now they've gone. It wasn't fair of you."

"Let us understand each other at once, Mrs. Twigg. This envelope and its contents were found in the pocket of Sergeant Cromwell when he was admitted to hospital, and were handed to me by the doctor."

"So, Mr. Cromwell took them. I can't understand why he should have done that. What reason could he have had?"

"Where did you get them, Mrs. Twigg?"

"They were the remainder of my mother's medicine in her last illness."

"You know what they are and their medical action?"

"They are heart tablets."

"You know more than that, surely. Dr. Tompion told you their exact therapeutic effects on the body."

This time she really turned pale, quickly gathered herself together, and faced him with flaring eyes again.

"I don't understand your activities at all, Superintendent. Have you been looking into my past life and environment? I could easily have told you all you wanted to know without your taking all that trouble. Besides, what have I done wrong to merit this kind of treatment? It isn't as if my husband had died unnaturally. As for Mr. Cromwell, why should I have tried to kill him? I was nowhere near the spot when he was shot."

"You forced me to make enquiries, Mrs. Twigg. You were so obviously hiding something when last I asked you some questions. I'd also point out that you then gave me the impression that your mother was still alive and living in London. Why did you do that?"

She was now completely put-out. She didn't know where to look and finally her eyes met those of Littlejohn in an effort of defiance.

"I don't see that you can make me explain. It was just a slip. I was confused. I'd been unwell and in bed, and I mustn't have known what I was saying."

"I suggest that you didn't wish to speak of your mother's death in case I enquired the cause of it and found out that she had died of coronary thrombosis and discovered what treatment she was given in her last illness."

There was a silence as she tried to understand what it was all about. She looked plainly bewildered, but Littlejohn also sensed a faint relief in her confusion.

In the back garden old Turner came into view. He was scything the grass round the old trees there, paused to hone his blade, spat on his hands, and resumed.

"Or, perhaps, Mrs. Twigg, it was that you didn't wish me to pursue any further the details of your life before you met Mr. Twigg. Is that it?"

This time the shot hit its mark. She was too terrified now even to make a show of protest or bluff.

"There were incidents in your past life which might have spoiled your happiness with Mr. Twigg had he learned of them?"

She shrugged her shoulders at last in despair or resignation.

"He's dead now and past caring. I admit the life I led might have surprised him. He was an upright, decent man, and, for some reason, he thought I was an angel. I've never met a man before who treated me that way. I played up to him. I never admitted I'd had lovers before. It was only natural, wasn't it? He could hardly expect me to have reached my time of life without a love affair or two, but he did, you know. He thought I was a little innocent, I think. He was so happy when I said I'd marry him, I hadn't the heart to tell him the truth."

"Did Cank know about your past life?"

"Do I have to answer all these questions? It's most embarrassing."

"I gather he did. How did he find out?"

"He went to London on business and looked up my old neighbourhood. He must have asked questions there, because, when he came back, there was a change in his behaviour towards me."

"He blackmailed you?"

"He asked for an increase in wages to begin with. He hinted that he'd heard things about my past life which my husband might not like to hear and suggested that I might increase his pay and that of his wife without telling Mr. Twigg."

"And you did?"

"What else could I do?"

"You could have told your husband."

"You didn't know Mr. Twigg. It would have killed him."

"And Cank is still extorting money from you?"

"I... I..."

"I think he is, Mrs. Twigg. Your husband is dead and Cank's source of blackmail in that direction has dried up. Perhaps now he's suggesting he knows something the police would be glad to learn about."

She turned deadly pale again and Littlejohn thought she was going to faint. He crossed to a decanter, poured two fingers of whisky in a glass, and handed it to her.

"Drink that. You'll feel better. And then, you can tell me everything. You'll feel better still then."

She gulped down the neat spirit, coughed, and sat back in her chair.

"I can't..."

"Did you know the cause of your husband's death?"

She replied quite calmly.

"He died from a ruptured stomach ulcer, which brought on very severe haemorrhage. Before they could get him to hospital it had gone too far."

She either didn't know the truth or else she was an amazing actress. She took it all quite naturally and spoke steadily now.

"Were you ever married before?"

A dead shot again! She crumpled up and then drank the remains of the whisky to restore her.

"Is he still alive?"

"I don't know. He left me years ago. I may as well tell you that someone told Cank when he called investigating my past. He is a loathsome creature and I've had to put up with him and his awful wife in this house just because of a foolish mistake I made over fifteen years ago. Alec Finebone was in the Air Force and I married him during the war. You know how things were. You never knew when death was waiting round the corner for you. He went out on a raid and was reported missing. I thought he was dead. He never came back to me. Cank said he was still alive. Someone had told him when he went to Strutt Street, my old home."

"Had he been seeking you?"

"Not exactly. He'd been seen down that way, but he hadn't made an effort to find me. He was quite a decent fellow and I know he wouldn't try to make it difficult for me. But, in the hands of Cank, it was dangerous. It was bigamy. I honestly thought Alec was dead. Else I wouldn't have married again. I swear it."

"You told Cank to be a bit more polite to me lest I suspect there was something of the kind, blackmail or the like?"

"Yes. Words to that effect."

"I see. Cank and his wife had better be sent packing right away, hadn't they? You're not so dependent on them that you need to put up with them any longer."

"I could go in a hotel, couldn't I?"

They were now talking like old friends. She seemed to have no idea that Littlejohn was waiting to fire a more appalling question.

"How many dicoumarin tablets did you save from your mother's prescription?"

"Four. I was just going to ask what you'd done with the other two."

"Why did you tell Dr. Tompion that you'd thrown them away?"

"Have you seen the doctor?"

"Yes. Please answer my question, Mrs. Twigg."

"I thought they might come in useful. One never knows when they might have been needed. It is an illness which comes on suddenly and I thought..."

"Did you think they might be useful in eliminating Cank in a way which would appear natural?"

She swallowed hard and looked at him pitifully like someone in the toils.

"I swear I never used them. I put them away and forgot them. I was desperate, I admit, but I couldn't bring myself to do that even to Cank."

"Did Cank know of the existence of these tablets?"

"I don't know, but I wouldn't be surprised. He was in everything. Nothing was sacred or secret from him."

"Isn't the village chemist's shop just opposite where Mr. Cromwell was shot?"

"I don't exactly know where it happened, but it's past the church, and I believe that's where the shot was fired."

"You're sure you weren't out at the time?"

"I swear I was in bed. You've got to believe me. Why should I want to kill Mr. Cromwell? He was my friend and doing his best for me."

"Have you a telephone where I can speak in private? I don't want Cank listening-in."

"In my bedroom. I'll switch it through and see that Cank doesn't come anywhere near. You know the way?"

"Yes."

Littlejohn looked up the number of the chemist in the directory in the hall and then went to the upstairs instrument. The chemist himself answered.

"Spofforth speaking..."

"Superintendent Littlejohn."

"Good morning; I've heard of you, sir, and I'm glad you're here, I must say. Shocking business about your sergeant, Mr. Cromwell. He was in my place, apparently just before it happened."

"Why didn't you tell the police, then?"

"I've been away until yesterday. My wife's not well and staying with her sister at the seaside. It was early closing the day after the shooting affair, so I closed for the whole day and went to see how my wife was. I left early and only heard what had happened when I opened next morning; that was yesterday. I rang you up and you were out and I rang again before I went to bed at eleven and they said you were still away."

"Very good, Mr. Spofforth. What did you want to tell me?"

"Just that he called here about eleven. The shop was shut, of course, but he knocked on the house door, which is adjacent. I wasn't in bed and as I'm sometimes knocked up when urgent prescriptions are needed, I let him in."

On and on. The monotonous voice droned over the telephone. A soporific voice, which might have made anyone nod-off in other circumstances.

"...He'd got some tablets he wanted to know about. I recognized them at once, but promised to confirm my views next morning, when I'd had a chance to examine them expertly. They were dicoumarin, a drug which..."

"Yes, I know, Mr. Spofford. What happened?"

"The name's Spofforth. There were four of them. Mr. Cromwell left two with me and kept the rest himself in an envelope. I asked him where he found them. He was evasive, sir. But there was one tablet that had been crushed. He said he'd trodden on it. I didn't quite understand what he meant, but, knowing his work might have been confidential and police, I didn't press the point. I examined the tablets after he'd gone. They were dicoumarin. He left the one he said he'd trodden on with me. I think that's all, sir."

"How long was he with you?"

"About half an hour. We got chatting about one thing and another. He's interested in bird-watching and so am I. We smoked a pipe together. Then I let him out. I don't know what direction he took when he left, but he paused, I know, in the shop doorway to light a cigarette and stood there for a little while, apparently thinking. Then I heard him go."

"Thank you so much, sir. That's very useful. I'll call to see you later, if I may. By the way, did you happen to hear a shot?"

"No. Nothing like that. I'm sorry. A pleasure, Superintendent. I'd like to meet you..."

Mrs. Twigg was waiting in the hall below, taking care that Cank didn't overhear what was going on.

"Do you mind asking Cank to join us, Mrs. Twigg? You are, I gather, prepared to discharge him and his wife."

"Most certainly, I am. I've told you what the hold over me has been and I've burned my boats. I'm in your hands, Superintendent. I hope it won't mean trouble. They send you to prison for bigamy, I believe."

She was resigned now and looked it.

"Probably not in this case. In any event, if you've told me the truth and are doing your best to help me settle this business, I shan't forget it, and I'll do all I can to help you, too. And now for Cank."

Still he hadn't told her the result of the autopsy on Richard Twigg, nor did he intend to do so, yet. That would come at a more appropriate time. They went in the living-room again. Mrs. Twigg hesitated and then rang the bell.

"Cank used to resent my ringing for him and I got into the habit of seeking him or calling for him."

The look on Cank's face when he entered confirmed what she had said. He glared at Mrs. Twigg and then at the bell-push.

"Yes?"

"I just wanted to tell you, Cank, that your services and those of Mrs. Cank are dispensed with as from to-day. I'll pay you wages in lieu of notice but you can start packing at once."

The rocket seemed to hit Cank full on the chin. His jaw dropped and then a cunning look came in his eyes.

"If that's the way you want it. All right. We'll go. But I'd like to speak to you in private first. I don't know if it's convenient right away. I'll see you later, then."

He turned to go, smiling to himself.

"Don't go, Cank."

The man spun round as Littlejohn spoke.

"I've one or two things to ask you before you start filling your bags."

"I've got to go and tell the missus."

"You'll do that later. You'll stay now and listen to what I have to say."

Cank turned and gave the pair of them a malevolent sneer. Littlejohn was reminded for all the world of the old gothic novels of a past generation. Cank seemed to exude an atmosphere of evil. The spirit of him seemed to hang about the house, an aura of corruption and wickedness. Even now, the man hadn't given in. He leaned impudently on one arm extended and resting on the wall.

"Come here."

Cank couldn't believe his ears. His narrow little eyes grew shifty and, as he slowly moved towards Littlejohn, he pulled himself up to his full height and thrust out his stomach in an effort of bravado.

"You dirty little blackmailer!"

Cank jumped to the defensive right away.

"Look here, I'm not goin' to be slandered and bullied by you or anybody else. I know the law and you've no right."

"Then you'll know you can be punished stiffly for blackmail."

"I don't know what you're talkin' about."

"Yes, you do. You've been holding Mrs. Twigg's past over her head for quite a long time. That's all over as far as she's concerned and, as she cannot bear the sight of you, you're being given notice to quit."

"I'll have the law on her. She can't do that to me. I've served her and the late Mr. Twigg loyally for years. Now he's gone she's chucking us out like a pair of old shoes. Well, I'm not standin' for it. Police or no police, I'm goin' to have my rights. Nobody's goin' to slander me and get away with it."

"Did you ever see these before?"

Littlejohn produced the envelope again and shook the dicoumarin tablets into his palm.

For a second, Cank was taken off guard; then he recovered.

"What's them?"

"They're the tablets you were examining when Mr. Cromwell suddenly entered. You'd found them in the bureau and, in your haste to put them back in the drawer, you dropped one on the floor. I don't think he'd have taken much interest in finding you rifling the old master's escritoire if he hadn't happened to put his foot on the tablet you dropped. When he found it, he naturally looked in the desk to find out what you'd been up to."

"He's recovered consciousness, has he, and told you? Well, I'll tell you why I looked in the desk."

"No. Mr. Cromwell's still not fit to speak, but my theory seems to fit the case. Go on, Cank..."

"You've tricked me. Suppose I said I know nothin' about the tablets? Which is true."

"No, it isn't, Cank. You're a liar. Now tell me what you were after or I'll run you in, now. There's enough in your unsavoury catalogue of crime to get you quite a stretch. Blackmail, for instance."

"So, Mrs. Twigg's been tryin' to turn you against me, has she? Well, as I said, I've always been faithful and discreet while I've been 'ere. There are limits. I might as well tell you the reason why I was huntin' around was that in my opinion Mr. Twigg died unnatural. There was somethin' queer about the way he died. One day he was in the pink; the next dead. It was wrong some way. So I searched to see if I could find anythin' suspicious. I was on the lookout for poison, I'll admit it. Well, I found the tablets. I'd naturally no right to start a row till I knew what sort of tablets they were. So, when I heard Mr. Cromwell outside the room, I just popped 'em back where I'd got 'em from. No harm in that, is there?"

"Where did you get all the information about Mrs. Twigg's past life?"

"I don't know what she's been tellin' you about me, but I never did her any wrong."

"Not out of benevolence, though, Cank. Just because she paid you to keep your mouth shut. Now tell me where you got your information about her."

"It wasn't very much. Mere gossip."

Cank, now wheedling and trying to paint himself as a faithful servant, was smiling, shrugging his shoulders, taking it all nonchalantly again.

"Suppose you answer my question."

"Mrs. Twigg's mother was ill, as you no doubt know. Mr. Twigg was always a good-hearted man, but he'd got so he never liked going very far from Rushton. He liked it 'ere and he'd his pals and a little routine every day. He sent me to London, instead of goin' himself. Mrs. Twigg wasn't well at the time. There was a letter to go—which I guessed contained money—some fruit, some flowers... He was a decent sort."

Mrs. Twigg said nothing. She still gazed at Cank with loathing as though she'd realized more than ever now the nature of the man who had been living under her own roof.

"Go on..."

"The neighbours was talkative. They told me quite a lot about Mrs. Laxey and Mrs. Twigg. I regarded it a mere gossip, if you get what I mean."

"I certainly get what you mean. You've held what you call gossip over Mrs. Twigg's head ever since. Perhaps you were too clever to ask outright for a lump sum. Instead, you took it in high wages. Am I right?"

"No you're not and if she says so, it's a lie."

"It's for Mrs. Twigg to decide what to do with you. If she prefers charges, you'll have to face a trial."

Cank waved his arms about.

"If she does, I'll make it damn 'ot for her. I know a lot of things that'll come out in court. She'll not be able to hold 'er head up in this neighbourhood after I've finished with her."

"There you go again, Cank. You're even having the impertinence to try blackmail under my very nose. What did you learn from the gossips of the Edgware Road?"

"All about 'er carryin's-on with a chap called Casadessus she worked for... and he wasn't the only one."

"I'm not asking about that. What about Mrs. Twigg's first husband? I believe you said he was still alive."

"I never did. I said no such thing."

Cank was now injured and innocent. His mean little eyes turned on Mrs. Twigg in reproach.

"'As she said I did?"

Mrs. Twigg was on her feet.

"You know you did. You said you knew where to get in touch with him."

"I never. I did you the kindness of tellin' you that Alec Finebone, your first 'usband, was dead. You know I did. I said he'd turned up in Strutt Street askin' about you years ago, and then he got a job as a test pilot an' crashed. I told you he was dead."

"You did no such thing. You said he'd been enquiring for me and there the story ended. You hinted that I'd committed bigamy in marrying Mr. Twigg."

Littlejohn interrupted the row.

"This is getting us nowhere. I'll leave you to settle matters between you. If you've any trouble with Cank, let me know, and we'll see he leaves the house peaceably. As for you, Cank, if you do leave, you'd better not go far. We shall need you. Better get digs in the village till you find a job and can give us a new permanent address. No monkey tricks, now."

"As if I would. But you've got me all wrong. I've always done my best. She just wants to get rid of me now the boss is gone. After all I've done, too."

"You mentioned Mr. Twigg's routine. What was it?"

"He was reg'lar as clockwork. Wet or fine he went out every mornin' for a meetin' with his cronies. He used to play a round of golf at one time, but he gave it up. He'd walk round the village. Any news of trouble... I mean sickness or poor people, he'd put his hand in his pocket. A proper toff that way. Four of them used to meet and, as the pubs wasn't open, they'd often have a cup of coffee together and play dominoes for an hour or 'ave a few rounds of cards and a talk and a smoke."

"Where?"

"Well, they used to go reg'lar to the *Weatherby*. They'd a table there they called their own. Sometimes one or two of 'em would stay on there for lunch. But after Mr. Twigg got married, he seemed to grow out of the *Weatherby*."

"Why?"

Cank leered and passed his hand over his loose mouth.

"Well... You know Mrs. Groves is a bit odd. Too free and easy and familiar, like, with the men. It's all right for a bit of fun if you 'appen to be unmarried, but a married man, specially Mr. Twigg, who's jest brought home his wife, he'd naturally feel he didn't want it. You get me?"

"Yes, I do."

"So, him and his pals started to patronize the *Green Door*, a café nearly opposite the *Weatherby*."

"What about the remainder of the routine, as you call it?"

"After his lunch, he'd have a nap and then...well... I'm really tellin' you the things Mrs. Twigg could tell better. He worked in the garden on nice days, didn't he? Or took Mrs. Twigg for a walk or a run in the car. That's right, isn't it, Mrs. Twigg? Then, in the evenin' he always went to the *Bull and Bush*, a mile away at Rushton Superior. His pals met him there for an hour and then they'd come back in one or another's car. That's so, Mrs. Twigg, isn't it?"

No reply.

"Who were these pals, as you call them?"

"Three retired men. One a bank manager called Temple; a chap called Wise, who farms near Rushton Superior as a kind of 'obby; and an ex-local auctioneer called Wainwright. They was a sort of little club and all good friends. To see 'em together did you good."

"What are their Christian names, Cank?"

Cank rubbed his stubbly chin.

"They've called 'ere from time to time and I've 'eard them address one another by their first names. Let me think. Henry Temple, Joseph Wise and Frederick Wainwright... Yes, that's it."

Harry, Joe and Fred, of the *Bull and Bush*!

"They still go to the *Green Door* and the *Bull and Bush,* do you know?"

"Mr. Wise hasn't been for a bit. He's been ill, but he's gettin' around again now, I believe."

"What's been wrong with him?"

"I heard it was coronary thrombosis. Surprising the number who..."

He didn't get any further. Mrs. Twigg, who had been listening to the conversation languidly, without saying a word, gave a faint cry and fell to the floor in a dead faint.

6

THE LANDLORD OF THE SILLY BILLY

It only needed a glass of water to put Mrs. Twigg right and then Littlejohn left her. He did so with puzzled feelings. The fainting fit hadn't seemed quite genuine. She had sagged down on a soft spot on the hearthrug and recovered too easily. Had it been that she had wanted to put a stop to further questions? Or, had the perpetual topic of coronary thrombosis begun seriously to upset her? The whole business seemed to be a muddle. Switching first to Cromwell, then to Twigg, with Mrs. Twigg rapidly becoming suspect number one and Cank running a close second.

Littlejohn took the small police car and drove himself to Manchester. On his way, he stopped at a country pub for lunch. There wasn't much peace there. There was a wedding-party in progress and they even sent a glass of champagne to Littlejohn's table, and he drank the health of the loving couple. The head waiter confided to Littlejohn that he was fed-up and going back to London as soon as he could, and the pretty waitress, finding him courteous and cheerful, told Littlejohn she was only there learning the ropes and wanted to be an air-hostess; perhaps he could help? As he left, the landlord asked him if he knew anybody who wanted to buy a good pub as he himself was fed-up, too, and anxious to get out.

In Manchester, Littlejohn met his wife and Mrs. Cromwell. They were both more cheerful. Cromwell had now recovered consciousness and was getting along nicely.

"But you can only stay five minutes; rest is essential," said the sister, a nice girl who was relieving the regular one whose day-off it was. She was dark and good-looking, but when she wasn't busy her face wore a scared, melancholy look. A young American doctor who had been in the hospital on study-leave for a year had written on his return to Texas to say that he couldn't settle down without her. Would she cross the Atlantic and marry him? She was off at the end of the month. She dreamed at night and had visions by day of vast sandy wastes sprouting enormous cactus bushes, and huge rocks like nightmare cinema organs, and chains of purple mountains peopled by gun-slingers and men who spoke in a strange, drawling tongue. Her education about her new home had been derived from the picture-house down the road, which she frequented when off duty.

"Have you ever been to Texas, Superintendent?" she asked Littlejohn, àpropos of nothing at all, and when he looked surprised, she told him it didn't matter and that he mustn't talk to Cromwell yet.

The surgeon arrived to have a word or two with Littlejohn. He had just finished an operating session and still wore his white gown.

"How is he, sir?"

"Getting along fine, now. He's a lucky man. Another fraction of an inch and he might have died, or, at least, been badly damaged for the rest of his life."

"Could I have a word with him? He needn't reply. I'm anxious to get hold of whoever shot him and I badly need his help."

"Let's go and have a try. A minute or so won't do him any harm. Don't press him hard."

"I won't."

Mrs. Cromwell and Littlejohn's wife discreetly withdrew from the bedside as the two men approached.

Cromwell's face lit up at the sight of the Superintendent and he tried to say something. He still looked pale and exhausted in his turban of bandages. Littlejohn tapped his hand which lay outside the bedclothes.

"Don't try to talk, old chap. We're all glad you're getting better and you'll soon be back with us. The doctor says I can ask you a question or two. Don't try to speak. Just raise your forefinger a bit if the answer's 'yes' and make no sign if it's 'no'. Get it?"

The forefinger twitched.

"You left your uncle's house and walked to the village chemist's. You were there half an hour, left, crossed the road, and then were shot?"

A pause. Cromwell's eyes were on Littlejohn's face but he didn't move.

"He doesn't know what's the matter with him," explained the surgeon. "We haven't told him yet."

Littlejohn repeated his question but instead of mentioning the bullet, said 'you remembered nothing more'.

The finger was raised.

"You found a crushed white tablet near your uncle's desk and went to the chemist to try and find out what it was."

The answer was in the affirmative.

"Did you suspect foul play against your uncle?"

The answer was 'No'.

"So, it was just the finding of the tablet which started your suspicions?"

The finger was raised again.

"And that was as far as it went? No suspects?"

No.

"Did you see who shot at you? You see, someone shot you. That is why you're here."

No, again. This time Cromwell seemed relieved. Now that he knew what had happened, a load was lifted from his mind, obviously. He even smiled slightly.

"You don't know anyone who might have wished to keep you silent?"

No movement of the finger.

"I think that had better be enough," interposed the doctor. "We don't want to tire him. I hope it's helped you."

"Very much."

He bent and patted Cromwell's hand again.

"You've been a great help, old man. Now you must rest. I'll be back to see you to-morrow. I'm staying here until I can take you home with me."

He left him with Mrs. Cromwell and, bidding his wife goodbye, too, set out for Rushton.

He drove abstractedly. Candidly, Cromwell's replies had given him no lead at all. The sergeant had simply found Cank handling the tablets from Richard Twigg's desk, come upon one of them crushed on the carpet, and taken it to the chemist to satisfy his own curiosity. Twigg had died from an overdose of the anticoagulant, but Cromwell hadn't known that. And, as he emerged from the chemist's he'd been wantonly shot. Shot by a weapon which, judging from the bullet, was almost a toy; a pop-gun, to use the surgeon's words.

Littlejohn felt completely at sea. It seemed as though the emotion of investigating the crime against his friend had got mixed up with the case and fogged his powers of perception and deduction. He felt hot and tired and decided that a cup of tea would do him good. He was near the *William IV*, the hotel at which he'd had his lunch and from which the owner and staff seemed anxious to part. Colloquially known as the *Silly Billy* by the natives, the place was rapidly becoming a road-house and Littlejohn pulled-in to get himself his tea.

The same waitress served him and asked him again if he knew

who could help her to become an air-hostess. He recommended that she should write to the airline offices. She said she would and brought him an extra couple of soiled-looking ice-topped cakes as a reward. He finally rose to go, feeling much better for the change. In the passage by the door, the landlord was talking to another man.

"Have a drink, doctor?"

"You know it isn't hours. Besides, I never take it when I'm driving. You ought to know that by now."

Littlejohn turned and saw that it was Dr. Clinton, of Wiston Purlieu. The doctor took no heed of him, but walked to where his car was parked, jumped in, and drove off without a word of goodbye to the landlord.

Shoesmith—for so he was named on the licensing sign over the door—turned to look for someone to complain to and his eye fell on Littlejohn.

"By God! If that chap wasn't such a good doctor and my wife won't have anybody else, I'd take a runnin' kick at the seat of his pants. I never knew such a rude blighter."

"Is your wife ill, then, landlord?"

"Arthritis. She can hardly walk sometimes. It's the district. Built on clay. Rheumaticky as hell all around here. If you know anybody as wants a pub, let me know. As soon as I can be rid, I'm off down south where it's dry. Then my missus'll pick up and we can get a new doctor. Clinton gets my goat good and proper. And yet, the women are mad on him. My wife thinks the world of him and many's the row we've had when I've expressed my mind about him. What women can see in some chaps beats me. Rude and uncouth, that's what I call him. But he must have some attraction for 'em. I can't see any..."

"Is he a ladies' man?"

"You might say yes and you might say no. I could tell you a thing or two, and it wouldn't be gossip either. I've had it from a good source."

The landlord closed his mouth tightly, apparently pondering whether or not to confide in Littlejohn. The Superintendent waited.

Then something seemed to strike the landlord. He looked a bit put-out.

"I don't want you to think I'm referring to my wife and the doctor."

"Of course not."

"He'd better not try his games on here. Strictly professional are his visits to the *William*. If I thought... Well... I'd kick him all the way back to Wiston..."

The landlord of the *Silly Billy* took out a packet of cigarettes, stuck one at an angle in the corner of his mouth, and gave one to Littlejohn, who lighted them both with a match.

They stood at the door of the inn looking across the sunlit fields to the hills, with clumps of fine old trees breaking the view on the rising ground.

"To look at Clinton and hear him talk, you'd think he hadn't any vices. Doesn't smoke, won't take a glass of beer, always prim and proper. That is, when he's in the company of the likes of me. I'm not good enough for him to smoke or drink with. He only does that with the gentry."

"He's a snob?"

"You're tellin' me. But I know a thing or two about doctor clever Clinton."

Shoesmith paused again. This time it was for effect. There was an aroma of whisky about Shoesmith which gave the reason for Clinton's distaste and his own funny mood.

"He carries on with a married woman, on the side. Or, at least, she was married till a few days ago, when her elderly husband kicked the bucket. Now Clinton will be able to make an honest woman of 'er. He's a childless widower. The pair of them can team-up and spend the old chap's money."

"Who's the old chap?"

"Fellow called Twigg, at Rushton Inferior. Worth a packet, they say. It was his missus. They kept it dark, 'er and Clinton between them, but sometimes, when they're desperate, caution goes by the board, doesn't it? They made a slip...or rather, she did. I got to know."

"How did it happen?"

Shoesmith paused and turned to Littlejohn with a stubborn look.

"Who *are* you, anyway? I like you, but I really shouldn't be shootin' off my mouth like this to a stranger. You might be a relative or friend of the doctor or his lady friend and then I might be in a mess. Slander, you know. I once knew a fellow..."

"My name's Littlejohn. Superintendent Littlejohn, of Scotland Yard. You'll have heard of the detective-sergeant who was shot in Rushton the other night. He's a colleague of mine and I'm here inquiring about it."

"You should have said so at first. I don't want to get mixed up with the police by talking too much. In any case, Clinton and Mrs. Twigg aren't concerned with your case, so we'll let it drop, if you don't mind."

Somewhere a stable clock struck five. There was hardly a soul about. Now and then a car passed, but there was nobody in for tea and the iced cakes looked like having to wait for yet another day.

"Look at this. Not a soul in for tea. I was done good and proper when I took over here. They said it was a gold mine. Must have cooked the books. I'm just making ends meet. Now, you wouldn't like a nice country pub to retire to, would you, sir? It could be worked-up, you know. Only the wife isn't too well. Else I'd have made a go of it. Know what they call this pub locally? The *Silly Billy*. It's me who's the Silly Billy..."

He lit another cigarette.

"If it hadn't been closing hours and you the police, I'd have offered you a drink on the house with me just to drown my disappointment."

"I think you'd better tell me the end of the story about the doctor and Mrs. Twigg. You see, the man who was shot was Mr. Twigg's nephew."

The landlord smiled bitterly and gave vent to his smoker's cough. When he'd recovered his wind and his colour, which had turned livid from his contortions, he spoke huskily.

"I seem to have landed myself in a bit of a mess talking too fast, don't I?"

A small, paunchy man with dark protruding eyes, fat cheeks and a little waxed moustache, he looked like a shrunken retired sergeant-major.

"This'll be in confidence. Not that it isn't true, but I don't want any bother. I've my customers and the goodwill of the pub to think of. Agreed?"

"Right."

"It's simple. I've got a pal who keeps the *Royal George* at Siseley, seven miles in the Chester direction. With the missus bein' what you'd call hors di combat...or it is hors di oovre?... I don't know which, but it doesn't matter. I mean with her not gettin' out, I stay with her in the day and, after we close at night, I take the car to Siseley and have a drink with the Stubbses at the *George*. I've got to get away from the place now an' then, else I'd go right off me chump. Well, it seems Clinton and the Twigg woman met there one day. It's well outside the eyes of the locals here and the doctor's patients. That's why they met there, I suppose. But, mind you, the doctor didn't like it."

"In other words, Mrs. Twigg made the rendezvous?"

"Eh? Oh, I see what you mean. Yes. She sent for 'im."

"Why didn't he like it?"

"Said it was dangerous. Stubbs overheard them. They was alone in the tea-room there in the middle of the afternoon with nobody else about. They wasn't there long. She wanted to tell him her husband had tumbled to what was goin' on."

"Rather a long way to go for such a short talk."

"Oh, you haven't got what I mean. Stubbs said she seemed crazy about the doctor. And him just a bit cool and afraid somebody might come along and catch 'em at it. But you know what women are when they're that way. They throw caution to the winds, don't they? Stubbs said from what he could gather she'd been callin' on the doctor as a patient and then they'd started carryin'-on together. The doctor was sayin' she couldn't call at his house any more. She was put-out and said she wouldn't give 'im up, and he said he'd think of somethin' and ring her up. She said not to use the phone. Somebody was always about listenin'..."

"That would be Cank, their servant. He's probably as good an eavesdropper as your friend Stubbs."

"He's a decent chap, is Stubbs. He said he was just outside the door comin' in for their order when he heard them talkin' quiet and confidential-like, and didn't think it right to disturb them. He only stood waitin' for a minute or two."

"A long two minutes."

"Eh? Then they closed the door. They'd been kissin', Stubbs said. The doctor was wipin' lipstick off his cheek and not lookin' so pleased, when they came out."

"Well, well."

"It always comes out sooner or later, doesn't it?"

"I suppose it does."

The would-be air-hostess appeared and inquired of Mr. Shoesmith how many dinners he was expecting to serve later. Mr. Shoesmith looked annoyed.

"How the 'ell do I know, Irene? Last night we prepared for fifteen and 'ow many turned up? Four. Saturday we got ready for twenty, and how many was it then? Well? Forty-one! Me rushing round the countryside for food and the customers waitin' and playin' merry 'ell. This place is haunted. *Silly Billy.* You can't do a thing right. All right. Get ready for twenty again. There'll either be four or forty-four..."

The air-hostess shrugged her shoulders without a word,

smiled at Littlejohn, and walked away, swinging her hips as though she were already in the gangway of a plane bound for foreign parts.

Littlejohn bade the landlord good-bye and assured him again of his discretion. Mr. Shoesmith delivered a parting shot by once more offering to sell the *Silly Billy* cheaply to Littlejohn.

"You know as well as I do, policemen make good landlords when they retire. They know the law and can 'andle people properly. Think it over and let me know."

The latest information was food for a lot of thought. On the face of it, it seemed to have little to do with Cromwell's affair. But it gave rise to many unpleasant ideas about the death of Richard Twigg and how far his young wife and his doctor had been involved in it. Littlejohn determined to tackle the doctor right away. The next signpost pointed the way to Wiston Purlieu and he turned down the lane to get there.

Wiston was obviously the metropolis of a fair-sized country area. An old town with a number of pleasant Georgian brick houses still remaining in the main street. Here and there the line was unpleasantly broken by a multiple store or a new chromium-plated shop-front. The shopping centre filled one busy main thoroughfare and the side-streets held two cinemas, a dance-hall, the fire-station and the town hall. The police station was nowhere to be seen, but later proved to be hidden by the lurid poster-boards of the picture-house which adjoined it.

Dr. Clinton occupied one of the old houses on the High Street. Littlejohn rang the bell and a housekeeper told him the doctor was not at home and, in any case, it wasn't surgery hours. These she indicated by a wave of the hand in the direction of a brass plate which gave full details.

So much for that. It would have to be Mrs. Twigg again. Littlejohn thought out how he would tackle her when he got back to Rushton Inferior, but there, too, he found the bird had flown. Cank answered the door of *Ballarat*.

"She's not in."

"I thought she wasn't well enough to go out of doors, yet."

"Well, she's gone."

Cank looked very pleased with himself again. He gave Littlejohn a cocky smile as he spoke.

"She went out half an hour ago. Said she thought a breath of fresh air would do her good."

"Have you packed your bags yet?"

"No. I'm not goin' now. The missus and Mrs. Twigg and me talked it over reasonable and proper, like, and it ended up by her sayin' she'd overlook the past and keep us on."

"Is that so? I'd better come inside, Cank. You and I have matters to talk over."

"Let me tell you, Superintendent, that my leavin' or stoppin' on here has nothing to do with the police. It's up to Mrs. Twigg and 'er alone, and I hope you aren't goin' to be awkward again about it."

"No. But I'll come inside. There are other matters. Lead on, Cank."

Cank made way for him to enter and then took him to the room at the back of the house in which they had talked earlier in the day.

"Is Mrs. Twigg likely to be away long?"

"I couldn't say and I didn't ask 'er. I know my place."

"I doubt it. Now, Cank, what further arguments have you used to force Mrs. Twigg to keep you on?"

Cank made an evil attempt to be suave and keep his temper.

"None whatever. You keep doin' me a great injustice, sir, with all these insinuations. I only want to be left in peace to do my proper work. Why keep tryin' to drive me out? I never did you any wrong."

"What can you tell me about the friendly relations between Mrs. Twigg and Dr. Clinton, Cank? You're always about the place when the doctor's here. How do they get on together?"

Cank was a bit stumped. He didn't know how much Littlejohn knew and now had to do some cautious stalking to find out.

"What do you mean, sir?"

"I think you know. Were the pair of them very friendly? Did they ever meet when Mr. Twigg was out on what you call his daily routine?"

"She was a patient of the doctor, of course, and they met in that respect. As for anything beyond that, I couldn't say."

Again, there was something evil about the demeanour of Cank, either his faint leer or his pose, which betrayed him, but which gave no loophole for a definite accusation.

"Did Mr. Twigg die at home?"

"Yes, sir. He was to go to hospital, but was too weak to move when the ambulance arrived. He died shortly after."

"Was Dr. Clinton here at the time?"

"Yes. He came and stayed about an hour, till Mr. Twigg passed on."

"We'll say until he *died*, if you don't mind, Cank. Did Dr. Clinton issue the death certificate?"

"I suppose so."

"*Did* he?"

"Yes."

"Then why didn't you say so straight out? Did you know he issued it?"

"Yes."

Cank licked his lips and rubbed his damp hands together.

"You said earlier that you suspected foul play. What did you mean, Cank?"

"What I said. He was took ill quickly and died quickly. I didn't like it."

"Did you tell the doctor?"

"No. It was no business of mine. The doctor had attended Mr. Twigg for ulcers in the past."

"It was your business, if you suspected foul play, to tell someone responsible about it. Why didn't you?"

"I thought the doctor ought to know."

"Yet you began to rifle the desk to find out if any poison still remained there?"

"I wanted to be sure before I talked."

"Mr. Cromwell was in the house, staying here. He was a police officer and, if you were in his company any length of time, you found him very genial, approachable, and easy to talk to. Why didn't you tell him?"

"It didn't strike me at the time."

"I suggest you wanted to keep the information for yourself to use as a lever against Mrs. Twigg to get your own way."

Cank gulped and rolled his head from side to side. His hands clenched and relaxed and then clenched again.

"I don't know why you keep pickin' on me that way, sir. I've only done what I thought was best. It's unjust and unfair to accuse me of blackmail."

The man twisted and whined until Littlejohn could stand it no longer. He seized Cank by the lapels of his coat and shook him. He could feel his hot evil breath on his face and it nauseated him.

"Now, Cank, tell me at once..."

Suddenly a car, Mrs. Twigg's two-seater coupé, pulled up at the gate of *Ballarat* and she stepped out. She looked hot and put-out and hurried to the front door.

Littlejohn flung Cank away. The man retired crab-wise for the door, pointing a finger at the Superintendent.

"You'd no right to manhandle me and you know it. I know the law and I'm goin' to Wiston the first chance I get and report this to the police there. You'd no right..."

He vanished to open the door. Littlejohn waited and could hear him talking to his mistress.

"That Superintendent's here again. He's been bullyin' and

tryin' to push me around. Well, I'm goin' to report him after dinner. He can't do that to Roger Cank... I've got my rights..."

Emily Twigg entered hastily. This time, she looked afraid, as though something had happened since last they met which had terrified her.

"Did you want me again, Superintendent?"

"I've been to see Mr. Cromwell."

"How is he?"

"Doing well. I was able to speak with him a bit."

She didn't register any fears on that score but stood waiting for what he had to say.

"I hear you have made your peace with Cank, Mrs. Twigg."

"Yes. What am I to do if they leave me? I can't run this place alone."

"I would have thought a spell in an hotel would be preferable to his company here."

Littlejohn crossed and closed the door almost in the face of Cank who was pretending to dust the cupboard in the hall. He returned and faced Mrs. Twigg.

"He didn't happen to threaten to tell me of the friendship which exists between you and your doctor, Clinton, Mrs. Twigg?"

She turned pale and staggered back, groped for a chair, and sat down. Her hands trembled so much that she could not remove her gloves, although she tried hard.

"I don't know what you mean."

"I'm sorry, Mrs. Twigg, but I know all about it and I'm afraid you'll have to tell me everything and about the circumstances of your husband's death. Otherwise, I shall have to ask you to come with me to the police station and make a proper official statement."

He felt sorry for her. She was completely bewildered and looked here and there as though seeking some source of help or relief.

"We were good friends..."

Almost a whisper, with, in it, a plea not to press the point, but to accept what she said as the whole truth.

"More than friends, Mrs. Twigg. He was your lover, wasn't he, and your husband found out?"

"I was often lonely and on my own. As time passed, my husband found better company in men of his own age. He was always good to me, but he left me a lot. Dr. Clinton was nearer my age and we had similar tastes... He was lonely, too... We went about together..."

She was groping for words, trying to avoid a full confession.

"But I swear it had nothing to do with my husband's death. He died of haemorrhage from an ulcer. I swear I didn't ..."

Another car at the gate. This time Dr. Clinton, who bounded out and almost ran up the path. Cank brought him in with a look bordering on triumph.

"The doctor."

Clinton didn't pause for breath. He marched right up to Littlejohn, fists clenched, lips tight, his eyes flashing behind his glasses.

"I'm told you've been wanting me. What is it? And why, may I ask, do you keep pestering Mrs. Twigg? She's been through quite enough."

"Calm yourself, doctor. Did you know I would call here? And why are you so anxious to prevent my questioning Mrs. Twigg?"

"I enquired in the village and was told you were here. I came at once. Mrs. Twigg is my patient and I forbid ..."

"*Forbid*, doctor? She must decide that. Either she and you answer my questions or you both come with me to the police station at Wiston."

Clinton jumped and then thrust his face into Littlejohn's.

"You don't mean to say you are, for some reason, committing the unspeakable folly of arresting us. Because I propose to ring up my lawyer right away. Neither of us had anything to do with the shooting of Cromwell."

"No, doctor, perhaps not that. But you signed a death certificate for the late Mr. Twigg."

"What of it? He died from natural causes."

"Last night, his body was exhumed by special order from the Home Office."

"What!!"

"He didn't die from a ruptured stomach ulcer, doctor. He died from internal haemorrhage due to overdoses of an anti-coagulant called dicoumarin. In other words, we suspect he was murdered."

All the stuffing seemed to ebb from Clinton. He suddenly sagged and became an old man. And with a cry of pain, Mrs. Twigg fell unconscious and this time it was a genuine case.

7
THE HOME LIFE OF A PHYSICIAN

Clinton took matters in hand right away and with professional competence. He opened the door, revealed Cank standing there listening intently, and brought him in the room. Caught in the very act, Cank was completely out of countenance.

"Get Mrs. Cank and the pair of you take Mrs. Twigg to her room. Tell your wife to put her to bed. She's fainted. I'll see her before I leave."

Cank was in a hurry to get away and do as he was bid. Mrs. Cank appeared, gave Littlejohn a pitying reproachful glare, as though he had caused it all and much more besides, and helped her husband out of the room, with Mrs. Twigg between them, now half recovered and able to stagger along with some assistance.

Clinton closed the door behind them and returned to face Littlejohn.

"And now, Superintendent...?"

Clinton's manner had changed completely. It was still distant, but more cordial. He had shed his professional manner, his air of resenting the intrusion of a stranger in the affairs of his patient. With Mrs. Twigg out of the way, they were now meeting on equal terms.

"I suppose you know all about me by now, Superintendent?"

The doctor said it calmly and without irony. It was like an opponent playing an opening gambit, from which all the other moves will originate.

"Hardly, sir. I've heard a lot about you. I'm particularly interested in your late patient, Mr. Twigg, and his death."

There was a silence, disturbed now and then by the humming of the motor-mower in the back garden and the noises of passing cars.

"You think I killed Twigg?"

A brutal question, but fair enough.

Littlejohn made no excuses and remained as calm as the doctor.

"Until early this morning, I had no interest in Richard Twigg. My one concern was that someone in this village had shot my colleague. Almost fortuitously, enquiries have led me to discover that the death of his uncle, which brought Cromwell here, was not from natural causes, or, at least, not as certified by his medical attendant."

Another pause. Both men were standing face to face, a yard apart. Clinton was as tall as Littlejohn, but lacked his breadth and strength. He was thin and his shoulders stooped. A clever face with a high forehead, and receding dark hair. Aquiline features, and a clean, well-groomed look about him. An intelligent, penetrating look, and a precise, authoritative way.

"What time is dinner at the *Weatherby?*"

Littlejohn looked hard at Clinton. It was the only way to keep amazement from his face. An irrelevant, almost infantile question, the kind used to make conversation when interest is flagging.

"Any time. Half-past eight will suit me. Why?"

"It's almost seven... Could we talk elsewhere? What about letting me drive you to my place at Wiston? I've no surgery tonight. I don't care to stay here any longer than I need. There are eyes and ears everywhere since Twigg died. Especially those of the Canks. We could be private at my house. Besides, you'll fetch up there sooner or later. You might as well come now."

Was it a confession, or an offer of friendship? Littlejohn couldn't make out, but Clinton didn't wait for an answer.

"I'll go up and see that Mrs. Twigg is all right. Then I'll join you. I won't be above five minutes."

Littlejohn sat down and lit his pipe. The doctor climbed the stairs at a leisurely pace, stayed a minute or two, and then descended. He went to his car and returned with a small case under his arm. Then he mounted the stairs again, presumably to give Mrs. Twigg a sedative. He was back almost at once.

"Ready?"

They might have been going for a joy-ride.

Conversation was casual on the way. Clinton, far from being tense like someone suspected, was more friendly. He even smiled in a rueful kind of way and offered Littlejohn a cigarette. It was of a brand Littlejohn had not met before; long, fat, and in rice paper. Like everything else about Clinton, it was expensive and fastidious. The car in which they were travelling was of the fast, costly variety and well-kept.

The road ran between tall hedges punctuated by old trees which spread a leafy canopy right across the road. Large houses here and there, many almost hidden by gardens. It was the time of day when the scent of trees and flowers is at its best and the birds, stimulated by the setting sun, were shouting an evensong so loud in parts that it was difficult to make conversation without raising the voice.

"You aren't from London? I mean, you don't originate from there?"

It could have been that Clinton was civilly trying to make

conversation. On the other hand, Littlejohn fancied there was something friendly in it all. He had been wondering about Clinton's origins, too, as though, in different circumstances, they might have become friends, interested in each other.

"No. I was born even farther north than this; Ulverston way."

"I come from these parts myself. A place called Tarporley."

"We're both countrymen, then?"

"Yes. My father was a country doctor."

They rode on in silence and soon were passing down the main street of Wiston to the house Littlejohn already knew. Clinton put his hand in his pocket for his key.

Now that he knew Clinton, Littlejohn was not surprised at the interior. Comfort and well-being met him at the door. Everything harmonious and in good taste. The old house had been modernized and given the benefit of up-to-date improvements without spoiling its original beauty. It was not a large place. Two good-sized entertaining rooms and kitchens below, a wide staircase with shallow treads and wrought-iron balusters. Thick carpets on the floors, good pictures on the walls, nothing which offended the eye. Wherever it had been possible, windows had been added or existing ones enlarged without in any way impairing the old style of the house, which, as a result, on this spring evening seemed to be bathed in light.

"Here is my study."

A large room facing the setting sun and overlooking a lawn and flowerbeds. An Adam fireplace, converted into an electric heater and, above it, a Sickert picture. Books covered the rest of the available space on the walls. A large period desk and chair faced the window. Little else. Expensive, you would have said, but in such good taste as to be modest. Hardly the set-up of a country doctor.

"What would you like to drink, Superintendent? Sherry? Whisky?"

He opened a cabinet and handed Littlejohn his drink in an old wine-glass with an air-twist stem and a Jacobite emblem carved round the rim.

"I daresay you wonder about all this, Superintendent, and where I deal with my patients. I inherited this place. It was my mother's family home, furniture and all. My waiting-room and surgery are at the bottom of the garden and accessible from the street which passes along there. It was the old stables and coach-house."

Clinton seemed to want to tell Littlejohn everything. They were both beginning to forget the real purpose of their being together. A patient dead and a wrong death certificate issued; the patient's wife and the doctor making love together before his death. And the doctor and the policeman drinking excellent sherry and lolling comfortably in the doctor's study.

The house was silent. The housekeeper must have been out. Littlejohn remembered that Shoesmith had told him that the doctor was a widower. His eyes strayed round the room and fell on a photograph in a silver frame on the desk.

"My wife... She was killed in a hunting accident two years ago."

A beautiful face, a woman with the innocence of a child in her large eyes. Extraordinarily naïve and simple, and yet with gravity and integrity of natural goodness. Littlejohn wondered how Clinton had come to be mixed-up with Mrs. Twigg.

"Smoke your pipe if you wish. I've seen you about Rushton with it. Cigarettes won't be much in your line, I know... There are some on the table, though, if you wish..."

Another pause whilst Littlejohn filled and lit his pipe. Clinton stood at the window, his hands in his pockets, looking down the garden in the direction of the surgery. Suddenly he turned and looked straight at Littlejohn.

"You must admit you would have had to come here sooner or later. It's better to have it out in private instead of at the Twiggs' place. I'm more friendly and at home in my own study."

Littlejohn finished his sherry and stood up, too.

"When you signed the certificate of death, doctor, did you really believe that Twigg had died naturally?"

Clinton filled up Littlejohn's glass and his own with a steady hand.

"Yes. I give you my word. He had suffered from stomach ulcers all his life; he told me when he first consulted me. That would be five years ago. He recently had another attack. The X-ray showed plainly that there was a large ulcer at the lower end of the stomach. I can find you the film if you wish. I have it in the files. I put him on a diet and treatment, and was prepared in the event of no improvement to send him to see a surgeon. Instead, I was called-in after he collapsed. He vomited and passed blood in large quantities. The reason was obvious. Or so I thought. The ulcer had burst and there was haemorrhage. He died before we could move him or even arrange a transfusion. That's all there is..."

He slowly drank his whisky and sat down at his desk.

"You ought to have told me you intended to exhume and have an autopsy. I ought to have had a chance to put my side of the case."

"That was not in question at the time. You were perfectly entitled to your opinion and, if it was honest, to give the certificate accordingly."

"Honest? I don't like the sound of that."

"In my colleague Cromwell's pocket, at the time he was shot, a few tablets of dicoumarin were discovered. He had, in turn, found them in Mr. Twigg's desk. He had just been to the chemist in Rushton Inferior and had them identified when he was shot. Now, sir. What inference would you think someone like me would naturally draw? It led me to investigate Mrs. Twigg, to find that her mother had suffered from thrombosis and been given dicoumarin by her London doctor. The tablets were never returned after her death. They were retained by Mrs. Twigg."

"But surely, you don't think...?"

"What else can I think? I know the drug is widely used these days, but who else would have interest in using it to poison Twigg?"

"But the motive?"

"He left her all his money. That is number one. Number two, is that Mrs. Twigg married a man much older than herself and then fell in love with someone else, someone her own age. I believe she fell in love with *you*."

Clinton remained calm; he even looked bored.

"That often happens in my profession. Women take a fancy to us. It is all part of the day's work."

"Yes, I know. But you don't respond by becoming the lover of every one who, as you say, takes a fancy to you!

Clinton clenched his fists, looked ready to rise in a fit of rage, and then subsided and poured himself another drink.

"You've heard Emily Twigg and I are lovers? That is quite untrue. I could have been her lover had I wished. It sounds caddish to put it that way, but I must defend myself."

He looked round the room, at the books, the pictures, the furniture, the dying day beyond the broad windows.

"I love this house. I love my work, my success, and even my failures. I have no intention of giving it all up or losing it through any woman. I won the love of the woman I wanted and, for a year or two, was supremely happy. I shall never feel that way again about any woman. I'm not saying I've lived like a monk since she died. But I refuse to become involved or have my private life violated. That is why whoever told you that Emily Twigg and I were lovers is a liar."

"She called here from time to time...not as a patient?"

"That is true. I always saw to it that Mrs. Harriman, my housekeeper, was here."

"So, according to you, sir, Mrs. Twigg was, to put it vulgarly, doing the chasing? And you were running away?"

"One comes up against such problems in a doctor's day."

"She recently had a meeting with you at a country public

house some miles from here... What was it about, sir? You were seen there together."

"She had called here a time or two whilst shopping in Wiston. Mrs. Harriman gave her coffee. It was becoming too frequent and I told her I was sorry it would have to end. People would begin to talk. She then said her husband had heard of our friendship but that she didn't care. I said it would be better if we ended it. She later telephoned me to meet her at the *George*, a country inn some miles from here, as she had something important to say. It turned out to be yet another plea not to leave her in the lurch, as she called it. I told her we mustn't meet again for some time. That was all..."

Clinton looked round the room again, as though weighing against it the blandishments of Mrs. Twigg and finding her wanting.

"I like peace and quiet. I like my work and when it is over—if it ever is—I am quite happy here with my books and my collections. I don't want public limelight. Just a calm life. That's all."

In cold print, it might have seemed reasonable. Just a busy man wishing to be left in peace and his leisure undisturbed. But as he said it, Littlejohn fancied he detected a desperate note, almost one of violence, that of a tame or amiable animal which, suddenly in fright or when taken unaware and its existence threatened, grows vicious or wildly aggressive.

"Another sherry?"

"No, thank you, sir."

"That is why I felt I must bring you here to make my explanations. Having seen my life and home, you will better understand why I must not be disturbed and why I would not make any false step which might upset a useful existence or threaten my personal or professional honour."

He looked sharply at Littlejohn to see if the Superintendent understood his point. Littlejohn was calmly smoking his pipe again.

"Of course, all this doesn't *prove* I didn't kill my patient just to get his wife free for myself. Nor does it prove that your colleague, having become suspicious about it all, I didn't shoot at him to silence him. It does, however, put you in a better position for understanding my motives and my aim in life."

Again, the questioning look. Littlejohn felt that a response was expected.

"If what you say is true, doctor, I can well see that no suspicion could attach to you."

"I have nothing to hide. Ask any questions you like. I know that poison doesn't often admit of an alibi, but I want to convince you that I could have no motive in killing anyone."

"I'm very grateful to you, doctor, for being so straight-forward about everything. Thank you for your hospitality, too. It has been a pleasure to meet you at home."

"Come again. You must be very lonely carrying on a case on your own."

"It's in the hands of Inspector Tandy, really. I'm only involved on the personal count of my colleague's accident."

"So Tandy will be calling on me, too?"

"The result of the exhumation and autopsy will, of course, be raised, but as far as I can see, if you are as straightforward with the local police as you've been with me..."

"Pah! Tandy isn't like you. He's no imagination. May I ask you a question, Superintendent?"

"Fire away, sir."

"Did you ever think of taking medicine?"

"You mean becoming a doctor?"

"Exactly."

"Yes. I left school during the 1914-18 war. I intended studying medicine. I couldn't get a place in the universities. So many men returning from the war had enrolled under state grants. So, I joined the police force."

"I thought so. Instead of seeking alibis and clues, you always seem to be trying to diagnose something. Have you succeeded, yet?"

"No, sir."

"Good luck, then. And now I'll drive you back to Rushton."

They said little on the way. It was now dusk and there were more cars on the roads. Parties returning from dining out; now and then a car towing a boat back from an evening's sailing on the local meres; families having a run-round in the pleasant weather. The doctor pulled-up just outside the village.

"Could you walk the remaining few hundred yards, Superintendent? If they see me riding around with you, the villagers will wonder what it's all about. Their hobby is gossip. I never knew such a place for putting two and two together to make five or six."

"Of course, sir. Thanks for bringing me so far. By the way, are the people in the house opposite the *Weatherby* patients of yours? The Beetons..."

"Why, yes. How do you come to be interested in them?"

"My room overlooks their place. She is an invalid?"

"In a way. It's mainly nervous. He's away a lot and she spends a fair share of her time alone. The introspective kind, you know. They're devoted to each other and the sooner he can afford to retire and give her the pleasure of more of his company, the better it will be for both of them."

"Are they natives of the village?"

"She is, I think. She's owned and lived in that house as long as I can remember. She was a maiden lady until she met Beeton about seven years ago. They are as devoted to each other as a pair of young lovers. What makes you so interested?"

"She watches all that goes on at the *Weatherby* and particularly all my comings and goings. I expect it helps to pass away the long days until her husband returns."

"I guess so."

"One final question before I say good-night, doctor. Don't

answer if it's a breach of trust. Have you many patients for whom you are prescribing dicoumarin at present?"

"Quite a few. But it may help you to know that I control it carefully. Those who need such treatment are subject to daily visits and I only leave enough tablets for a day's dosage. Not enough to cause rapid death such as you say Mr. Twigg suffered."

"Thank you, sir, and good night."

"Good night. Call on me soon and good luck on your case."

Mrs. Groves was waiting for him in the hall.

"You naughty boy... Dinner's been waiting for hours. I've arranged for them to grill you a steak. The joint is quite cold. You are a great trial, Superintendent."

"I'm sorry."

"It's all right. I heard you'd been seen with the doctor. Is it Mrs. Twigg who's ill again?"

"No. He just invited me home for a drink. A very nice fellow."

"You think so? I'm surprised at his sudden gush of friendly hospitality. He only drinks, as a rule, with the county people. By the way, Inspector Tandy has been on the telephone. I said I'd ask you to ring him up when you got back. You'll just have time while we're cooking your meal. Don't be long."

It was almost dark as Littlejohn washed and tidied himself in his room. The air was heavy with the scent of flowers and the bellringers were practising again. An old lady of the village was going to celebrate her ninetieth birthday the following Sunday, and a peal was to be rung in her honour. The ringers sounded to be having a rough time.

He stood in the dark interior of his room looking through the window. There was a light in the dining-room of the house opposite and, as he looked, it was switched off. A moment later, the bedroom light went on, revealing Mrs. Beeton in a house-coat and ready for bed. She crossed to draw the curtains and before doing so, looked out, down the street, and then across to Littlejohn's room. She stared hard, trying to penetrate the gloom and then shrugged her shoulders and pulled the cord which shut her off from the world.

Over the telephone he learned from his wife that Cromwell was still getting along well. He arranged for Mrs. Littlejohn to bring Mrs. Cromwell to Rushton Inferior next day for a change and said he would call for them in the car in time to get them back at the *Weatherby* for lunch. Then he rang up Tandy, who had left his home number.

Tandy and Buck had been working hard. They'd visited doctors for miles around and discussed dicoumarin and patients with them. Clinton hadn't been available, but they hoped to see him to-morrow.

"You needn't worry on that score, Tandy. I've already seen him and his explanations were satisfactory. You heard about the post-mortem?"

"Yes, sir. Very hush-hush, but confirms your theory."

"Yes."

"But there's one thing that we found out. It was almost my last call. There's a Dr. Flowerdew lives semi-retired at Cropton, in the country a few miles from here. He does a bit as locum for other local doctors now and then. I asked him about the... the drug... I've got it written down in my book. Dicoumarin, that's it. He hadn't used it for some time. I asked him how long. It was before Mr. Twigg died, because Dr. Flowerdew hadn't been doing much since. He checked his own stock and then I just casually asked if he'd any in his drug-case in his car. I always remember those drug cases because they're the ones that cause us most trouble. Always gettin' lost or pinched..."

"Yes?"

"He went to his car and unlocked it. The case was there with all the drugs in it except the dicoumarin!"

"Had he any idea where he'd lost it?"

"Not a single one. He's nearly eighty and a bit woolly. Can't say I'd like him about me if I was bad. So, I went carefully through his movements around when Mr. Twigg was taken ill. It was mostly on the other side of Wiston, but he'd been once to Rushton Inferior about that time. There'd been a farewell party to the county medical officer who was retiring and Flowerdew had been at the dinner."

"Where was it held, Tandy?"

"At the *Weatherby*, where you're staying at present, sir."

8
THE BULL AND BUSH

It was dark by the time Littlejohn finished his dinner. A hasty meal, much to the annoyance of Mrs. Groves, who wished to stay and talk, but in the hour before closing-time, he wanted to make a call at the *Bull and Bush* at Rushton Superior, a mile away. He didn't tell Mrs. Groves where he was going, which made her all the more put-out.

"Do you *never* rest? We've seen very little of you since you came here, Superintendent. The guests have commented on it. You ought to give us more of your company."

"I'll have to spend a few days in a more sociable way as soon as the work is finished."

"Are you any nearer finding out who shot poor Mr. Cromwell? I do hope you'll bring them to justice. And, by the way..."

She lowered her voice and asked the question coyly, the chubby infantile cheeks flushed, the china-blue eyes wide open.

"By the way, there was a reporter here this afternoon. Is it true there's also a mystery about poor Mr. Twigg's death? He actually asked me if they were going to exhume the body. Whatever is it all about?"

So something had leaked out already, but the less said the

better for the present. The press would deal with it soon enough. Mrs. Groves could be silenced without even telling a lie.

"We've no intention of exhuming the body, so put your mind at rest on that score, Mrs. Groves. And now I must be going. I've a call to make."

"I'll have some cold supper ready when you return. We can have it together in my room. I couldn't sleep without a bite at bedtime and I'm quite sure after all the work you do, you'll be just the same..."

The *Bull and Bush* wasn't hard to find. A mile from Rushton Inferior along the road which passed the Twiggs' place. As he drove by, Littlejohn turned to look at the now familiar *Ballarat*. There was a light in Mrs. Twigg's bedroom and another in the lounge on the ground floor.

There was a string of cars outside the *Bull and Bush,* which was a favourite calling-place in the district because they sold good beer. A low-lying, black-and-white timbered house with a swinging sign over the door illuminated by a bright lamp. The *Skelton Arms* had a lot of elaborate heraldry. This, too, must be a pub with a nickname like the *Silly Billy*. A broad passage with a door leading off each side and a bar at the end near the back entrance. As soon as you opened the front door a gust of beer, loud voices and cooking food greeted you. There was a dining-room upstairs and it was fashionable for people from Wiston and other nearby towns to dine there. A potman emerged from the bar with a tray of drinks and made a flat-footed way to the door on the left.

"Is Mr. Temple here to-night?"

"Eh?"

"Mr. Temple."

"Aye. He's a regular. Comes every night. Just wait a minute while I get rid o' this lot, then we'll see about it."

He disappeared through the door, was greeted by a cheer of fruity voices which must have been waiting a while for his ministrations, and then he emerged, mopping his brow with his cloth.

"It's gettin' too much for me. More and more comin' for drinks and no fresh staff. I just can't cope, sir."

He turned his watery eyes on Littlejohn, so liquid that they looked about to float from their sockets and run down his cheeks. A little, bald man with a shaggy black moustache, he had been enjoying the same grumble for years.

"Mr. Temple, you said. He's a special and frequents the snug. You a friend of his?"

"No. I just wanted a word with him."

"Well, you might as well go in the snug, unless it's private and you'd like me to bring 'im out."

"No, thanks. Show me the snug, please, and point him out to me."

There was a door behind the bar with a small sign over it. *The Kennel.* This was formerly the landlord's office, but with the growth of the *Bull and Bush* it had become too small. Here assembled half a dozen regulars who came every night. The potman led the way.

A cosy room with a couple of round tables, comfortable chairs, and a shaded light. A small fireplace without any fire. A carpet on the floor. A quiet, isolated little place where the specials could talk and drink in peace every night. By day, it was used as living-quarters by the landlord and his wife.

"Gentleman wants a word with Mr. Temple," said the waiter, and, in keeping with his grouse about being busy, he hurried away again, mopping his bald head with his cloth.

Four men were sitting at a table in one corner and from their group a tall man with a good shock of white hair and a small silver moustache rose and came to meet Littlejohn. He wore grey tweeds and was well-groomed. A man getting on for seventy and with clear grey eyes and a round, pink, healthy face. He had been the manager of a large bank in Birmingham and had retired to

Rushton Superior six years ago. He was on a good pension and enjoyed every minute of his leisure.

"Well... You're Superintendent Littlejohn, sir, aren't you? You were pointed out to me in the village only yesterday. Come and sit down with us."

He shook hands firmly and led Littlejohn to his table and introduced him to his friends.

"This is the landlord, Charlie Bragg, and these are Mr. Wise and Mr. Wainwright."

Charlie Bragg got up to go, excusing himself on the score of being busy. A small, grey-haired fat man, addressed as Major by his inferiors on account of service in the territorials at some time or other. The other two rose as well. They were both tall and looked healthy. Wise was thin and aquiline, with fair hair sprinkled with grey. A clean-shaven intelligent face, and a gentle, almost finicky way, which manifested itself in the cut of his tweeds, the excellence of his linen, his tie and his shoes, and the way he had of pondering his words before he spoke. Littlejohn had been told he farmed for a hobby and had plenty of money. He certainly didn't look like a born farmer. Neither did he shake hands like one, but gave Littlejohn a flabby clammy salute and sat down again.

Wainwright was cumbersome and talkative. His hands were large, his features heavy and swarthy, and he bore all the signs of a heavy drinker. His glass was half full of whisky; the rest were drinking bottled beer.

All three looked over sixty, but Wise best kept his youthful looks. He had an almost ageless appearance, the kind you merely guessed at, and only his hands, with their hard-looking protruding veins, betrayed him.

"Sit down and have a drink, Littlejohn. What will it be?"

Wainwright, the auctioneer, was first in the field. He might have been on his rostrum persuasively taking bids.

"Beer? Right. Where's Carrie...? Carrie...! Another round, and beer for our friend here."

He smiled across at Littlejohn, and gave him his famous and well-known *what am I bid?* wink.

"I knew you'd find this place sooner or later, sir. Best beer in the county. Drink spirits meself. Doctor forbade beer. Not that it's much hardship. Always a spirit man. Thanks, Carrie."

A dark girl with an opulent bosom and a generous figure laid out the glasses. Wainwright slapped her behind as she left and she turned and gave him a smile, half rebuke, half encouragement. Littlejohn noticed that Wise was the only man who really noticed her, however. Wainwright slapped most girls instinctively; Wise was the sort who followed them with his eyes and pretended not to be doing so. As for Temple, he was so placidly enjoying his retirement that he hadn't time to be disturbed by even a pretty figure and a provocative face. He also had a jealous, wealthy wife and a reputation to keep up.

"Good health."

Wise drank and put his glass down.

"Good health to you all, gentlemen. I hope you're better, Mr. Wise."

Wise raised his eyebrows.

"You know I've been ill? Yes, I'm improving, thanks. This is my second appearance since my last attack. I feel a lot better."

"It's not difficult to get all the news of everybody in the locality, Mr. Wise. Everybody in Rushton knows everyone else's business."

Wainwright was curious, too. He barged-in in his usual aggressive way.

"But you've not come here to sample the beer or gossip, have you, Super? You're after something more than that, or I'm a Dutchman."

The people at the next table were beginning to take an interest. Conversation there had ceased and eyes were turned on Littlejohn. These were obviously some more bigwigs of the locality, also privileged to enjoy the *Kennel* every night. There wasn't going to be much privacy there. Wise seemed to sense this and, after excusing himself, rose and left the room. As he went, Littlejohn thought he looked more like a country squire than ever. He wore riding breeches and beautifully polished boots.

Wise was back almost right away and the landlord with him.

"I believe you four gentlemen want to talk privately."

Charlie Bragg breathed an eager blast of brandy over Littlejohn as he addressed him on behalf of the rest.

"Well, there's another room on the floor above, just like this. You know it, don't you, Fred? You can use it if you like. It's empty. We keep it for little private do's now and then. If you care to come..."

He led them out. The people at the other table looked a bit disappointed and shouted good-byes and other greetings.

It was getting towards closing-time and, as the little party led by Bragg made for the foot of the stairs which led up to the private room, a number of locals, farm labourers and other working-men, were emerging from the taproom on the right of the door and bidding each other noisy farewells Among them was Turner, the gardener from *Ballarat*, who also did jobbing work for the Beetons opposite the *Weatherby*. Turner wasn't drunk; just merry enough to feel a gush of good-feeling towards Littlejohn as their paths briefly crossed.

"Good evenin', sir. So you've found your way to the old *Bull an' Bush*. I mush say I'm glad. The beer 'ere's ver' good."

Turner's face assumed a sad expression in keeping with his next question.

"And how's your poor friend? The one that some murdrin' thief took a shot at in the dead o' night?"

"He's improving now, Turner. Thanks for the inquiry. I'll tell him you asked for him."

Littlejohn's friends had, by now, left him behind, and Wise

called down the stairs rather acidly that he would find them in the room to the right at the top.

Turner hadn't finished.

"You might also tell the gentleman... he was a proper gentleman... that I'm keepin' for him the geraniums and fuchsia cuttings I promised him. Don't forget, sir. We used to have a little talk now and then about gardenin'. The gentleman said he hadn't much of a garden where he lived in London, but asked me advice about window-boxes..."

Turner nodded gravely.

"Now if there's anythin' I like, sir, it's a nice window-box. So I told him how to start an' what to do, and I promised him some geraniums and fuchsias of which he seemed very fond. I got 'em in the greenhouse at the Beetons'. That's where we did the talkin'. I can't bear talkin' to anybody at the Twiggses. That feller Cank all the time watching round the curtains. An they've not got no fuchsias or geraniums at the Twiggses. All roses and 'erbaceous stuff, they like. I showed 'im over the Beetons' greenhouses twice. If ever you get a chance, I tole 'im, you get a greenhouse... A good place to sit in an' smoke a pipe at the end of the day. An' he said I was right. A very nice gentleman..."

It looked like continuing for some time, until a clock struck a quarter past ten and Turner, remembering what one he described as 'my ole bag o' trouble' would do to him if he got home after half-past, bade Littlejohn a respectful good night again and went off in the dark.

"I ordered some more beer for you, Super. That all right?"

Wainwright and his two pals had settled down in the upper room and had left a seat and a full glass for Littlejohn. The place was more dismal than the one below. Difficult to say why, but the light was more glaring and, cleared of all its occupants, the floor seemed dreary and dead. As the door into the main room opened, a waiter could be seen tidying the empty dinner tables and screwing up the cloths.

"Now, what was it you wanted to ask us about?"

Wainwright was the spokesman and Temple and Wise were more diffident and ready to let matters take their course. Their companion couldn't wait. He wanted the bidding to start right away.

"I suppose it's about our late friend Twigg, Superintendent. Your colleague, I believe, was related to him."

Temple looked at his watch. He was an early-to-bed man. It was getting near his time. He was preoccupied with his health and determined to draw his pension for a long time.

"Yes. I'm anxious to get to know all I can about Mr. Twigg and my friend, Cromwell. It seems so stupid for someone to have shot Cromwell. He wasn't even known in the village and could have done nobody any harm."

"In my view, he must have run up against a poacher or somebody else up to no good, and they just took a pot at him. It was as simple as that…"

Wainwright rose as he said it and shouted through the door at the waitress in the dining-room.

"Bring more drinks, Lucy. Make mine a double. It'll be time in a minute or two and then we won't get any at all."

"Yes. It's as simple as that," he said as he sat down again.

"Except that the bullet wasn't the sort a poacher or prowler would fire. It was from a small revolver a woman might use."

They all looked at Littlejohn astonished.

"Well, I'll be damned! That's a queer one."

Wainwright emptied his glass. Wise was absorbed in studying his signet ring. Then he spoke.

"How can we help?"

"You were all three bosom friends of Mr. Twigg. You met most nights for a drink and a talk. Did he ever give you the impression that he had enemies?"

They all shook their heads and looked more bewildered than ever.

"It isn't Twigg, though, who was shot at. He died a natural death, didn't he?"

Temple's clear eyes were naïve in their questioning wonder.

"I'm trying to get some background, sir, about the Twiggs. It will help. You see, my colleague can't talk to me yet. I don't know a thing about what caused all his trouble."

Wainwright laughed hoarsely. The drink was loosening him up even more than normally, and he was prepared to talk all night now.

"Richard was a right decent chap. Wouldn't do anybody any wrong. I don't think he ever made an enemy. Exceptin' Mrs. Groves, at the *Weatherby*... Remember Mrs. Groves, Wise...? Remember, Temple?"

Both Temple and Wise didn't seem disposed to talk much about it.

"She set her cap at him good and proper. The four of us used to go to the *Weatherby* for morning coffee. We had to pack it up and find another place. It was getting embarrassing, wasn't it, chaps? Mrs. Groves would have had Richard at the altar in no time. You're staying there, Super?"

"Yes."

"You'll know Mrs. Groves, then? You know the sort she is. The sort of silly, coy way she has. Baby-talk to the men and such like. She tried it on us and Twigg was fool enough to start giving it back to her. Answering her in her own coin. She thought he'd fallen for her. He was a bachelor at the time and she an eligible widow. She got in the habit of asking poor Twigg into her office. Said she wanted advice and she was on her own and helpless. The usual stuff. We had to rescue Twigg and take him elsewhere for his coffee. Then he went off on his cruise and came home with a wife. Mrs. Groves didn't half carry on about it, didn't she, chaps? She was heard to say she could take Twigg up for breach of promise, the things he'd said to her in the past and the shabby trick he'd played on her. A regular hymn of hate..."

"But not enough to make her wish him harm."

Wainwright emptied his glass, wiped his mouth and laughed.

"Do him harm! She'd have murdered him. All this baby-mine, helpless little girl stuff is put on. She's as wicked and hard as nails underneath, isn't she...? Isn't she, Wise?"

Wainwright was getting irritable with his companions for not supporting him.

"That's true," said Wise thoughtfully. He looked at his gold wrist-watch.

"Time I was off, too. I'm still under the doctor, you know."

"Clinton, sir?"

"No, Cruickshank. You've met Clinton?"

"I was at his place to-day. He asked me to call for a drink."

"Indeed! You're honoured. He's a bit standoffish."

Wainwright, now half-seas over, waved impatiently.

"The Super's not come to see us for small talk. He's here on a case. We were talking about Ma Groves. A tartar, a proper wicked tartar, I was saying she was. Her first husband died early in life, nagged and worried to death. She spent his money like water and made a regular fool of him. You want to watch Groves, Super. She might have taken a pot-shot at your colleague."

"Why?"

"Don't ask me. She was quite capable of it. Perhaps did it to spite Twigg, even if he *was* dead. Payin' off old scores, if you get what I mean."

Temple emptied his glass and stood up.

"If you ask me, Superintendent," he said, "that shot wasn't intended for Mr. Cromwell at all. It was meant for somebody else. It stands to reason. According to everybody, Cromwell was a right good sort. Who'd want to kill him? No. It was meant for somebody else. By the way, how is he?"

"He'll pull through."

"Good. I'm glad. It wasn't meant for him. Take my word. Some jealous wife or other mistook him for somebody else."

Wainwright laughed gruffly.

"Good Lord, Temple, you've been readin' detective stories. I never knew you'd such an imagination. You'll be sayin' it was one of us next."

They all rose and said good night.

Wainwright was loath to part.

"We don't seem to have been much help, Super. Sorry. Just gettin' down to business when it's closing-time. Come again. We'll have another session. Temple might be able to help you solve the case. Good old Temple. I didn't know you were so interested in crime."

Wise and Temple looked uneasy. Wise was eyeing his highly-polished boots and Temple twisting his little silver moustache.

They were right. It hadn't been much of a session after all. Littlejohn wondered if it would be any better after the full report of Twigg's autopsy reached the newspapers. They would have something to talk about then.

Wainwright was taking the other two home in his car. He shunted it unsteadily from the car-park and they all bade Littlejohn good night. Back at the *Weatherby*, Mrs. Groves was waiting for Littlejohn with a large plate of ham sandwiches.

"Ah, there you are, Superintendent. I'm so glad to see you. I'm starving. Let's settle down..."

9
THE ROYAL GEORGE

An almost farcical situation. Littlejohn sitting opposite Mrs. Groves in her private room at eleven o'clock at night, eating sandwiches and drinking coffee. There was a fire of logs on the open hearth, a cat on the rug, a budgerigar talking to himself in a cage in one corner. Now and then, to attract attention, the bird would ring a little bell or climb a little ladder in the cage and call out his name.

"Percy! That's me!"

The pair sitting at the table might have known each other all their lives.

The *Weatherby* was a place where most people went early to bed. The younger regular boarders, like Valentine, Miss Broderick and Miss Marriott, of course, had a late night or two every week. But the holidaymakers, people there for a quiet week or fortnight, were invariably in bed by eleven. There wasn't much to do after dark.

"I wouldn't be surprised if Mr. Valentine and Miss Broderick don't make a match of it one of these days. They go out together quite a lot. I like to see young people enjoying themselves."

She took a large mouthful of another sandwich and smiled over the top of it at Littlejohn.

"I suppose your regulars now and then do fall in and out of love with one another. It must be strange watching the relationships between your guests."

She stopped chewing for a moment, as though ready to say something. Then she changed her mind and took a drink of coffee.

"Did you know Richard Twigg very well, Mrs. Groves?"

She didn't even wince. She just kept on chewing her sandwich, looking at him with her china-blue eyes and like a cat ready to start purring.

"He stayed here for a month or two whilst he was hunting for a house in the village. He said he'd no intention of marrying then. He just liked the neighbourhood and wanted to settle here."

"Were you and he very friendly in those days?"

They looked each other full in the face again. The cat was purring on the hearth now and the bird was ringing his little bell. It might just have been a little family gathering with the humans exchanging experiences about what had happened since they last met.

"Yes. We were good friends. He often came in here, just as you do, and had a bite with me after he'd been to the *Bull and Bush* with his friends. Have you been up to the *Bull and Bush* to-night, Superintendent?"

"Yes, I wanted to talk with the old friends you mention."

She rose and took the tin of chocolate biscuits from the old corner-cupboard, opened it, and offered it to Littlejohn.

"No, thanks, Mrs. Groves. I'll smoke my pipe, if I may."

"Yes, do. It's so homely to have a man and the smell of tobacco in the room again."

She took several biscuits, put them on a plate, and began to munch them with relish.

"I suppose they told you a lot of things about Richard Twigg?"

"Not as much as I expected. I got there a bit too late. They'd been drinking rather freely and the party was ready for breaking-up when I arrived."

"Did they tell you they used to come here frequently. Sometimes for dinner at night, and very often for coffee in the middle of the morning, especially when it wasn't fit for a game of golf?"

"Yes. They told me that."

A pause.

"Then, suddenly, they stopped coming and went to the cafe across the way. Did they say why?"

The eyes were open wider and there was a pathetic question in them.

"Yes."

"They used to make fun of me, I found. Spinsters and widows are often the butts of those kind of men. It's cruel. Especially as it's so wrong, so untrue. Mr. Wainwright was particularly rude. His wife died two years ago and he should have thought better of women."

She busied herself with a biscuit again and then poured out two more cups of coffee.

"You were angry about it, Mrs. Groves?"

"Both angry and hurt. It was unkind, especially as I was only trying to make Mr. Twigg comfortable during his stay here."

"Didn't they come for some time after Mr. Twigg married?"

"Not for very long... Were they talking about me at the *Bull and Bush*, then?"

It was obvious what all the little suppers were about. Mrs. Groves catching him every evening with coffee, sandwiches and a warm cosy room, and then pumping him about the case and her own share in it. All the same, it was convenient. He could, by being frank and not hiding anything, perhaps learn much.

"They talked about a lot of people, yourself included."

"What did they say about me?"

The voice was wheedling and the blue eyes childishly appealing.

"Percy! That's me!"

The budgerigar rang his bell and uttered a string of unintelligible words. Mrs. Groves rose and covered the cage gently with a cloth.

"That will do for to-night, Percy."

"Good-night one and all. Percy, that's me!"

Silence, except for the gentle breathing of the fire and the tick of the brass carriage-clock on the top of the desk in the corner.

"Tell me what they said. I won't take it amiss, I promise."

"They said you considered breach of promise, because Twigg had talked of marrying you."

She flushed and then the colour drained from her face.

"How cruel of them to say that!"

"I was as much to blame as they were. I didn't ask them outright about Twigg's relations with anyone, but I tried to get to know as much as I could about his life here since he came."

"It was quite true. One night, sitting just where you are, having his supper with me, he said how nice it would be to settle down, and he asked me what I thought about it. It wasn't an outright proposal of marriage, but could have been taken as such."

"And when he married, did you remind him of it?"

"I did. That's why he and his friends never came here again."

"Is it asking too much to inquire what you said? Did you threaten him?"

"No. I reminded him of what I said on the night I've just mentioned. He talked of settling down. I told him plainly that he'd never settle down with anybody like me. I was too old for him."

"Why?"

"Nothing much that goes on here gets past me, Superintendent. People might think me frivolous, perhaps a bit simple, but I've lived a very experienced life, believe me. I wasn't blind to the tastes of Mr. Richard Twigg in the way of women. He liked them young and good-looking. During his stay here, there were quite a few lady boarders of charm. He made a fool of himself about one or two of them; others liked his blandishments and played up to him. Mr. Twigg was very popular in certain parts of the village, but I knew him better than most. In his time, there were one or two bedrooms he'd have made free of, if I hadn't kept my eyes open and taken the necessary steps."

She rose, cleared up the dirty dishes, and removed them on a tray.

"Yes... I told one hussy to pack her bag and go next day. Another, I put in the next room to mine, so that I could keep an eye on her. So, when Twigg married a good-looking girl half his age, I reminded him of what I'd said. He didn't like it. He grew offensive and abused me. I told him not to come in here again. Now you know."

It was all said so calmly and yet, somehow, Littlejohn found it hard to believe. Mainly, he had to confess to himself, because of Cromwell. It was difficult to think it of a member of Cromwell's family, his favourite uncle. Of course, there are always black sheep...

"Did they say anything more?"

"No. And what was said was in no way making fun of you or maligning you, Mrs. Groves, believe me."

"I'm glad to hear it."

She didn't seem inclined to retire. She took up some knitting and started to cast on stitches automatically. Littlejohn made no move either. He felt that something vital was forthcoming and was anxious to know what it was.

"It looks like being a late night. I'm waiting for Mr. V. He's gone to a dinner in Wiston and it will probably be about one when he turns in. I never retire until the last of my boarders is indoors."

"You hold dinners here sometimes, too, I believe."

"Very rarely. You see, we haven't a licence and it means bringing in all the wines."

"Someone was saying you had a medical dinner some time ago."

"Yes. When the medical officer retired. There seemed a lot of events at the same time and they couldn't get a room at the usual places. Why? Has someone been telling you all about it?"

"Yes. It was mentioned."

"In what way? Was the menu discussed, or the guests? I'm rather curious."

"As a matter of fact, the police at Wiston heard that Dr. Flowerdew, who was present, had some drugs stolen from his car on that night. Where do they park their cars as a rule when they come here?"

Littlejohn looked up at her. She was eyeing him differently. The usual infantile look of innocence had gone. Then, the smile was back.

"You were saying?"

"The car-park?"

"Oh, yes. It's behind the house. We use it when we're busy. The one at the side with the garage, where your car is parked, is usually enough. What's that about Dr. Flower-dew?"

"He seems to have had some drugs taken from his car when he was here that night."

"He's an old fool. Well past eighty and he oughtn't to be trusted with dangerous drugs. What did he lose?"

"I heard it was dicoumarin, a drug of the anti-coagulant class, used now in coronary thrombosis."

"Whoever could have taken that?"

She paused and suddenly spoke again.

"It's all a lot of nonsense. I'll bet he lost it himself. His memory's failing. He's not to be trusted. I'm surprised anybody takes any notice of him at all."

Another pause. Littlejohn was feeling tired and ready for bed. And yet, it was so cosy there by the fire and there were other questions he might ask.

"How long have you been running this hotel, Mrs. Groves?"

"Twelve years."

"You are a native of these parts?"

"No. I came from Gloucestershire. My husband was mayor of the town where I was born. I didn't see much of life until I was married. Then I saw quite a lot."

"Why?"

"We ran the largest hotel in town. My husband was president of the Licensed Victuallers' Association for a number of years. We travelled abroad together for conferences. When he died, I felt I just couldn't carry on that great hotel. Twenty-eight bedrooms, you see. But I couldn't live without people about me. I like people. So, I came here. It was advertised and I bought it."

"Were the Beetons living opposite in those days?"

"She was. She was a Miss Spicer. A maiden lady of means. Then, one day, it will be seven years ago, she went away and returned with a husband. She'd met him on a holiday and they were married before they came back, and settled here in her house. Mr. Beeton, to put it vulgarly, just came here and hung his hat up. It was as simple as that."

"He travels frequently?"

"Yes. He's often away. He works for a firm of foreign exporters, I believe, and has to go abroad quite a lot. Mrs. Beeton has been ill for a long time. Nerves and arthritis, I believe. It would be far better if her husband stayed at home and looked after her. She has plenty of money and could well afford for him to retire."

"But he doesn't care to?"

"Exactly. He said he would rather earn a living for the pair of them. Said people would think he'd married her for her money, otherwise. Which doesn't seem to be the case. They're very fond of each other. So much so, that if one of them died, I don't know what the other would do."

She gave him an ironical look.

"You seem very interested in the Beetons. Surely they're not suspect in your case."

"No. I'm just a bit curious. From my room I can see all that goes on at *Rushton House,* and Mrs. Beeton seems to spend a lot of time watching this place."

"I didn't know. But then she must be lonely, poor dear, cooped up there on her own, with nobody but a woman from the village to mind her when he's away."

Another pause. The clock in the hall struck half-past twelve.

"You're sure none of your boarders was abroad when my colleague was shot, Mrs. Groves? You've heard of nobody being about or hearing a shot?"

"No. If I had, I'd have been the first to tell you, Superintendent. The local police inquired, too. They were all in bed by eleven that night. I remember, and I told Inspector Tandy so, too."

"Have any of them been here very long?"

"Not very. Mr. Valentine, about a year. The rest less. Some of them, like the Bachelors, are only here for a fortnight. They come and go. Last week a Polish gentleman, visiting Manchester on business; this week two Spaniards. They're due to-morrow. Yes, they come and go. It's all very interesting."

By now the air was almost blue with the smoke from Littlejohn's pipe. It curled up and round the lamp above their heads and then slowly vanished.

"I think I'll say good night, Mrs. Groves. I've another busy day to-morrow. Mrs. Littlejohn and Mrs. Cromwell will probably be coming for lunch. It's not good for them to be penned-up in Manchester, and it's quite safe now to get about a bit. Cromwell is out of danger. You'll be able to find us all a meal?"

"Of course. I'd like to meet your wife. You said, by the way, that your colleague is out of danger?"

"Yes."

"And he doesn't remember a thing about who tried to kill him?"

Again the childish smile had vanished. Littlejohn was beginning to regard it as a kind of stock-in-trade, an act Mrs. Groves put on like a mask to hide her feelings from her guests.

"So far, he doesn't remember anything. Of course, we can't question him yet. He's not well enough. But he was probably taken quite unaware and won't know a thing about what occurred."

She seemed greatly relieved, and picked up a biscuit and ate it rapidly, like someone who has been on hunger-strike and suddenly gets his own way and begins to tuck-in again.

As they said good night, there was the sound of a key in the lock. Valentine entered as Littlejohn reached the first landing. He was obviously full of wine and spoke loudly and familiarly to Mrs. Groves.

"'Ello, my old dear. Needn't have stayed up. Let meself in. Lose your beauty sleep keeping all these late nights."

"Now, Mr. V., go quietly to bed, like a good boy. You'll wake the house talking so loud. You wouldn't want to do that, would you? Be off with you, now."

"I haven't paid the taxi. Couldn't sort out the change."

As Littlejohn undressed he heard the taxi move away. Then Valentine staggered upstairs noisily. From the Bachelors' room came the sounds of voices. Mr. V. must have wakened the children.

Littlejohn was up early for breakfast. Miss Broderick, looking fresh and pretty in a blue tailor-made, was alone in the dining-room eating her meal, the morning paper propped up against her teapot.

Mrs. Groves was about and greeted him with surprise.

"I thought you'd have had breakfast in bed after your late night. Bacon and eggs again; or what about an omelette? I'll make it myself."

It was a lovely fragrant morning with the sun shining in through the window from a blue sky which looked to have been shampooed. The village was busy. The postman on his rounds; the cafe opposite opening up, and a woman in the shop adjoining putting bread in the window. The greengrocer next door had just returned from market with his vegetables and fish, and was unloading his van.

Littlejohn paused at the map in the hall after finishing his breakfast, and found out the road to Siseley. Then he took out the car and made for it. After leaving Rushton he turned off the Wiston road into a network of by-ways barely wide enough for two vehicles to pass in. Tall hedges broken here and there by fine old trees. The dew was heavy on the grass verges. Now and then, a lorry carrying milk-churns passed with difficulty. Hardly the kind of day to encourage anybody to work.

He arrived at Siseley just after ten. A pub, the *Royal George*, a few black and white houses, some of them thatched, and a village shop, all clustered round a church with a squat tower. There was a pond in the middle of the village with ducks swimming on it. A van, made into an itinerant grocer's shop, was standing in front of the houses and a bunch of women had gathered around it, gossiping and buying things.

The *Royal George* was closed, and Littlejohn sat and enjoyed the morning, smoking his pipe until the church clock struck half-past. Then a man emerged from behind the pub and opened the front door.

Herbert Stubbs was quite a distinguished little man in his own way. The hunt often met at his inn and he laid claims to being county on the strength of it. He was thin and middle-sized, with a hatchet face, a large, hooked nose, and two gold teeth showing prominently whenever he opened his mouth. He was in his shirt sleeves and wore riding-breeches and a yellow waistcoat. He greeted Littlejohn on the doorstep and shook hands right away.

"Come inside. You from the police? Shoesmith of the *Silly Billy* told me he'd been talking to you and mentioned a little incident that happened here not long ago. He shouldn't have brought me into it really. It was nothing. I mean, nothing to bother the police about. The doctor was obviously bored about the whole thing."

Littlejohn couldn't get a word in edgeways. Stubbs led the way into a little parlour as he talked and waved the Superintendent into a chair.

"What'll you have, Superintendent? It was in this very room the pair of 'em were. It's a bit off the beaten track here, you know, and these lovin' parties can meet one another on the q.t. But there, I'll get you some beer. A pint? Right."

Stubbs could be heard at the pumps in the next room and began to talk again as soon as he left the counter.

"You'd be surprised the things that go on. I've a reputation for being a discreet man and the missus is the same. People trust us, for some reason, and, as there's hardly anybody ever about except at night, these little meetin's take place."

"You seem to know all about me and what I'm after before I open my mouth, Mr. Stubbs."

"I'm sorry. Perhaps I talk a bit too much. That's what comes of being alone most of the day. Only the missus and the maid to chat with, and it's quite a treat to find a caller, especially in the morning."

He sat down with Littlejohn. A pleasant room, furnished in oak, with blue upholstered leather chairs here and there. Chintz curtains at the windows.

"I've done my talkin' now. It's your turn, Superintendent."

"So, Mr. Shoesmith told you all about me, Mr. Stubbs, and what I'm after. You say you've a reputation for discretion. I hope you'll exercise it in this case, too."

"My word on it. What did you want to know?"

"You said the doctor was a bit bored. That right?"

"Yes. The woman did all the running, if you get what I mean. The doctor seemed to want to be going. I'm not surprised at that. I suppose he's a reputation to look after, although he's no patients here. I know him through seein' him at the hunt ball."

"You know her, too?"

"Yes. I've seen her there, too. But she wasn't making eyes at the doctor that time. Her husband wasn't with her, of course. He wasn't what you'd call a dancin' type of man. She came on her own in her car, but there was somebody there expectin' her. Not many there knew that, but I saw 'em in the garden. The missus and me do the catering for the hunt ball. It's held at Norseley Grange, where there's a big ballroom, and his Lordship lets them have it free. When the rest are dancing and enjoying themselves in the place, I'm here there and everywhere seein' there's plenty of grub and drink flowing. I saw these two in the garden. They'd kept it dark from the rest. To see them in the hall, and even dancin', you'd have thought nothin' of it. But out among the trees where we'd a few tables and some coloured lights, I happened across 'em in the dark. Kissin' and cuddlin' and sayin' soft things to one another."

Littlejohn smiled as he filled his pipe. Stubbs was an excellent man for coming-across people and overhearing what they said. It seemed to happen in the ordinary course of business with him.

"She's a bit of a hot-line, if you ask me. Married to an old man, she fancies her chances with the younger ones. And ready to take 'em, too. There was none of the... well... you'd call it passion, wouldn't you...?"

"I don't know, Stubbs. What do *you* call it?"

"Passion. There was none of that between her and the doctor, like there was between her and the chap she had with her at the hunt ball. Red-hot, they were. In spite of the fact that he was a much older man, too. But virile, he was, believe me. They was almost eatin' one another up with it."

"You knew the man she was with?"

"Of course. He's a member of the hunt and often used to stop here with them. Hasn't been out lately, though. Been ill, though I hear he's picking up again, now. He's a gentleman farmer out Rushton way. Name of Wise."

10

FRIENDS FALL OUT

Before he left Siseley, Littlejohn entered the telephone box near the village green and put through a call to the Wiston police. Out of the corner of his eye he could see Stubbs watching him through the window of the *Royal George*, obviously wondering what it was all about and why the Superintendent hadn't used the instrument in the pub.

"Hello!"

A bored voice answered at the other end of the line. The police clerk soon changed his tune when he learned who was speaking.

"Yes, sir. Inspector Tandy happens to be in. Excuse me. I'll get him."

"Any news, sir?"

Tandy couldn't wait for an exchange of civilities. He sounded disappointed at Littlejohn's questions.

"Yes, I know who Wise's doctor is; I've seen his car at Wise's gate of late. He's been ill, you know. It's Dr. Cruickshank, of Wiston. Yes..."

"Yes, sir. Flowerdew has acted as locum for him now and then. Why? Have you traced the anti-clotting tablets?"

Littlejohn thereupon asked the date of the last Siseley hunt ball and if Flowerdew had deputized for Cruickshank recently.

Both inquiries were easy to answer. Tandy had been to the hunt ball himself last December. And as for Cruickshank, he'd been away to the Bahamas for a month in March, and Flowerdew had taken on part of his work; in fact he had attended Cruickshank's patients in Rushton Inferior and Superior. They were near his home. Yes, he'd probably attended Wise.

Tandy delivered a parting shot.

"The news about Mr. Twigg's death and the autopsy were given to the newspapers last night, sir. The reporters had got on to it somehow and there didn't seem any sense in keeping on denying it. The village should know all about it by now. It'll be in the late morning editions. That'll shake 'em a bit."

At Rushton Inferior, the atmosphere had certainly changed when Littlejohn got back. Mrs. Groves, for one, was annoyed with him and let him know it.

"You might have told me last night. I would have kept it secret till you said I could tell people. You are a very naughty man."

Two reporters from London had booked rooms at the *Weatherby* and another couple from Manchester were staying at the village pub. One was sitting in the lounge writing near the window with one eye on the street. Another was in the telephone box dictating to his paper. And a press photographer was emerging from the chemist's.

Mrs. Groves kept flitting from one to another, smiling and chirping in her usual fashion. Then, the chairman of the Rural District Council arrived and asked for Littlejohn. At the mention of the Superintendent's name, all the newspaper men abandoned what they were doing and crowded round.

But the Chairman was going to have his say first. He was an old man with a grey goatee beard and nicotine-stained teeth.

"I hope you'll soon find out who's done this dastardly thing. It gives the locality a bad name. Who are all these men in raincoats?"

"Reporters."

"Good God! The whole of England will be reading about the affair for days now. The village will be crowded out with a lot of undesirables full of morbid curiosity. Are you anywhere near solving the case?"

"It's officially in the hands of Inspector Tandy, of Wiston, sir. He'll be able to give you a report."

The Chairman was obviously suffering from nerves, like everyone else in the village. First a shooting affair; now a death from poisoning in a very subtle manner. They wondered who'd be next.

"I don't want panic to spread in the neighbourhood. I hope you arrest somebody soon."

The newspaper men couldn't wait any longer.

"Give us a break, Super. Any news or clues?"

"Will you go away!"

The Chairman hadn't finished with Littlejohn.

"It's out of my province to give you orders, but you must solve the case at once. Everybody's suspicious of everybody else. If this goes on nobody will dare to go out after sunset. As for Tandy. Well, I did hear that you've rather left him out in the dark. He doesn't know quite what you're doing."

Littlejohn had had enough.

"I'm sorry, sir, but I must go. I'm merely here to look after my colleague who was shot the other day. He's in hospital in Manchester and I'm due to see him shortly."

The newsmen were swarming round the telephone again.

"Panic breaks out in the little village of Rushton Inferior. This pretty spot has a killer in its midst... Got that? Put it under headlines, it's hot news. And say Superintendent Littlejohn of the Yard is in charge of the case... Got it?"

Turner passed the door trundling a barrow. He'd let it be known he was the murdered man's gardener, closely in his confidence, and ready to talk for the price of a pint or two. So far, nobody had bitten, so he was pushing his vehicle here and there in case they did.

Littlejohn made for the door. The Chairman called after him.

"Please keep me informed."

Cromwell was asleep when Littlejohn arrived at the infirmary and he didn't care to wake him. The sister gave a good report. The sergeant was making good progress and perhaps to-morrow would be able to talk to the Superintendent for a bit.

"He seems anxious to have a word with you. He kept worrying the night sister about his dead uncle. Something about his having a weak heart as well as a bad stomach. Sister thought he was growing a bit delirious and gave him a sedative. However, perhaps, as I said, you'll be able to put his mind at rest to-morrow."

Then Littlejohn went to pick up his wife and Mrs. Cromwell and take them back with him to Rushton.

The afternoon was hardly a success. Mrs. Cromwell was worn out with worrying about her husband and how the children were getting along in her absence. She hardly knew what she was eating at lunch, and kept looking at her watch as though anxious for it to be visiting-time at the hospital again. Even Mrs. Groves's false gaiety did nothing to improve the atmosphere. The newspaper men, having discovered that Cromwell's wife was in the village, kept trying to get a story from her, as well. It took Mrs. Littlejohn all her time to keep Mrs. Cromwell in good spirits. And then the Chairman turned up again and asked for Littlejohn.

"Any more news?"

The Superintendent took his guests back to Manchester at five o'clock. He had hoped to get accommodation for them at the *Weatherby* and Mrs. Groves had been eager to find it, but it was obvious Mrs. Cromwell wouldn't be happy so far from the infirmary.

"I'm sorry, Tom. It hasn't been a very cheerful afternoon for you. Things will be better in a day or two."

He felt a bit nettled. His wife wasn't looking too good either. A few days in Rushton would have made all the difference.

He got back to Rushton in time for dinner. The place seemed to have altered. All the peace and quiet had gone since the news of Twigg's murder had got about. Mrs. Groves seemed to be keeping out of his way and the maid attended to him at dinner. He wished one or two others would keep away, too.

"Any news?"

First one and then another newshawk accosted him, and a photographer snapped him leaving the *Weatherby*. One had the cheek to ask if it would be any use going down to the hospital to see Cromwell.

To mend matters, it started to rain. The sky turned to dirty grey and night came on early. It was quite dark when Littlejohn got out the car and set out for the *Bull and Bush*.

Charlie Bragg met him in the passage.

"Glad to see you again, Super. If it's Mr. Twigg's old pals you're wantin', they're in the *Kennel* all on their own. It's a sad night for them. The news is terrible, isn't it? Poor old Twigg. Bumped off, was he? Whoever could have done it? I guess you'll soon know, if you don't know already. This way..."

Bragg had been drinking again and staggered as he walked.

"The Superintendent, gentlemen..."

Wainwright was on his feet right away. He shook hands with Littlejohn and took him by the arm.

"Good job you're here, Superintendent. They need a man like you to find out who murdered poor old Twigg. Staggering news... Did you know about it before? Perhaps that's what really brought you to Rushton?"

"No, sir. I merely came to see my friend after the shooting."

"Wonder if the same chap committed both crimes. Perhaps a maniac... What do you think?"

Temple and Wise were quiet and thoughtful. They greeted

Littlejohn cordially, too. They seemed to derive comfort from his being there.

"Glad you've come, Superintendent. What will you drink?"

Wainwright brushed Temple aside.

"On me. Where's Carrie? Carrie! Carrie!!"

The girl arrived.

"Three beers, and the usual for me."

They gave him a chair by the fire. Outside, the rain was falling in sheets and a wind had sprung up and was plastering the rain on the windows.

"But how could anybody want to murder poor old Twigg?" went on Wainwright. "And the way it was done, too. That was a crafty thing, wasn't it?"

Littlejohn looked sharply at Wainwright.

"The way it was done? Is there something in the papers about that, too? I haven't seen one."

"No. It just said there'd been a post-mortem and there was every reason for suspecting Twigg had been poisoned. But it seems Cank has been talking. He got drunk in Rushton Inferior this afternoon. It was the newspaper men who'd been plying him with whisky and pumping him. Cank said something about a drug being used that made poor old Twigg bleed to death internally and that it might easily be mistaken for, say, a burst ulcer. Is that true?"

"We'll have to wait until the inquest."

The waitress brought the drinks.

"Poor old Twigg."

Wainwright couldn't get over it.

"Had he any enemies?"

The other three men looked at Littlejohn incredulously.

"What, Twigg? No. One of the best."

"But you were telling me last night that Mrs. Groves had a rod in pickle for him."

Temple suddenly woke up.

"But surely she wouldn't want to murder a man for that? She got over it years ago."

"Yes, that's right. I can't see Mrs. Groves having brains enough to concoct such a cunning idea... At any rate, where would she get the drug from? I believe it's hard come-by. Your health, Superintendent."

Littlejohn didn't answer the question about dicoumarin. He was anxious to get more information about Twigg.

"Did he get on well with his wife?"

Wise looked up and took a swig of his beer.

"They seemed to hit it off very well."

Wainwright wasn't going to let that pass.

"They might be described as comfortable enough, but you know what happens when an old man marries a young woman. He's apt to get jealous and she often tends to turn her eyes to younger stuff once the newness of the marriage has worn off."

Wise flushed.

"You know there was nothing of that kind with the Twiggs."

"Wasn't there? What about Clinton? He and Twigg's missus were very thick with each other. Only quite recently they've been seen about together."

"Did Twigg know of this, sir?"

"Yes, he did. He didn't seem to mind much. 'Provided it's only the doctor,' he once said. He said it here. The other two will bear me out."

Temple nodded.

"I remember it. I recollect we thought it was a bit odd. We asked him why such implicit trust in the doctor. He simply said, perhaps his wife liked a bit of fresh company now and then, especially if it was a younger man's. It would keep her alive... Those were his words."

"He trusted the doctor?"

"He said he did. He liked him. Said he wasn't the philandering sort."

"Did he trust his wife, Mr. Temple?"

Wainwright butted in.

"I'm not so sure about that. Are you, Wise?"

"Why bring me in it? I know nothing about it. He never mentioned such things to me."

"But you were here once or twice when he actually talked about leaving the village and going to live at the seaside, because his wife seemed to be getting bored... He'd had a drink or two and spoke more freely than usual. You were here, Wise. Don't you remember?"

"I must have forgotten. Anyhow, it doesn't matter now. Twigg's dead and past caring."

"I remember it."

Temple nodded and ordered more drinks.

"You see, Littlejohn, Mrs. Twigg's a damn good-looker, even though she's no longer a chicken. I'll bet she had a few adventures before she took up with Richard. She's that sort."

Wainwright's eyes sparkled at the very thought of it.

"Of course she's not. You're simply talking for talking's sake. What do you know about Mrs. Twigg before she met Richard?"

"Keep your hair on, Wise. No need to get annoyed. We're men of the world and we know her kind when we meet them. Personally, I was disappointed when Twigg brought her home. It was asking for trouble and now the poor fellow's got it."

"You're drunk."

"Look here, Wise, we're all friends together here and we say what we like. I'm not drunk and you know it. I suppose you're peeved because it seems disrespectful talking like this of the dead. But you ought to remember that poor Richard's been murdered and our friend Littlejohn here is going to find out who did it. We ought to talk to him freely. It'll help him."

"I said you're drunk, Wainwright, and you've no right to talk about a woman like that in the mess."

"Well, I'm damned! The man's come all over gallant! Why the

sudden change, Wise? You were as sorry as we were because we thought Twigg's new wife wasn't up to his standards. Don't say *you've* fallen for her, too."

Wise pulled himself together.

"Don't be idiotic, Wainwright. What would a man of my age be doing chasing skirts? I'm not that sort, either."

"Twigg did, and he could give you ten years. You never know, Wise, what a man's going to do. Age doesn't matter in these things, you know. Does it, Littlejohn? Your glass is empty. Carrie! Carrie, same again all round."

"Well, I can't make head or tail of it."

Temple, who had drunk more than usual, looked completely befuddled.

"Well, I can. There's only one person could have done it. And that's Mrs. Twigg herself. It's obvious..."

Wise rose to his feet.

"You're at it again, Wainwright. Give the woman a chance. Why should she kill her husband? He treated her well and they got on well."

"Sit down. The party's not over yet. We've things to discuss. You were asking why Mrs. Twigg did it. I'll tell you. Twigg told me he'd left her all his money, unconditionally. That's motive enough, isn't it? He was a rich man. Temple there will tell you. He used to ask Temple's advice on investments. Didn't he, Temple?"

"That's right. He did. Once he asked me to run my eye over his investment list. I was staggered. He was worth about seventy-five thousand pounds. He'd a flair for speculating on the stock exchange. That's in confidence, of course."

"And there's another reason, too. You both know, as well as I do, that Twigg was getting as bored with his wife as she was with him. He married her under romantic conditions, didn't he? Cruising in the Mediterranean. But life's not a long cruise, is it? They'd got to live together, hadn't they? Well, it didn't come off. You chaps know it didn't. Twigg much preferred our company to his wife's by the time he died. Now don't tell me he didn't. He counted the hours to our meetings. Any time he could arrange some little excursion or an extra meeting, he jumped at it. He was bored to death with her. But not only that. She was bored to death with him, too. With Twigg out of the way, she could have a whale of a time. All that money and still not too old to enjoy it, still damn' good-looking. She'd motive, excellent opportunity, too, to put the stuff in his food or drink, and by God, she was hard enough to do it, too. Twigg was good to her, but if she wanted to get him out of the way, nothing would stop her. Suppose she'd got another lover on the q.t...."

Wise was on his feet again.

"I'm going. I've had enough of this. It's not fair to put a rope round her neck, especially in front of an officer of the law. It's not good enough. Give her a chance, for poor old Richard's sake. What do you suppose Twigg would have said if he'd known you were going to try to get his wife hanged for his death?"

"He'd have thanked me. You and Temple weren't as close to Twigg as I was. We were both men of the world and we talked about the things of the world. There wasn't much went on that Twigg didn't know about. He wasn't born yesterday and he wasn't blind. He knew all about the men in Mrs. Twigg's life, before, *and* after he married her. You don't think he was fool enough not to make inquiries about her past before he asked her. He knew he certainly wasn't the first."

Wise shrugged his shoulders and struggled into his raincoat. Outside, the rain was still beating on the windows. In the back room somebody was singing in a drunken voice and soon they heard him being put out into the dark. Then there was a hush.

"I'm off, then. It's ten o'clock, or as near ten as dammit. I'm still under the doctor, you know."

"Flowerdew?"

Wise jumped at Littlejohn's laconic question.

"No, Cruickshank. Why? Do you know Flowerdew?"

"I've heard of him. His name cropped up because a few weeks ago, he lost a phial of tablets of the drug which was used to poison Twigg."

Dead silence. Wise was breathing heavily.

Wainwright spoke first.

"That's funny; and yet it isn't, you know. Old Flowerdew is past it. He's eighty if he's a day and though he's still very lively, he tends to forget things. I told Wise when he was attending him that I wouldn't like to be at the mercy of a doctor in his dotage..."

"He only came three times when Cruickshank was away. I was well on the way to recovery then."

"He gave you dicoumarin tablets?"

"Yes. I gather it isn't a drug they dish out *ad lib.,* so to speak. They give you a few at a time to be sure you don't take too many."

"Did you know there were some such tablets in Mrs. Twigg's possession when her husband died?"

Another dead silence.

"Yes. I may as well tell you, my colleague had found them and was just returning from the chemist's, where he'd been inquiring about them, when he was shot."

"But how did she get those, if, as Wise says, they're doled out one or two at a time?"

"They were some her late mother used. It seems the London doctor who prescribed them was more liberal and less cautious than your local men."

Wainwright thrust out an accusing forefinger here, there and everywhere, stabbing the air uncertainly.

"What did I tell you? She did it. You'll find it was Mrs. Twigg. I've given my reasons why, and I stick to them."

"You're drunk."

"If you say I'm drunk again, Wise, I'll take a poke at you, invalid or no invalid. I say Mrs. Wise did it, and when Cromwell found out, she shot him. You'll find I'm right."

"She had an alibi in the case of Cromwell."

"All rot! Anybody can have an alibi. Who gave it to her? You'll find it's a phoney. Ready to bet on it? Wise? Temple? Ready to bet?"

"It's time you went home, too, Wainwright. You've had enough. You're drunk."

Wainwright rose solemnly and strode and faced Wise.

"That's the third time you've said I'm drunk. Well, I'm not, and I resent your keeping on saying it. We've been friends a long time and I like you, but there are limits. If you keep insulting me in front of the Superintendent, I shall hit you, and I mean that. You're not behaving like a pal and I shall cease to treat you as such if I have one more derogatory word from you."

Wainwright tottered on his heels. Wise was right, but his friend was in no mood for the truth about it.

"Admit I'm sober and shake hands."

Temple was getting alarmed. He was a man of tact and peace and wanted no brawling. Besides, he liked their little meetings every night and morning. It would be a shame to break the habit and for him to have to start all over again.

"You two stop arguing. It'll be all right in the morning. We've all drunk more than usual. It's the shock of poor Richard's murder that's done it."

Wainwright turned sad eyes on Temple.

"You, too, say I'm drunk, Temple. I'm surprised at you. I valued your opinion more than any man living. Now, you let me down. You side with Wise here, and you know what Wise is. He is a rotter and a petticoat chaser... No, no... Don't deny it, Wise. And don't clench your fists, ole boy. If you try to hit me, I shall be there first and then they'll have to take you to the hospital again. You accuse me of being drunk. I, in turn, accuse you of being a petticoat chaser. My weakness is for drink; yours for women. Fair's fair, isn't it? We're tellin' the truth about one another, aren't we?"

It was fantastic to see the two men facing each other, old friends suddenly turned enemies. Wise looked as though he daren't turn and leave the room. His eyes goggled and he gazed fascinated at Wainwright, who was now intoxicated by the fear he saw in his old pal's eyes.

"You called me a drunk... Now call me a liar, Wise. Call me a liar. Go on. Say it..."

Charlie Bragg thrust in his head to see what all the fuss was about, the raised voices, the way Wainwright was thumping the table.

"What's all the row about? It's ten-thirty and time you drank up, gentlemen. Saving your presence, Superintendent. No offence. But these gents have drunk too much to-night and ought to be on their way home and to bed."

A small crowd had gathered at the landlord's back. One or two familiar faces among them. Old Turner again, a man with a wooden leg who swept the road and did jobbing gardening here and there, and the taxi-driver Littlejohn had seen calling for Mr. Beeton in the house opposite the *Weatherby*. Finally, the room to the right of the door, the one labelled *Parlour,* opened and the sheep from it began to mix with the goats of the taproom. Among the patrons of the *Parlour* was the Chairman of the Rural District Council. He was smoking a cigar. His eye caught Littlejohn's and bore the eternal query: Any news?

The landlord closed the door to keep the row between Wise and Wainwright private.

"Call me a liar... Go on. And then I'll tell the Superintendent something that isn't a lie. Something I promised Twigg I wouldn't mention, because he said he wanted more proof and then he'd deal with it himself. It was about something that happened at the last hunt ball at..."

Wise's mouth fell open and his eyes goggled. He seized Wainwright by the lapels of his coat.

"I say, old chap, I'm sorry. I didn't mean to insult you. If I said you're drunk, I'm sorry. You obviously couldn't be talking so well if you were drunk. My mistake. I apologize in front of all these gentlemen. Shake hands and be friends, old man. I didn't mean to be offensive."

He held out his hand, contrition written on his face and drooping from every limb.

Wainwright couldn't believe his eyes. He looked at the outstretched hand and then at Wise, shook it, and slapped Wise on the back.

"Don't mention it. Suddenly changed your mind, though, didn't you, ole man? Must have felt like me. I felt I couldn' afford to lose your friendship, but you shouldn' have provoked me. Anyhow, all's well that ens well, ole man... And now, we'll go home and sleep it off and forget it."

Temple drank the last of his beer and mopped his forehead. A near thing! Now, all was right, pals again, and the party to be resumed to-morrow night. He sidled up to Littlejohn.

"I've never known this happen before. It must be nerves, through the news about Richard. It's turned us all up, I must say. Well... Good night, Superintendent. You'll always be welcome when you care to join us."

Through the greenish glass of the door of the *Kennel*, faces kept peering in. The news of the row had gone round and people were anxious to see the select patrons of the pub quarrelling, like the men from the taproom, from the same cause which was behind every tavern brawl—they'd had too much. Carrie and the waiter were leaning against the wall of the lobby unperturbed; they were used to this kind of thing in the public bar.

Charlie Bragg looked relieved, too. These were good patrons and he didn't want to see the nightly party broken up.

"That's good, gents. Friends again. It's against the rules, but..."

Then he remembered Littlejohn.

"Against the rules to serve after hours, but we'll all have a drink on the house to-morrow. Whose turn is it to-night to see Mr. Wise home?"

"Mine," said Temple.

"He's not driven his car after dark since his illness, you see. So one of his friends sees him home. It's only five minutes away..."

Bragg told it all to Littlejohn, seeking some topic of friendly conversation and proof of what good pals they all were.

"Ready, Wise?" said Temple.

"Yes."

Littlejohn followed them to the door and, after they had passed through it, he took Wise by the arm.

"I'll see you home to-night, sir. Mr. Wainwright is certainly not fit to drive a car at all. In spite of your apology, he *is* drunk, you know, and I'm sure he'll agree it's hardly safe to try to drive, especially as there's a policeman here. So I'll take you, and Mr. Temple will take Wainwright, and Mr. Bragg will garage Wainwright's car till morning."

"Look here..."

Wainwright was going to start all over again. Littlejohn took him by the arm.

"I know you'll agree, Wainwright. You and I aren't going to quarrel... If you enter your car, I shall book you, so you can please yourself."

"Well, I'll be damned! You drink my beer and enjoy my company, and then threaten to charge me before the bench on which I'm a ruddy J.P. Superintendent, you're the bloody limit!"

He burst into roars of laughter, followed Temple to his car, and left Littlejohn to take the bewildered Wise safely home.

11
SALTS OF LEMON

"Perhaps you'd care to come in and have a nightcap, Superintendent?"

Wise's place was between Rushton Inferior and Rushton Superior, a modernized Georgian farmhouse, standing back from the road and approached by a long drive fringed by old trees. Littlejohn could see nothing much beyond the patches illuminated by the headlamps of the car, but it was enough. A well-kept, tidy little manor run for his comfort and pleasure by a man who wasn't dependent on farming for his fortune.

The house itself was the same. It was creeper-covered at the front and the heavy door stood back in a semi-circular portico with four pillars supporting the top and three steps leading up to it. A light shone from the roof of the porch and two of the large oblong sash windows of the front were illuminated.

Throughout the journey the two men hardly spoke a word. Wise merely gave directions how to find the house and Littlejohn was occupied in carrying them out. Finally, he invited the Superintendent to come in for a drink.

The interior was just as imposing as the outside. A blast of warm air met them as they entered. Although it was spring and the days were warm, the chilly nights were provided for by central heating. Thick carpets on the floor of the hall, good pictures on the walls, and solid period mahogany furniture. A broad graceful staircase curved upwards from one side.

Wise took Littlejohn's hat.

"My housekeeper's gone to bed. We'll have to look after ourselves."

He opened a door to the left and stood aside for Littlejohn to enter.

A large, beautifully panelled room with oak beams in the ceiling. It must have been Wise's office, and was furnished as a study as well. Comfortable easy chairs, a large desk, books mainly on farming and kindred subjects on shelves on the walls, an agricultural almanac. A row of trophies—silver cups and the like, won at shows—a baize-covered notice-board with the year's prize-cards from many events and in many colours pinned on it. Framed photographs of horses and cattle all over the walls, and above the fine fireplace an oil portrait of a lovely hunter, graceful with a shining black coat, set against a background of wooded fields in the traditional manner of equine pictures.

"Whisky?"

Wise poured out a couple of glasses from a decanter set on a silver tray.

"Sit down, Littlejohn. I take it you're in no hurry... Good health..."

"I'm glad you came, Littlejohn. I've been seeking the opportunity of asking you if there is anything I can do to help you. If so, please don't hesitate to call on me."

Wise had something on his mind. He was a bit awkward and chose his words carefully. There were long pauses in his conversation.

Littlejohn met his questioning look with a bland expression.

"In what way do you think you can help me, sir?"

Wise cleared his throat, seemed about to speak, changed his mind, and took a drink of his whisky.

"Is there anything I can tell you about Richard Twigg?"

Littlejohn felt there was quite a lot. Wise was by far the most intelligent of the group of men which gathered in the *Kennel* at the *Bull and Bush*. Wealthy, business-like, wellbred, he seemed to have all it took to be a happy man, and yet... Here he was with his legs sprawled out and his highly-polished shoes toasting in front of the electric fire, looking worried to death. A man whose occupation should have found him in perfect health, yet suffering from the current illness due to tension and civilization, coronary thrombosis. A worried man, a man judging, too, from the way he lived, with a soft streak in him.

"You live alone here, sir?"

Wise looked surprised. He'd just offered his help in the case of Richard Twigg and here was Littlejohn asking him a lot of questions about himself. He tried to damp it down by being a bit off-hand.

"Yes. I have a good housekeeper. My wife died ten years ago. I never married again."

"You've always been a farmer?"

"No. I own an engineering works not far from Wiston. I'm chairman, and other people look after it nowadays. It's the family business. I moved in here during the war. It belonged to my family and was rented to farmers. When it became vacant, I came to live here. I like it so much that I've gradually turned over the works to men who are better qualified to run it."

There was asperity in the way he said it, as though he resented inquiries on his private life and, as he finished the last sentence, he nodded as though to ask: Is that enough for you?

"You were an old friend of Mr. Twigg?"

"I've known him ever since he came here. We met at the golf club. He was a member there from the first. I liked him. Gradually, the four of us came to making a regular evening rendezvous at the *Bull and Bush*."

"May I ask where you all were on the night a shot was fired at my colleague, Cromwell?"

Wise gave Littlejohn a queer look, half question, half protest.

"You don't think any of us would take a shot at a man like Cromwell? Why, we didn't even know him, except by name. Twigg mentioned him a time or two. He seemed proud to have a nephew in Scotland Yard."

"All the same, just as a matter of routine, where were you all?"

"Twigg was dead, by then. The rest of us were at the *Bull and Bush* that night. We parted at the usual hour of ten. I understand that Cromwell was shot-at between eleven and midnight. I'm afraid it's a bit difficult for *anybody* to give an alibi for such an hour. I, myself, was in bed, and I'm sure Wainwright and Temple were, too. I can only ask you to take my word. I've no proof."

"I don't doubt what you say, sir."

Littlejohn paused to take a drink.

"Twigg was a queer sort of chap, wasn't he? Don't you agree?"

"I... I..."

"You knew him well, sir, didn't you? You spent every night with him. You were a friend of his."

"I agree, but what do you mean by queer?"

"He didn't marry till late in life. He'd travelled a long way and made his fortune. Then, he settled here in comfort with a lot of good friends. One day he goes off on a cruise, and returns with a wife a lot younger than himself. She was charming and attractive. Quite a lot of men in the neighbourhood found themselves interested in her. Twigg began to get suspicious... Did he ever talk about it at the *Bull and Bush*? Did he get confidential in his cups?"

Wise looked at the shiny toe of his shoe and took another drink. Then, he reached over and filled up the glasses again.

"Well... He did mention the doctor... Clinton, I mean. But he seemed to think it rather funny. He said the doctor was quite smitten on his wife. He sounded proud about it. You see, Clinton's a bit of a snob. The idea of Clinton falling for Emily struck him as extraordinary."

"Do you know if he mentioned it to his wife or Clinton?"

Wise looked uneasy. He couldn't quite make out where the questions were leading to now.

"I think he did. He pulled his wife's leg about it. He said so."

"He didn't threaten her?"

"No; I don't think so. He was proud of her good-looks and perhaps it pleased him to think the doctor admired his good taste in women."

"Was Twigg a bit of a martinet?"

"What do you mean by that?"

"Was he normally strict with his wife?"

"I think he was, a bit. I'm sure he kept an eye on the company she kept."

"Was he mean or generous with her?"

"Oh, generous. She never seemed short of money and he gave her all she wanted. Speaking of his being a martinet, though. Once or twice I've found him a bit put-out when he's found her out of the house when he returned home. He asked me once if I ever saw her about the village or the neighbourhood. I think he was trying to find out what company she kept."

"Did he strike you as having found out about, let us say, the male company his wife might be keeping?"

"I can't say. There was local gossip about her and Clinton. I'm sure there wasn't anything serious in it. She was a Londoner, after all, and used to London ways. More free and easy, perhaps, than country people. Clinton's the same, you know."

"Twigg left her all his money, I hear."

"Yes. At first he seemed to take her little peccadillos with a smile. But he *did* mention altering his will. Just casually, he spoke of it one evening. He wanted to be sure that, if she married again after his death, the next husband didn't come into all Twigg's money."

"Is Clinton your doctor?"

Wise looked surprised at the sudden change of subject.

"No. As I told you before, I have Cruickshank, of Wiston. An older man and I prefer him."

"Let me see... Isn't he the man whom Flowerdew acts for when he's away."

"Yes. Why?"

"I've heard of him. And of Flowerdew. When did Flowerdew visit you, sir? I heard Cruickshank had been away."

"Easter week. Cruickshank always goes away then."

"Was that the time the local county medical officer left, as well?"

"Yes. But I don't understand what all this is about, Littlejohn. What has the local medical officer to do with Flowerdew and my illness?"

"Only that Mrs. Groves told me about the party the medical men of the district gave in honour of the departing county M.O. She seemed proud of the dinner she put on for them."

"Yes. He left Easter week. Flowerdew went. I remember his telling me when he called here one day. He's like a child now. A party fills him with infantile delight. Free drinks and food, especially the first, and he's in his element."

The clock in the hall slowly struck twelve.

"Good heavens! Midnight! I'd better be off, sir. Thanks for entertaining me and giving me a drink."

"Don't mention it, Littlejohn. I hoped I'd be able to help you. But I don't seem to have done much. Call again, if you're ever at a loose end. Come in the daytime and I'll show you the farm. I'm very proud of the farm and my stock."

"I'm sure you are, sir. It's a delightful place. I'll be sure to come again."

Mrs. Groves was sitting up waiting for him, as usual. He'd

forgotten her custom and was afraid she was going to ask him in her room for supper again. Instead, she met him with a reproachful look.

"You're very late again, Superintendent... The phone has been going for you. Three times, if not four..."

"I'm sorry you've been bothered. Who was it, Mrs. Groves?"

"Your wife. I don't know how she puts up with such a hateful man, who stays out so late at night."

It was said in the usual arch way she always used, half serious, half nonsense.

"Finally, she left a message. Could you go to the hospital in Manchester, first thing in the morning? She says that Mr. Cromwell is much better—which I'm glad to hear—and may be able to talk to you for a minute or two."

"That's good news. Thank you, Mrs. Groves."

"Glad to be of service. And now, I've got a ham sandwich for your supper in my private room... and some coffee, so come along."

"He's had a very good night."

Littlejohn could hardly eat his breakfast for eagerness to see Cromwell and when, after picking up his wife and Mrs. Cromwell at their hotel, he arrived at the Royal Infirmary, he found quite an atmosphere of revelry around the private ward in which they had installed Cromwell. The sister was beaming as she met the little party of visitors.

"He's able to talk to you a bit to-day. But, mind you, only a word or two. He's not to be tired at all. He's not out of the wood yet, by any means. I've known them have a relapse and haemorrhages through overdoing it. He mustn't be tired."

Cromwell was still wearing his turban of bandages, but he looked a lot better. His old smile was returning, a sure sign that he was improving. He asked about the children and expressed his regret for causing his wife so much trouble and anxiety.

"You'd think he'd shot himself, wouldn't you?" asked Mrs.

Cromwell, who, in her delight, looked more like her pretty self again and was beginning to talk about taking her husband home very soon.

"I don't really know what it was all about, sir," said Cromwell when he and Littlejohn got a word together at length. "It must have been an accident. Perhaps I was mistaken for someone else."

"You had some tablets in your pocket, old man. They were anti-coagulant and rather deadly. How do you explain them?"

"I found one on the floor near my uncle's desk. Cank had, I'm sure, been rifling the desk and dropped one. I wondered what he'd been after. I opened the desk and found a few in an envelope. I was curious. So I called and asked the chemist. It was very late, but I found him up. As I left the chemist's, someone must have shot at me, or else I met the shot intended for someone else."

"Don't worry, old chap. I think you probably were mistaken for somebody else."

"You don't think it was connected with my visit to the chemist's?"

"I don't know. I'll find out and let you know."

"I felt puzzled after talking with the chemist. What was my uncle doing with anti-coagulant tablets? The chemist said they were used for coronary thrombosis. My uncle hadn't that. He died from an ulcer."

"His wife's mother had used such tablets and it might have been these were left over from her treatment. I'll take the matter up."

Littlejohn skated lightly over it all, not wishing to worry his colleague or leave behind ideas which would trouble him.

"I hope they'll soon let me out of here. I want to get back to work. As for this accident, it's just a bit of bad luck. I stopped a shot perhaps fired by a poacher... I don't know. Anyhow, I'm not worried so long as I can take up where I left off, sir."

"You'll soon be all right."

It was obvious that Cromwell, before the shot laid him low,

had not harboured any suspicions about his uncle's death or Mrs. Twigg's behaviour and private life. He had simply inquired about the dicoumarin as a matter of curiosity.

"Is Cank still with my uncle's wife at *Ballarat,* sir?"

"Yes. Why?"

"I don't like him. If I'd stayed on, I'd have persuaded her to get rid of him. He's a dark horse and is up to no good."

"In what way?"

"He's some hold over Emily, but I couldn't find out what it was. She seems afraid of him. I'll have to speak to him and Emily when I'm up and about again."

"Anything I can do?"

"You can find out, if you can, sir, what sort of hold Cank has over her. That is, if you've time. I suppose now that I'm nearly in circulation again, you'll be off back to London."

"I'll stay another day or two. Just to make sure you're behaving yourself."

The sister was back.

"Enough for one day. No sense in tiring the patient the first time he's allowed to speak. It's time to go."

There were arrangements to make, too. Mrs. Cromwell would be able to go home to-morrow and see the children, returning every other day to her husband without needing to stay overnight. Mrs. Littlejohn was going back with her.

"How long will you be before you're home, too?" she asked Littlejohn.

"A day or two."

"You know who fired the shot, then?"

"Not yet."

"Or how Mr. Twigg met his death?"

"I know how, but not who did it, yet. By the way, Cromwell doesn't know his uncle died an unnatural death. They've kept the news from him. As far as Cromwell is concerned, there's no mystery, no case at all to solve at Rushton."

"I'm glad. It will keep his mind at rest."

On the way back to Rushton, Littlejohn pondered the case with exasperation. It was the most barren investigation he'd ever come across.

It would be easy enough to tackle the matter of Uncle Richard's death. His wife and her lovers could account for that and it might, by taking a chance, prove easy to break down one or another of them and get a confession or a vital lead out of them. Wise, Clinton, Mrs. Twigg—and Cank thrown in for good luck. It might be any or all of them. And sooner or later, the truth was bound to come out. But the shooting of Cromwell with a pop-gun, or as near as dammit to one, was another matter.

Was it a mistake, or an accident? Or did somebody think Cromwell knew more than he actually did and try to silence him?

In the latter case, Mrs. Twigg would fill the bill, or Wise, or Cank, or...

The whole thing was a mix-up. In any event, whoever had murdered Richard Twigg had done himself a bad turn in taking a pot-shot at Cromwell. For the shooting affair had caused Littlejohn to travel north and had almost fortuitously brought the murder to light.

He was no nearer seeing daylight when he arrived back at Rushton Inferior.

Something had obviously happened in the village since Littlejohn left early that morning. There was a queer atmosphere hanging over the place, even before he noticed or heard anything. People standing in knots by the roadside, talking together, heads close, faces awe-struck. A police-car passed him almost as he reached the *Weatherby*. There was a screech of brakes, the vehicle stopped, reversed, and drew up alongside Littlejohn's own car. Tandy was inside, with Sergeant Buck at the wheel. Tandy leapt out and hurried round to the open window of the Superintendent's car.

"Never rains but it pours, sir. Another tragedy, accidental or deliberate. I don't know which, yet. It's Cank this time. He's taken a dose of salts of lemon, and, although they got him to the cottage hospital as soon as they could, he's died. I've just come from the bedside. I'd hoped he might say something before the end, but he was in so much pain, he never spoke. A horrible death..."

"How did it happen, Tandy?"

"It seems he's troubled with indigestion and relieves it by taking a biggish dose of bicarbonate of soda. Well, he had an attack a little more than an hour ago, went to the packet of bicarbonate, took a large spoonful, put it in hot water, and swigged it off. He'd got it all down before he found out it wasn't bi-carb., but something else. The doctor soon recognized what he'd taken. It was salts of lemon. It was too late, though. They couldn't get a doctor quick enough."

"But how could Cank have made such a mistake?"

"He didn't. Our worthy Bloor made a remarkable discovery whilst waiting for the ambulance. You know, sir, how this refined bicarbonate's sold. In a bag, contained inside a cardboard carton with the name on. It seems salts of lemon is sold in the same way. Somebody had removed the bi-carb. bag and put a salts of lemon one in its place. Cank had taken a dose before he knew what he was doing. After all, how was he to know...?"

"And Bloor spotted it?"

"Yes. He saw the stuff didn't quite look like bi-carb., and called the doctor's attention to it."

"Clinton?"

"Yes."

"I wonder why Cank didn't spot the difference."

"Pain probably made him in a hurry to get relief and he went to the usual box, hardly noticing what was in it. How could he be expected to? I suppose he'd taken dozens of doses from that or similar packets."

"So... It looks like another murder?"

"Very much so. Could you come along and take a look over the place, sir? We'll be glad of your help."

The Chairman of the Rural District Council had just spotted Littlejohn and was making for him, intent on another third-degree. The Superintendent pretended not to see him, slipped in the clutch of his car, and drove away after Tandy, in spite of the fact that he hadn't yet eaten a meal and didn't look like getting another for some time.

12
THE RELEASE OF MRS. CANK

The murder of Cank was in line with the rest of the recent unsavoury events in the pretty village of Rushton Inferior. It might have been committed by any one of a dozen people. Mrs. Cank said she had been out shopping in Wiston when it happened and had arrived home to find her husband rolling on the floor in agony. She'd been away over half-an-hour and anybody might have entered the back door and substituted salts of lemon for bicarbonate of soda. Everybody, according to her, knew about Cank and his bicarb. He was an addict. Took to it like a lot of men take to drink. He kept it in the kitchen cupboard and everybody from the milkman to the doctor had seen him take it to soothe his innards.

"He might easy 'ave done it all his-self. Made away with 'is-self and tried to make it look as if it was me as did it... I wouldn't put it past 'im."

Beyond the grief and prostration expected of a widow in such circumstances, Mrs. Cank didn't seem in the least upset. When reminded of her husband's death, she broke down and wept and wailed, and immediately forgot it when she talked of him, and began to belabour his memory venomously and speak ill of the dead. She seemed glad to be rid of him.

"I's go down to live with me sister in Gloucester," she told Littlejohn. "Cank was insured and I'm supposed to get the money. With me widow's pension and the bit I've saved, and 'is insurance monies, I'll manage. That is, if he's not willed his insurances away from me, which I wouldn't put past 'im. But to be took so sudden before I could see 'is affairs proper in order is a very bitter blow, sir."

She wept and moaned and then began once again to make arrangements about going to the better land, which, judging from what she said of it, was situated in Gloucestershire.

Tandy and Buck were busy about the place, asking questions of all and sundry. It seemed that Turner had actually been within shouting distance of Cank when he made his mistake in choosing his medicine. Only Turner had been mowing the lawn with a motor-mower which made such a racket that he couldn't hear anything else, added to slight deafness, which precluded altogether Cank's groans reaching him.

"What did 'e want takin' salts o' lemon for? Anybody'd know the difference atween them and soder. Even a child would know. It's my believe Cank committed suicide. Guilty conscience. I do believe it were Cank as killed 'is master and shot the detective. Then he poisoned his-self..."

Buck spent half an hour with Turner, who was delighted to leave his gardening for a discussion of murder at the rate of three shillings an hour. Tandy, meanwhile, was talking to Mrs. Twigg in his most consoling manner, which was his most dangerous.

"Believe me, Mrs. Twigg, some people have to bear an undue weight of trouble. I'm heartily sorry for you. Whatever could Cank have been thinking of?"

Littlejohn and Mrs. Cank were sitting in the kitchen talking things over.

"Such a nice gentleman, so sympathetic," she later told her sister in the golden Gloucester days.

"My only worry about Cank is, will 'e go to 'eaven?" said Mrs. Cank, throwing her fat body to and fro in a rocking chair. Every time the chair went back, her dropsical legs left the ground and Littlejohn held his breath lest she should turn a somersault over the back. "You see, I was alwiz brought up religious. Still go reg'lar to meetin's in Wiston. Pentecostal Wrestlers, I belong to, and I've tried so 'ard to get Cank to think of 'is immortal soul and be saved. But 'e never would. 'I don't believe in God,' he used to say. It worried me. And then I stopped worryin'. I thought out things and it came to me that bein' married to Cank throughout eternity would be more than I could bear. I'd rather be in 'ell if he was to be in 'eaven and claim me there as his lawful-wedded wife. It might sound wrong of me, but it's the truth."

"Was he a hard man, then?"

"Nobody knows 'ow 'ard he was. Except me. Often's the time I've thought of runnin' away from him. But I didn't, on account of me marriage vows. I promised for better or worse and it turned out worse. I'm glad he's gone before me. A few more years of this life and he'd 'ave dragged me to hell with him. Now, I've a few years left to make me peace before I die."

It seemed unnatural to try to make the woman talk about what life with Cank had been like, but it was obvious it had turned her brain a bit.

"Look!" she suddenly said, ceasing her rocking and drawing up the sleeve of her blouse. The arm was covered in heavy blue bruises.

"Whatever...?"

Littlejohn sat up aghast.

"He did that to me, because I said I'd tell the police. He twisted me arms and said he'd give me some more if I so much as went near the police."

"What had you to tell us, Mrs. Cank?"

Her bulging eyes were full of fear and she twisted her fingers together.

"I feel 'e's still about, listenin' round doors like 'e used to do, and that 'e might come back and ill-treat me if I don't do as he says..."

"You've nothing to fear now. Nor had you before. We'd have looked after you."

"Would you, sir? He'd have beaten you, though. He'd have got even with me. Told me once or twice he'd kill me..."

"What were you going to tell us that he was afraid of our knowing?"

"*He* wasn't afraid. He wasn't afraid of nothin' or nobody. All he wanted was to keep on in his evil ways and nobody to stop him. My mother always said I'd rue the day I married Cank, but he bewitched me and 'ad 'is way with me, like he did with everythin' else, including Mrs. Twigg."

"Mrs. Twigg?"

"Yes. He'd only to ask 'er for money an' she paid up. I'd hear him ask her and then he'd come in the kitchen and count it. Twenty pounds a time, sometimes more. And if he wanted anythin', he'd just to say the word. That's how we got the telly."

She pointed to a large television set in one corner.

"How did he manage to get his own way with your mistress?"

"I've heard him say if people knew the things he knew, there'd be trouble. That was enough for Mrs. Twigg. She did as he bid her."

"Did Mr. Twigg know when he was alive?"

"No. Cank used to say if he told Mr. Twigg all the 'istory about his lovely wife, she'd soon be out of the house. That was if Mr. Twigg didn't kill 'er."

"What was it all about?"

It was like drawing blood from a stone. The woman couldn't get used to the idea of Cank's not being there and kept looking fearfully around in case he should appear and start his evil tricks again.

"I don't know, sir. Honestly, I don't. Cank never told me anything. 'You got no brains,' he used ter say of me. 'Can't think for yourself, so I got to do it for the both of us.' That's what he said. He never told me what evil things went on in his mind. And I thank the Lord he didn't. Else I'd 'ave been damned the same as he was..."

It was a case of weeping at her widowhood and rejoicing at her freedom, with Mrs. Cank.

"You know, don't you, Mrs. Cank that poor Mr. Twigg was poisoned, too? He was murdered, you know."

She stopped rocking and remained stock-still for a moment, horror all over her face and rigid body.

"But the doctor said it was nacherall."

"Don't you read the newspapers? It was all in there, how they found out later it was a mistake and he'd been poisoned after all."

"I never read the papers. I can't read proper. That's why I like the telly. Because I can't read. Sometimes Cank would read to me bits about things, things that pleased him. Robberies and murders, horrible things that used ter frighten me. He'd laugh at me then..."

"Who murdered Mr. Twigg?"

"I'm sure *I* didn't. I know nothin' about it. I liked Mr. Twigg. Used to stop and have a joke with me and bring me sweets and things now and then. I cried for days after he was took. If ever a man'll go to 'eaven, it was Mr. Twigg..."

"Did you ever see anything suspicious going on? Anything like putting something in his food or drinks?"

"Suspicious?"

She looked blankly at him. It was painful getting her to understand. She was so obviously bemused by her past life, and that on top of a naturally sub-normal mentality, kept her in a dark world struggling to see through the fog.

"Did you ever see anybody...?"

She'd got it.

"Mrs. Twigg used to put him his tablets in his tea. Once when I come upon her in this kitchen where she was making tea for the two of them, she'd poured him out a cup and was puttin' in his tablets."

"You caught her at it?"

"Yes. She looked up and saw me there and I thought she'd have killed me for comin' on her so quietly."

"What did she say?"

"'You started me,' she sez. 'Don't ever again go creepin' about the house.' And she said Mr. Twigg's digestion 'ad been very bad and she was just givin' him his tablets."

"What kind?"

"Little white things."

"When was this?"

"Just before he was tuck ill with his bleedin' ulcer."

"Why didn't you tell the police when they were here to question you all?"

She looked impatiently at Littlejohn, as though he, in turn, were slow-witted.

"What did I show you me arms all bruised for? Didn't I say that Cank told me what he'd do if I so much as opened me mouth?"

"I see. You told him about it, did you?"

"Yes. After Mr. Twigg died."

And Cank had gone straight away to hunt for the tablets and Cromwell had come upon him just as he'd found some of them. That had started it all.

"Can you remember the night Mr. Cromwell was shot?"

"Of course. I cried hard and prayed hard for him that night. I liked Mr. Cromwell. Sich a gentleman, he was. Smilin', full of fun, and a good word for you. 'And how's Mrs. Cank, my little chickabiddy.' That's what he used to say when he met me about... I remember the night well. We didn't know till mornin', but I remember 'im goin' out and never comin' back."

"Did your husband or Mrs. Twigg go out after him?"

"No. I'm sure of that. Mrs. Twigg stopped in her bed. She wasn't well and I took her tea up two or three times that night. She was undressed and settled for the night. My husband didn't go out. He stopped in to watch the telly. After we got the telly, he hardly ever went out after dark. We'd sit there, all quiet, for hours and hours, me on one side and 'im on the other, and the telly between us."

"Did your husband have a private drawer or box where he kept his special things? His money and papers?"

She looked at him suspiciously.

"He didn't leave no will. All his money'll come to me. He once said so when in a good mood. Offen after that, he threatened to leave it to the dogs' home, but he never did."

"It's not the money, Mrs. Cank. I just wanted to know if he'd happened to find Mr. Cromwell's notebook. It's been lost and I thought Mr. Cank might have come across it and put it away till he got well again."

"I don't know nothin' about it. You wouldn't take away the money, would you?"

"Of course not. It's nothing to do with me. Had he a box or something, then?"

"Yes. A sort of strong money-box he kept locked in a drawer. He never let the key out of his sight. I've got it now. His keys was in his pocket when he died. I'd a right to them."

She looked quite aggressive and her soft, stupid brown eyes suddenly flashed.

"Of course, you have. But could you show me the box?"

She hesitated. It was obvious her mind was on the valuable contents.

"All right, if you'll keep it to yourself, then. You've been kind to me and talked to me more like a yewman than most. I'll get it..."

She left him and made off upstairs. After an interminable time, she returned, breathing heavily, carrying an expensive strong-box which she placed on the table and opened with a key on a bunch she took from her skirt-pocket. The box had cost Cank a pretty penny when he bought it. It wasn't the kind you could open with a tin-opener, nor pick the lock with a hairpin.

It was plain from the start why Mrs. Cank had been a long time away. She'd obviously removed the money and valuables, for there were nothing but odds and ends of papers in the box.

The first thing Littlejohn saw was Cromwell's shiny black notebook. Cank must have taken it for perusal and, after Littlejohn had missed it and asked for it, he hadn't dared to return it to the pocket of the coat still hanging in the wardrobe. Littlejohn looked at the last entries in the book. They merely consisted of the train times and other travel particulars to which Littlejohn had seen Cromwell refer when—it seemed very long ago now—they had said goodbye in his room at Scotland Yard. Cank, expecting some reference perhaps to the dicoumarin, had been disappointed, but daren't put the book back in its place. Littlejohn slipped it in his pocket.

"This is the sergeant's little book, Mrs. Cank. Your husband must have been looking after it for him. I'll take it."

"I don't mind. Is that all, sir?"

There were other papers. A few life policies of the penny-a-week variety. Birth, marriage, and death certificates for various members of the family. Savings certificates, and two bank-books; one in the Post Office with a balance of six hundred pounds; the other in the Wiston Savings Bank, with a thousand pounds deposit. Then, a building society book, with nine hundred to credit. Cank's ill-gotten gains! And presumably, Mrs. Cank had removed a lot of pound notes on the way.

Littlejohn turned over the papers briefly. Finally, an envelope, with a circular inside.

"Mind if I look at this, too?"

"It's nothin', is it?"

"Just a circular..."

STERNDALE & COMPANY, LTD.
BOND STREET, W.1.

We are still interested in purchasing antiques of all kinds for export to America...

It was the address on the envelope, however, which interested Littlejohn.

Casadessus & Co.,
Antiques,
12, Hampole Street, W.1.

The name and address had been scored out in pencil and the envelope re-directed.

Mr. Frederick Wainwright,
Yew Tree House,
Rushton Superior,
Cheshire.

Littlejohn paused and gently balanced the envelope in his fingers. The postmark on the face was a mere smudge, but whoever had re-addressed the letter had stamped the date on the back. It was the 20th of the previous December.

"Your husband used to be a postman here, Mrs. Cank?"

"Years since, yes."

"Has he ever helped them since?"

"Sometimes at Christmas when they was pulled-out with the mails. Last Christmas, he did it. Sam Foley, the local postman, fell ill with pneumonia right in the Christmas rush. They had some of the boys from Wiston Grammar School deliverin', but with Cank 'avin' been a postman and knowin' all the places and rounds, the main postmaster from Wiston asked him, as a favour, to do the sortin' and put the boys on the right road. He was there near on a week, till the rush ended and Sam got back."

"I'd like to keep this circular, if I may."

He showed it to her and she handed it back without even reading it.

"It's no use to me."

"May I telephone, please?"

"You know where it is, sir. In the hall."

He could hear Tandy and Mrs. Twigg talking on his way to the instrument, which he lifted softly and asked for Scotland Yard.

"I want you, please, to look up the firm of Casadessus and Co., 12, Hampole Street, W.1. Find out who owns it, if they're still there. Otherwise, look up the records. As much information as you can. It's urgent, so please ring the Wiston police with any news."

Tandy entered and disturbed the seance, just as Littlejohn got back to Mrs. Cank.

"Well, that seems to be all, sir. I take it you've had a good talk to Mrs. Cank... Please accept my condolences, Mrs. Cank. It must be hard to lose your man after being together all these years. It's hard when the time comes..."

Mrs. Cank wept to show it was hard and then they left her.

"Can't make head or tail of it," said Tandy. He pushed his hat on the back of his head and looked in a fog.

"It seems very much to me as if Cank made a mistake himself. He put the salts of lemon in the wrong box. Or else, the grief or strain of recent weeks preyed on his mind and he committed suicide. It can't have anything to do with Mr. Twigg's death, can it? Are you any nearer finding out who did it, sir? Because, if you are, we might kill all the birds with one stone. Cank's death, too."

"I think you ought to proceed in the usual routine way, Tandy. Keep on gathering information and comparing notes. Question the suspects..."

Sergeant Buck, who had been standing by, thought it time to

put in his own motto. He stabbed the air with a fat forefinger, almost poking Tandy in the eye.

"I'm keepin' my eye on Turner. He positively 'ated Cank. Said he was glad he'd made away with himself. Good riddance, and all that. Turner thinks Cank took poison because of a guilty conscience. He says Cank murdered Twigg. He can't produce any evidence of it, but he says he feels it in his bones. That makes me suspect *him*. He's trying to lead us astray. He could have nipped in the kitchen any time and poisoned Cank's bicarbonate of soda."

He paused and looked wise.

"That's clever of you, Buck. You've nearly solved the case already."

Tandy's voice was full of heavy sarcasm, which was his only medicine for keeping Buck in his place. Buck's expression of dejected resentment was comic. He lowered his eyes and kicked the ground with one foot like an angry horse. Then he brightened up.

"What about Mrs. Twigg herself as a suspect?"

"Come on, Buck. Let's be getting along to the police station. You'll be suspecting me next."

Littlejohn made his way back to the *Weatherby*. He'd missed his lunch and afternoon tea as well. Mrs. Groves met him with the usual rebuke.

"Why don't you let me know when you're not coming back to lunch? You're a most difficult man to cater for. You can have a double afternoon tea and think yourself lucky I'm so nice to you..."

The childish laugh, the pink cheeks, the expression almost like that of a dummy in a shop window showing off the latest fashions with a sugary grin on its lips.

"I hear there's been another tragedy. You never tell me anything. I always have to ask you. Cank, isn't it? Poisoned himself? No? You don't know? Well, who should know if the police don't...? I'll order your tea. You don't seem in a very good mood."

Littlejohn went to his room for a bath and a change of clothes. As he took off his tie and glanced across the street, he saw Mrs. Beeton, sitting at the window, looking like an invalid, staring out. Her face, even from that distance, looked pale and waxy, with a haunted look of one who expects herself or someone dear to her to die at any moment. The figure of the district nurse materialized at her side. She must have been there to make the bed and tidy up, for she helped Mrs. Beeton from her chair and took her back to the gloomy interior of the room.

It was past six when Littlejohn finished his bath and dressed again. The village had grown quiet and, after the rain of last night, looked well-washed. The scent of flowers was heavy on the air again. People passing by, aware of the afternoon's tragedy, seemed to walk on tiptoes and speak in low voices. There was a parish meeting in the Sunday School, too, and the councillors were gathering. These, added to another meeting of members of the Women's Institute, who were holding a garden-party on the following Saturday, livened the place temporarily.

Downstairs, the restaurant was filling-up for dinner. A few people had driven out from nearby towns and Mrs. Groves was going to be busy cooking the omelettes for which she had a local reputation. The Chairman of the Rural District Council was there and, when he saw Littlejohn, he made for him almost ferociously. He was smoking a cigar and looked important. All eyes turned on him.

"I'd like a word with you, Superintendent. Let's go across to the *Brown Cow* for a drink."

His goatee thrust fiercely before him, he led the way to the pub across the road and chose a seat in a quiet corner. All eyes there, too, turned on him. The local elections were due shortly and the Chairman was anxious to show his mettle.

"What will you drink, Superintendent?"

"A *Pernod*, please."

The Chairman's eyes opened wide. He looked disgusted at the man who drank such dissolute stuff.

"Sure?"

"Yes, please."

"A dry sherry for me and a *Pernod* for the Superintendent."

Littlejohn didn't know quite why he'd asked for it, but he felt he'd like to shake the Chairman's equipoise a bit.

"I suppose you've acquired the taste on your travels. Can't stand the stuff myself. In addition, it's not supposed to be good for you."

"Can I help you, sir? My dinner's almost ready."

The Chairman looked as if food at such a time was a mere trifle.

"There's been another murder here this afternoon, Superintendent. Matters can't possibly go on like this. You've been here several days and I'm sure you've found out quite a lot. I hope you'll act soon and put us all out of our anxiety. If you don't make an arrest quickly, there will be panic. There's a feeling abroad that there's a lunatic about. Now, it's poison in a poor man's dose of indigestion mixture. Where will it be next?"

"I'm sure I don't know, sir."

"You don't know? And, if I may say so, you don't seem to care, Superintendent."

Littlejohn sipped his drink and looked the Chairman full in the face.

"My dear Chairman, you don't seem aware that one of my men was shot in this village and the sole reason for my visit was to find out who did it. That is still my main object. Your own police are responsible for the rest, although they've asked me to help and I'm gladly doing so. I suggest you ask Inspector Tandy about the case. He's officially in charge and is a very good officer. One thing I would like to know, though. Who has asked you to take up this matter officially? The villagers themselves...or is it some body of influential people who look to you for a lead?"

"I'll have you know that I represent the ratepayers of the villages in this locality, and several of them have asked me to do what I can to expedite the eradication of this terror which is among us..."

"People like Mr. Wainwright and Mr. Wise, shall we say? Men who sit on the same Bench as yourself, sir?"

"Yes. The Justices are vitally interested in the matter. It concerns the law and is of importance to us."

"You may tell them, then, sir, that I hope in a few days to have solved the case. In fact, I am waiting for the right time to make an arrest."

"Waiting?"

"Yes, waiting. You must allow me to judge when it can best be done."

"Meanwhile, there may be more murders! It's ridiculous."

"There will be no more murders or crimes whatever in this case."

"Can you assure me on that point? There is no madman about?"

"I give you my word. No more crimes; no madman. In fact, if it will comfort you and those you represent, sir, I'll tell you that each of these crimes, the death of Mr. Twigg, the shooting of my colleague, the poisoning of Cank... They're all separate. Each committed by a different person. Touched off by each other, first Twigg, then my friend, then Cank, but each by a different criminal. There will be no more in this series. Of course, there might be an odd burglary, unconnected with the Twigg series, now and then, but probably no more murders. You can report me as saying that, if it pleases you."

"You choose to be sarcastic, Superintendent."

"And you, sir, choose to meddle in matters which are no concern of yours. You can have no authority to badger the police, who are doing all they can to free you and your villages from the current wave of crime. And now, sir, if you'll allow me, I'll go and get my dinner. Thank you for the *Pernod*. I got the habit of drinking it when I worked with the French force. It is quite harmless. You must be thinking of absinth."

The Chairman was not seen in the villages of Rushton Inferior or Superior again during the whole course of the Twigg case.

13
DIVINE JUSTICE

Just after eight, as Littlejohn had again returned to his room for some tobacco, he saw the invalid opposite sitting at the window, apparently enjoying the pleasant evening and the last of the dying day. He realized that, by now, he knew almost everyone in the village except Mrs. Beeton and her husband. They lived very near the scene of Cromwell's catastrophe and, judging from the lights often showing late at night, might possibly have seen or heard something when the sergeant was shot.

The elderly woman from the village who looked after Mrs. Beeton during her husband's absences from home was standing at the gate of the house, gossiping. She was obviously on her way to settle Mrs. Beeton for the night. The Superintendent hurried down to join her. In the hall of the hotel, the maid he met told him her name was Mrs. Prentice, and she was the widow of a one-time postman.

Mrs. Prentice was a small suspicious woman, who eyed Littlejohn warily when he bade her good-evening. The neighbour to whom she was speaking made an excuse and sheered-off, leaving them together alone.

"You look after Mrs. Beeton, Mrs. Prentice?"

"Yes."

She looked him up and down as though asking what it had to do with him.

"I wanted a word with her, if possible. Is it too late now?"

"No. She'll only lie waken in bed for hours after I've settled her. But I'd better go with you. There's nobody there yet. Her husband's due home about ten. It's a flying visit, I gather. He was on the telephone this afternoon and said he was just callin' to pick-up a bag of clean clothes and then off first thing in the mornin'. He travels, you know."

She had grown suddenly garrulous, as it had dawned upon her who Littlejohn was. She was delighted to let the village see her in earnest conversation with him. Some of them looked down on her because she had to 'do' for people for a living. This would show them she was of some little importance.

"Mr. Beeton is in foreign trade, I believe."

"Yes. Travels in all sorts of things. He's away sometimes for weeks at a time. Then he comes home for a few weeks. Sometimes, when he's busy, he can only stay a night, and then off first thing. It all depends on the state of trade, I reckon."

"Was he at home on the night the police officer was shot?"

"Yes, he was. I recollect he mentioned it the day after when I came to clean up. Why?"

"I wondered if he and his wife might have remembered anything that happened then. Their house is very near where it occurred and they may recollect something that would help us find out who fired the shot."

"You could come in and speak to Mrs. Beeton. She's an invalid and often bedridden, but she's quite right in her head and easy able to talk with you."

"Do they write to each other a lot when he's away?"

"No. It may seem funny, but, you see, he flies a lot in aeroplanes and, as he says, letters will only follow him round and never reach him on account of the speed he travels at."

"They're happy together, in spite of her illness?"

"I never knew a 'appier pair. He dotes on her and she can't wait for the time he comes home."

"Has she been an invalid long?"

"Gradually over the past three or four years. It's arthritis, really. She's got she can hardly move and never goes out, except when he has his long leaves and lifts her into a car and takes her off for a run."

"They've been married long?"

"About seven years. She's lived in the village all her life, and I knew her as a young woman. Knew her dead father and mother, too. There's money there. Thought she'd live and die an old maid. She was that sort. Then, she went on a 'oliday and came back married. She waited a long time but she made a good choice. He's a charming man and dotes on her."

"Does she have many visitors?"

"Not now. She used to be in everything in the village, but since she got married and then took ill, she's not cared to see many callers. Just me and the district nurse and one or two very old friends who call for a little time. No entertainin' of any kind, though."

"Neither of them has any relations?"

"I don't think so. She was the only child in her family and, as for him, nobody seemed to know anything about him or has found out anything. He just came and lived with her in her home after they married, and he insisted on earning his own living rather than live on her money, which, I must say, does 'im credit."

"Has she mentioned the shooting affair to you?"

"No. She didn't know about it till I told her."

"Who are Mr. Beeton's employers? Do you know?"

"I don't. I never meddle in matters which don't concern me. What good would it do me to know?"

"The doctor visits her now and then?"

"Dr. Clinton, yes. About once a fortnight. He isn't able to do her much good, except give her things to ease the pain in her legs and back when it's bad. The weather affects it terribly... Well, if you're wantin' to visit her we'd better be going up. I've her supper to get ready. Just a light one; milk and biscuits. You could have a quiet word with her while I'm boilin' the milk if you like."

"Thanks. I'm ready."

She took a key from her purse and opened the front door. The house was of the Victorian variety, spacious, well-built and neat. The hall was full of good old furniture and spotlessly clean. A heavy staircase mounted on the right as they entered. There was a faint odour of sickness about the place. The air of closed rooms, never used; the smell of disinfectants and medicines; the stuffy atmosphere of draughtproof windows.

"You might tell her I won't disturb her. I've been visiting everyone near the scene of the crime and would appreciate a brief word with her if she'll be so good."

He was a bit uneasy about meeting Mrs. Beeton face to face. He knew her well by now. The pale invalid's face, the thin yellow hands and arms, the tired glance which his own had intercepted across the street. He wondered what she would say and do when she learned he was here in person.

Mrs. Prentice knocked gently on the door of a room at the head of the stairs which, according to Littlejohn's calculations, was the one with which he was most familiar. She entered and was away for a minute or two, perhaps straightening the room or making the invalid presentable. Then she returned and bade him come-in.

The room was illuminated by the fading daylight. Littlejohn was surprised how much he had been wrong in constructing it in imagination from the samples he had seen of it from over the way. Like those strange holiday places which, visited for the first time, completely and for ever destroy the pictures we have made of them for ourselves in our minds. This was a brighter room than he had thought. Light paper, light furnishings, colourful pictures on the walls, everywhere evidence of good taste and an effort to make a sick-room as pleasant as possible.

Mrs. Beeton was sitting up in bed in a pink bed-jacket and a nightdress which ended round her throat in a lace collar, and with long sleeves with lace round the cuffs. She herself looked the same in bed as staring at him across the street. She had the pale sickly complexion of some nuns who give you the impression of being perpetually immured. Her hands were bony and thin and her hair, cut rather short, was almost white. The eyes were large and grey and, set in the small lined face, looked larger than they really were. She asked Littlejohn to be seated and indicated a saddle-backed armchair by the bedside.

"I'll just go and get your milk, Mrs. Beeton," said Mrs. Prentice, and she tiptoed from the room silently, just in the same strange sickroom manner that Littlejohn had found himself adopting as he entered and walked to the bed.

"Please excuse my disturbing you, Mrs. Beeton."

"Mrs. Prentice has told me what you want. I'm afraid I can't help you very much. Neither my husband nor I was disturbed by what happened."

Her voice was strong enough, but, now and then, the elision of a word or two gave an impression of tiredness or weakness. She kept her large eyes gravely fixed on him.

"You say you didn't hear anything between eleven and twelve on the night my colleague was shot?"

"That is right."

"Nor your husband?"

"No."

"You sleep well?"

"Moderately. I may or may not have been asleep then. I can't remember. In any case, vehicles pass here at all times of the night and sometimes there are backfires and other noises. I couldn't say."

"You usually have the window open?"

"Yes. Always."

"You were both in bed?"

"Yes. The room through that door is my husband's. He always sleeps with it open, so that he can hear me if I call. He certainly would not hear any shot or commotion in the road unless it were very loud."

"Your husband travels a lot?"

"Yes. He is a foreign representative for a London company and spends much of his time on the Continent."

"What is the name of his company? Perhaps I know them."

"Cassell, Priest and Company. They have wide connections in France and the Middle East."

"His movements are regular?"

"Not exactly. They are always receiving requests for a representative to call and he has to go, often at a few hours' notice. It just depends on the plane service. For instance, I expect him home about ten to-night, but he's only calling to see me for a few hours and take a change of clothing. He will leave for Manchester airport first thing to-morrow."

"Bound for London?"

"Yes, and then to Morocco."

There was a pause. Mrs. Beeton passed her hand over her eyes.

"I'm tiring you, Mrs. Beeton?"

"No. It's just my eyes. The light is fading and I can hardly see you."

"You spend a lot of your time alone?"

"Most of it. I read a little and sometimes I am well enough to sit up. I even do embroidery now and then, when my hands are a bit better and I can move the fingers. It's arthritis, you know. My husband has had all the best specialists' advice, but I don't improve. He is a wonderful husband to me."

"You married late in life?"

"Yes. I was a real old maid when we met... on a holiday... But I'm boring you. You called for help and I begin to tell you the story of my life. It's owing to not having much company or people to talk to. Is there anything more?"

It had now grown so dark that he could only see a kind of silhouette of her sitting in the bed and the faint light of her eyes.

Mrs. Prentice was back with a tray on which was a steaming glass of milk and some biscuits.

"Here's your supper, Mrs. Beeton."

"I must go now, and thank you for seeing me and talking to me, Mrs. Beeton, and I hope I haven't tired you. Perhaps you'll think over the events of the night of the shooting and, if you have time, mention it to your husband when he arrives. You may remember something helpful."

"I'm afraid not. But I shall be glad to see you again soon and tell you if I do think of anything. Now, I shall know you when I see you at your own window. Are you here for long?"

"Until the case is closed. My colleague is much better and I hope he'll soon be able to return to his home in London."

"I'm so relieved... so glad. It was very sad. Mrs. Prentice tells me he is a relative of the late Mr. Twigg who died recently. I see from the newspapers that his death, too, is causing the police a lot of trouble."

"Yes. I fear it was murder."

"How dreadful!"

Mrs. Prentice was drawing the curtains. Across the way, the maid was in Littlejohn's room with the light on, turning down the bedclothes and spreading out his pyjamas.

"Good-night, Mrs. Beeton."

"Good-night, Superintendent, and thank you for being so considerate. I hope your friend continues to make progress..."

He crossed back to his hotel. The road was lined with the cars of diners-out at the village pub and at a fashionable restaurant just outside, an old mansion converted into a road-house from which the faint strains of a string band could be heard. The last gossips were standing around in knots, chatting and joking, and the village lads and girls were clustered round the old stocks near the church, laughing and flirting.

Once inside the *Weatherby*, Littlejohn made for the telephone-box and asked for Scotland Yard. Mrs. Groves, passing with omelettes for late diners, saw him and waved a free hand at him.

"Littlejohn here. Please find out if there's a firm of Cassell, Priest and Co., Exporters, in the city. I want to know if a man named Beeton travels abroad for them. Try to find out where the managing director lives, and ask him if Beeton travels a lot and where to. Is he abroad for long periods, say a month at a time, or more, or less? Get as much information as you can about these trips. It may mean ringing up the nearest police-station to where the managing director lives and getting them to call on him. I want a reply to-night and I'll wait up until you ring me back here. Rushton Inferior, 22435. Got it? Thanks very much."

Then a call to Manchester Airport, at Ringway. The police-office.

"Kindly find out the schedule of flights to London tomorrow morning. Is there a passenger named Beeton due to leave for London on one of the early planes? If he's not booked for that, check the other schedules. Let me know tonight, if you please. If the office staff have gone, you'll have to contact them, but perhaps one of the night services will help you. Do your best and ring me back here. Rushton Inferior, 22435."

At about ten o'clock, after most of the dinner guests had gone, Tandy made a late call. He was tired and dishevelled and said he'd worked from lunch-time without a meal. Littlejohn insisted he be given one, and Mrs. Groves found him some cold pork and pickles which the Inspector set-about with gusto. They talked together in the quiet corner where his table was laid.

"I can't make head or tail of this Cank business. I've been to the chemists all round here and I finally struck one in Wiston where Cank used to buy his bicarbonate of soda. Last time he called for supplies, he bought some salts of lemon, too. He said he wanted to clean a panama hat. The chemist said it seemed a bit queer. Salts of lemon is an old-fashioned cleaner. There are much better and safer ones on the market now. But Cank insisted, saying he was used to it. Both salts are made by the same firm, and packed in similar 4 oz. cartons, but the salts of lemon are marked POISON. What did Cank insist on salts of lemon for? Was he going to poison himself? Because, if he was, he might have chosen an easier way out. He died horribly, as I said earlier to-day."

"Did anybody else use the bicarbonate, or was it Cank's own packet?"

"His wife used it now and then, but Cank was the real addict. He took about a packet in a fortnight, his wife said."

"Could he have been planning to kill his wife and make it look like suicide? Suppose he changed the inside bags about, and left it for her to take a lethal dose. Then he'd have changed them back and it would look as if she'd killed herself. She's a bit dim-witted, you know, and probably wouldn't know the difference."

"But surely, Cank would be on the look-out. If he'd done that, he'd watch it next time he took a dose himself."

"Perhaps he forgot. He might have been in his usual hurry when his dyspeptic spasms seized him, and the thing was done before he could stop himself."

"I don't know... It's all very funny."

"Wait! Suppose he did plan to get rid of Mrs. Cank."

"Why?"

"For years Cank has been blackmailing Mrs. Twigg. He knows something about her past. Then, one day, Mrs. Cank sees Mrs. Twigg putting a white tablet in Mr. Twigg's tea. She tells her husband and, after Twigg's death, she expresses the intention of informing the police. He bullies and beats her and frightens her into silence, but he knows now he can't trust her. She's a religious woman and is constantly fighting her conscience. Sooner or later, she'll tell."

"But Cank won't suffer. It's Mrs. Twigg who'll be arrested."

"And with her goes Cank's little goose that lays the golden eggs. He's bled her white and, now he knows about the poison in the tea, she's completely at his mercy. He's not going to let his wife, whom he despises, stand in his way. He plans to poison her and make it look like suicide."

"So...?"

"He changes the bag of bicarbonate for the bag of salts of lemon. The name bicarb., is still on the outer carton, but the bag inside contains poison. All he has to do now is wait for Mrs. Cank to have dyspepsia. Then, she, having taken a dose of the poison, looks to have tried to commit suicide. Probably he'll see to it that help doesn't get there in time. He has a good case for suicide, you see. His wife's neurotic and hates him; thinks he's the devil incarnate, and talks about it. She's fed-up and says she'd rather die than go on living and being corrupted by her husband. Everybody thinks she's half-mad with religious mania."

"What then?"

"Have you got the result of the post-mortem, yet, Tandy?"

"No, sir. The doctor was just starting when I left an hour ago."

"Ring him up and ask him what he found in the stomach as well as the salts of lemon... Or, get on with your meal. I'll do it. What's his telephone number?"

"He'll have left now. Do you mind ringing the police at Wiston, sir?"

Yes, the report was at the police station. Contents of stomach? A bit difficult. The victim had vomited them all away. The poison was definitely oxalic acid.

Littlejohn returned with a disappointing answer, but they weren't beaten.

"Go and ask Mrs. Cank what she gave him for his lunch. He began to be ill just after. That's why he was thought to have taken the salts of lemon...to allay his indigestion. I'm waiting for some telephone calls, otherwise I'd have come with you..."

Tandy finished his apple tart and left. Not long after, the telephone rang. It was Ringway Airport.

"We've checked the booking for to-morrow, sir. Name of Beeton. He's booked a seat on the 6.50 plane for *Birmingham*, not London. It goes on from Birmingham to London, but Beeton is only booked to Birmingham, sir."

"Please get me a seat on the same plane, will you? If it's booked up, tell them I must have one. Police work and urgent. You'll see to it, won't you?"

"Certainly. A pleasure, sir."

"And thank you for your prompt help."

Scotland Yard came on half-an-hour later.

"We've traced Cassell, Priest and Co., sir. Exporters, as you say. Managing director is a man called Priest, who lives at Cobham. He was in when the police there called. He says Beeton is on their staff. He goes over to France mainly. Paris, Lyons, and Marseilles. He's not away for long at once. Overnight mostly. The rest of the time he puts in at Birmingham. They have an office there and one in Manchester, where he also looks after their shipping. They aren't in a very big way and Beeton serves the three places."

"Splendid! Good work. Thanks for being so quick about it."

Littlejohn was drinking a last cup of coffee with Mrs. Groves when Tandy returned. The Inspector didn't know whether to laugh or weep about the latest news.

"It's funny, sir, if it wasn't so tragic. It was just as you said, and more besides. It looks as if Cank tried to poison his wife by swopping the bags, substituting salts of lemon for bicarbonate. Mrs. Cank didn't know. But Cank likes Cornish pasties and *she* doesn't. She made him a large one to-day. I asked her if she used bicarbonate of soda in it. Yes, she did. She makes her own baking-powder. Tartaric acid and bicarbonate of soda. She did it to-day and put Cank out."

"Good Lord! Divine justice."

"But that's not all. Her conscience had been troubling her

again and she confessed she wasn't in the village, but indoors when it all happened. She lied in a panic because she thought we'd blame her for the disaster. When he began to be ill, she mixed him a cracking big dose of what she got from the bicarbonate packet, and poured it down his throat! She's as dumb as they make them and wouldn't know the difference."

So Cank was hoist with his own petard.

14
THE FAMILY MAN

Littlejohn's trick of thinking last thing of the time he wished to awake the following morning, worked again. He opened his eyes at half-past five, got up, and washed and shaved. Then he sat by the window and watched through a chink in the drawn curtains for things to happen at *Rushton House*.

At just after six, the curtains of the upper room were pulled back, and Mr. Beeton looked out to see the kind of day. It was slightly misty and the sun was shining. Not a soul about.

Beeton then began the routine with which Littlejohn was now so familiar. The pottering around, the packing of the bag, the careful way of stowing away the personal articles of travel, the snapping-to of the catches, and the locking of the case. Then, the pale face of Mrs. Beeton appeared round the curtains, too, looking out. She turned to say something to her husband and then apparently got back in bed. But first she glanced uneasily across at the closed curtains of Littlejohn's room and seemed satisfied to see them thus.

The little drama continued, the same repertoire. Mr. Beeton entered the space illuminated by the rising sun. He had a cup in his hand now and was eating as he stood looking out. He seemed to like his toast! Now and then, he glanced over his shoulder at the figure in the bed. He took a cup from the thin hand, filled it again from a pot on the dressing-table just to his right, and passed it back. The pair were quietly breakfasting together.

Act 2. The taxi arrived. Littlejohn could hear it on the road far away, gradually drawing nearer. Beeton looked out, said something to his wife, bent to kiss her, and then disappeared. The taxi drew up, the driver rang the bell, and Beeton opened the front door, his hat on his head, his coat over his arm. The taxi-driver took his bag and put it in the taxi. Mrs. Beeton waved from the upper window and watched them depart. Then she drew the curtains and the little scene was over.

Littlejohn descended softly. The hotel was quiet. Only the dripping of a loose tap somewhere and the tick of the clocks. Instinctively, he tapped the barometer in the hall which stood at 'Fair,' and it rose a fraction. Good flying weather. He let himself out and went for his car, which he had left in the park behind the night before. Soon he was on the way to Ringway Airport, a matter of ten miles away.

The Superintendent hated disguises; they made him laugh and, had he been forced to use them, he would have felt self-conscious. Now, however, he put on a pair of dark glasses, in case Beeton had seen him before.

There were plenty of travellers astir. Business men on their way to London for a full day's work after an early arrival. At the desk, he calmly showed his warrant-card. The girl in charge nodded and handed him a boarding-ticket.

"The plane was booked-up, sir, but you can sit at the back if that will suit you."

"Fine."

He entered the restaurant and ordered coffee and toast. Beeton was there eating another breakfast of rolls and tea. He looked quite calm, hardly noticed Littlejohn, and began to read the morning paper. Then the loudspeakers announced the flight and they made for the plane. Beeton went along leisurely, his lips pursed in a whistle, swinging his arm and slapping his thigh with his newspaper. He didn't seem to have a care in the world.

At Elmdon Airport, Birmingham, it was just the same. A free and easy manner, a whistle on his lips. Beeton passed Littlejohn without a glance, claimed his bag, and took a waiting taxi.

A small unmarked police-car had been laid-on for Littlejohn. "Just follow the taxi ahead. Don't hurry or let him suspect we're behind him."

The taxi in front continued its peaceful way towards the city. Then, just as the houses began to thicken, it suddenly stopped.

"Pass it and stop in the next road off..."

It was a bit of a surprise, but Beeton suspected nothing. He dismissed his cab after paying the fare, walked for a few hundred yards along the main road, and then turned off and made his way through a maze of side-streets. Littlejohn followed. He had now taken off his dark glasses, his coat and his hat, and was strolling casually in Beeton's footsteps. Still his quarry went ahead. Then he entered an avenue of small semi-detached houses with gardens in front. New property in which the occupiers were struggling to make lawns grow and flower-beds flourish in the thick clay soil. *Evershed Avenue.* Every house painted a different colour outside. Green, blue, red, cream... A perfect rainbow of decorations. Beeton stopped at a house marked *Little Meadow*, a pious hope, a figment of imagination, but by no means real. He took a key from his pocket and opened the door. A smooth-haired fox terrier dog met him and started to jump and prance around him in delight. He shouted something and closed the door.

The street was beginning to wake up. Workpeople were on their ways and hurried to join the buses which passed the end of the road.

Littlejohn sauntered along smoking his pipe. An electric milk-van arrived, the man running in and out delivering full bottles and collecting the empties from the doorsteps. He stopped at *Little*

Meadow and left two bottles. Littlejohn met him higher along the street.

"Is there a house called *Little Meadow* about here?"

The dairyman removed his fag and smiled happily.

"Yes. Just by the second lamp along there... Name's on the gate. You looking for the Hardcastles?"

"That's right. Are they at home?"

"Yes. He's back from his travels, too. There was a note ordering two bottles. They usually only have one when he's away. He goes abroad a lot."

"Yes, I know. He asked me to call if ever I was in Birmingham. It's a bit early, but not too early, I hope."

"You'll be welcome. Nice people."

"I only know him. I've not met his family."

"Wife and two unmarried daughters. Rather plain girls, but they'd make good wives. I must be gettin' along. Don't forget. The one by the next lamp but one."

Littlejohn strolled comfortably down the road and rang the bell of *Little Meadow*. It was a spring affair and rattled on the back of the door. A pause. And then a woman appeared. About thirty or so, and obviously one of the plain daughters spoken of by the milkman. She was all smiles, probably expecting the postman, but her face grew serious when she saw who was calling.

"Good morning. Is Mr. Hardcastle at home?"

"Yes. He's only just got in. He's been abroad and travelled back home overnight. Who shall I say it is?"

"Mr. Littlejohn. I'm a business friend. He told me to call one day. Sorry I'm so early, but I'm leaving Birmingham this morning."

"Come in, then. I'll tell dad."

She was tall and had a good figure, but was as plain as could be. Her hair and complexion were uncared for and her hands spoke of what might have been drudgery. She looked to have got straight up from bed, washed cursorily, and twisted her hair into shape in a hurry. But she kept smiling. It lit up her face and made you forget her defects.

She held the door open for him and he passed inside. He was bewildered indeed. He'd expected something funny, perhaps shady, about Beeton's existence, but never this. Hardcastle. Dad. *Little Meadow.* It was quite fantastic. And there was more coming.

The house was small and modern. Two entertaining rooms to the right, and a kitchen at the end of a lobby. Upstairs, presumably two bedrooms, a bath, and a boxroom. The kitchen door was open and the girl hastened to close it, but not before the two people there had taken a good look at their visitor. They evidently lived part of the time in the kitchen, for Littlejohn got a brief glance of Beeton, sitting at one side of the table, his coat and collar off, eating a meal of what looked like bacon and eggs. On the other side, a woman was also taking breakfast. A buxom woman, with her elbows on the table, chuckling at something Beeton had said. She, too, was untidy, after the fashion of her daughter, with a soiled overall over her blouse and skirt and her hair grey, bunched and anyhow. Beeton seemed quite at home and might have been mistaken for the lodger had the girl not called him dad.

"I'll tell him you're here. Will you come in the front room?"

It faced the street and gave a good view of all that was going on. A stuffy room, apparently little used except on special occasions. There was a large settee with two armchairs to match, all in faded loose covers; a table full of china knick-knacks, a light oak cabinet containing the best tea-set and all kinds of odds and ends of pottery and little figures. A large porcelain figure of an Alsatian dog on the window-sill, pictures of Switzerland framed on the walls...

The girl had gone to get her father. Beeton put in an appearance and now wore his collar and coat again. An empty curved pipe dangled from between his teeth as though he'd put it in his mouth to keep him in countenance. He was a pleasant, likable sort of chap, in spite of the mystery about him. He eyed Littlejohn uneasily.

"I don't know you, do I? And yet I seem to have seen you somewhere before."

No use beating about the bush.

"You've perhaps seen me in Rushton Inferior, sir. I'm from the police."

Beeton's pale puffy face slowly lengthened and then flushed suddenly as though he were going to have a stroke. Then he grew calm, removed his pipe, and shrugged his shoulders. A look of resigned despair replaced the smile he'd assumed when he entered.

"Don't say anything here, please. It would kill them. My wife's not well as it is. Her heart's bad..."

Looking at him, Littlejohn was amazed. Hardcastle was quite a different man from Beeton. The man before him had shed his assumed suburban polish and was now a modest middle-class workman, who ate in the kitchen of a two-up and two down, and took off his collar and coat the better to enjoy his breakfast. He even spoke differently, or rather, he had a different way of addressing you. The gentle way he used with Mrs. Beeton had been replaced by an almost cocky, self-confident manner of a man who is boss in his own house and knows what he wants. He was more at home in *Little Meadow* than playing a part in *Rushton House.*

"What are you going to do?"

"You'd better tell me all about it, Mr. Hardcastle... or should I say Beeton?"

"You can please yourself, only don't let *them* know. I couldn't stand it. I've known that sooner or later it would all come out, but I hoped one of us would die before it did. I wish I'd died rather than this happen. I can't talk here. We'd better go somewhere... Or are you going to arrest me? I don't know whatever to do."

He looked utterly bewildered and talked rapidly in his panic, his thoughts turning this way and that, as though trying to find a way out or a bolt-hole in which to escape. Beads of sweat shone on his globular forehead and his jaw trembled.

"You'd better make an excuse, then, to come out with me Mr. Hardcastle, although I can't see how this matter can be kept secret. I presume it's bigamy, or worse. You can tell them I'm a friend from abroad, if you like. But I warn you, I have my duty to do and you need not make any statement if you don't wish."

"Please cut out the formalities. I've heard 'em all before. I want to tell you everything and get it off my chest."

"Anything you say may be used in evidence, you know."

"I'm not being arrested yet, am I?"

"No. But I want a full explanation of all your queer carryings-on here and at Rushton."

"All right. Where shall we go?"

"That's up to you, Mr. Hardcastle. Is there a park nearby where we can take a walk?"

"There's a recreation-ground two roads away. We could go there."

"Very well. Come along."

"You won't say anything to *them,* will you?"

"No."

"You'd better come and meet them, then. My wife and daughter. I've another, a typist in the city. This one, Betty, stays at home doing the housework. My wife's heart won't let her do much. She's been bad a long time. I'll say you're a friend."

Littlejohn followed him into the lobby again and then into the kitchen. The women were there washing-up the breakfast dishes, Betty washing and Mrs. Hardcastle wiping them lazily. There was an atmosphere of torpid comfort about the place. She turned to meet Littlejohn.

"This is Mr. Littlejohn, a business friend of mine, Myra. He was on his way through Birmingham, and just thought he'd call.

We've a bit of business to talk-over, so we're just going for a stroll in the recreation-ground."

"I'm sure I'm pleased to meet you. Any friend of Martin's is a friend of mine. But you needn't go out. There's the front room. We won't disturb you, will we, Betty?"

"Of course we won't. I'm surprised at dad. Him and his funny notions."

She laughed outright, as though her dad were a huge joke, a joke which all the family enjoyed together. There was a general air of easy-going camaraderie about them all, marred now by Hardcastle's anxiety.

"Have you had any breakfast?"

"Yes, thank you. I had some in the city."

"You must excuse us being here and the place all untidy. Dad suddenly turns up and wants his meal and can't wait. We just had to set it here for quickness. We're not always like this, you know."

She talked to him comfortably, as though he were already a familiar friend.

"I'm sorry to impose myself on you so early. It's not fair."

"Don't mention it, Mr. Littlejohn. So long as you don't mind..."

A heavy woman, and slow and bad on her feet. And yet there were remains in the face, which might have been aged by pain, of a good-looking, a bonny young woman, good-tempered and with a sense of humour. The kind one would not care to hurt or harm. Hardcastle had certainly landed himself in a mess!

"Come back for a cup of tea if you've time, then. You'll see he comes back if he's time, dad?"

"Yes, Myra."

Hardcastle was keeping his end up well, but there were limits, and Littlejohn was anxious to get him away before he broke down and caused a scene.

"Shall we go, Martin?"

Hardcastle gave Littlejohn a grateful look.

"Yes. Won't be long, Myra."

"Well good-bye, Mr. Littlejohn, just in case we don't see you again. Come any time. Any friend of dad's is welcome here. You'll have to take us as you find us, you know. Homely people, no trimmings."

Hardcastle bade her good-bye just as fondly as, earlier, he'd parted from Mrs. Beeton. Except that he gave her a more rousing kiss on the mouth. She looked taken-aback and blushed. Then Hardcastle turned on his heel and made for the door, Littlejohn following behind, as though Hardcastle had forgotten him.

The recreation-ground was not far away. A piece of waste land, turned into a children's playground, tennis-courts, and a bowling-green by the local authority. The bowls and tennis sections were deserted, but already children on holidays were romping and shouting on the swings and other contraptions erected for their play and pleasure. There was a seat in a quiet spot by the bowling-green. The two men sat down. It was growing warm and the sun shone over the patch of pleasant grass and birds were singing in the bushes which separated it from the rest of the park.

"Now, Mr. Hardcastle... Is that your real name, by the way?"

"Yes."

He looked utterly dejected. His body had sagged and he had lost all his well-kept appearance. He turned his agonized brown eyes on Littlejohn.

"I don't know where to begin..."

"At the beginning."

"All I can say is, my name's Hardcastle. I'm married to Myra, and I have two daughters, Betty and Flo. I've been married to Myra thirty years."

Looking at him, all gone to pieces, Littlejohn couldn't believe it. He wasn't the type for an adventurer. In his black jacket and striped trousers he'd looked, at Rushton, like a prosperous business man with means and culture behind him. Now, he was a little clerk again, trying to keep his end up, respectable and decent. Nothing of the lady-killer or reprobate about him.

"The trouble is, I've always had ideas above my station. I always wanted to be more than I was, to have more money to spend than I'd got, to live above my means. I couldn't do it with Myra. She wouldn't play that game. She believes in being what she is."

Littlejohn understood. The modest untidy house, and the modest untidy woman. Myra didn't believe in putting on airs. You took her as she was, or not at all. Hardcastle and his high-flying would find no sympathy there.

"It's always been fascinating to me. I wanted to get on. I was a clerk with Cassell, Priest & Co., at their office here in Birmingham. Mr. Jabez Priest looked after this end when he was alive. He took a fancy to me, specially as I seemed to have a flair for foreign languages. I took French, German and Spanish at night-school, and though I say it myself, I could soon rattle them off like a native. It just came natural. I was their foreign correspondent and then Mr. Jabez put me on travelling. It took me abroad a lot. Everywhere, I went. France, Spain, the Middle East. Everywhere. I met people and it broadened my mind. I got more sophisticated and I wanted to better myself more and more. I envied the lives of the rich people I met in the course of my travels."

As he spoke, he bucked-up, seeing, in his mind's eye, the prototypes of what he wanted to be. It was as if he was trying to act now in the way he thought certain of his former associates would do.

"And then I met Elaine Spicer. It was on my way home by boat from Marseilles and she was coming back from somewhere in the Middle East. I've got a bit of polish through my travels and we were thrown together. There weren't many passengers aboard, and well... I could see she'd fallen for me. I was a bit better looking, younger you know, in those days. It's seven years since. We got from one thing to another. It turned out she was a wealthy maiden lady, good-looking, educated, and absolutely charming. We got on like a house on fire together. Before we reached England, I'd fallen for her, too. She seemed to embody all I wanted and could never have. It went to my head. I never mentioned I was married. I let her think I was a bachelor who'd never settled down."

"Did you marry her, too, or go through a form of marriage?"

"Yes. I've got to confess it. I committed bigamy. No use hiding it. It's bound to come out. You see, I hadn't the nerve and I thought too much of her... I loved her too much...to ask her to, well... to be my mistress. I asked her to marry me."

"So, you ran two homes?"

"Yes. For seven years I did it, and I never got found out. I expected it any time. It's been a nightmare, and yet, I found I couldn't give either of them up. I loved them both in different ways. Myra's the mother of my children and she's the sort who's restful and free and easy. I could come home to her, take off my coat and collar, and eat my meal in the kitchen. Draw up in my old armchair, smoke my pipe, and relax. With Elaine, there were all the things I'd dreamed about. A lovely house, good manners, good taste... All the things in my dreams, you see. It was like wakening up when I came back to Myra in Birmingham, and then going off to my dreams again when I get back to *Rushton House*."

"And when you were with one wife, the other thought you were on your travels abroad?"

"That's it. I had to have a regular schedule, you know. With Elaine's money, too, I was able to do less work. I could be at Birmingham for a week or so, with the family, living free and easy, and going down to the city pretending to do office work at our Birmingham branch. Then, I'd say I was off abroad, go to Rushton, and stay there a while telling Elaine I was attending to the Manchester end. I had it all worked-out like clockwork."

"And you were never suspected?"

"No. But that was because both Myra and Elaine were semi-invalids. That's what makes it so hard. If I broke with either of them, I'm sure it would kill her. Elaine's bedridden a lot. She got arthritis badly two years after we...we married, and has got worse. Myra's got a weak heart. She developed it during the war. Damp shelters and such gave her rheumatic fever and her heart got dicky. You see, being tied down to their homes, so to speak, and not getting about much, they didn't need, or they weren't able to get around with me or want to follow me. They just took things as they were. In that sense, I was lucky. I'm not boasting. I feel awful about it now."

"Did you never feel awful before you looked like being found out?"

"Now and then. I loved them both, as I said, in different ways. I wanted to be with Myra and my girls, and I wanted the stylish life and surroundings Elaine gave me as well. I'm just mixed-up. Always have been. Perverse and foolish, as the hymn has it. When I'm in Birmingham I tire of it and long for the style of Rushton and Elaine. Then, I want my girls and Myra when I get fed-up with playing the part I'm bound to play when I'm at *Rushton House*. I will say, though, that I've been a good husband to both of them. I've looked after them and treated them decent and gentlemanly. I've broken the law, I know, and I've got to take my medicine now. But I wish to God I didn't have to make the two of them suffer. Especially Myra. She's been my wife a long time and she's the mother of my two girls. I'm proud of the girls. And then, Elaine's always loved me, too, and put up with me all this time, though she must know she's a very big cut above me. She's never reproached me with anything. I got a pair of really fine women who love me, and I'm at my wits end to save them any grief."

He was pathetic in his remorse now, but Littlejohn was more amazed by his outlook than anything else. He was like an Eastern potentate with many wives, thinking they were both his, and proud of them both and their love for him.

"Where do we go from here, sir?"

The sad eyes turned on Littlejohn, pleading for a satisfactory solution.

"I'm afraid it's back to Wiston Purlieu, Mr. Hardcastle. You'll be charged there with bigamy and detained in custody for the time being."

"Can we do it without either of them knowing?"

"For the present. You'd better let your wife know you've found you'll need to make a business trip with me and must go right away. You'll know what to tell her. You've been doing it long enough. We'll go back to your home and pick up your things and get the next plane back. We'd better be moving."

"You're not arresting me? They won't know that?"

"Not if you behave. We'll just leave as we did when we came for our walk."

"What about Elaine?"

"Look, Hardcastle. For seven years you've concocted schemes for keeping your two wives quiet and apart. Concoct another now if you don't want them to know for the time being. It will come out, of course, as soon as the case comes for trial and you'll then have to make your peace or otherwise with both parties. I'm sorry for you and I don't want to be hard on you, but you do see that you've broken the law and I'm an officer of the law."

"I don't know what will become of Myra and Elaine. I suppose I'll be sent to jail for what I've done."

"I'm afraid you will. Where did you marry Mrs. Beeton?"

"At a registry office in London."

"And why Beeton? Didn't she know your name was Hardcastle?"

"It was something funny on the boat when we met that started it all. It was one of the Italian Line and the steward called me Mr. Beeton. You see my name's Martin Beeton Hardcastle and I travelled as M. Beeton Hardcastle. It sounded better... sort of hyphenated name. I did things like that then. In keeping with my high falutin way of life, you know. Lots of people do it. I suppose it was too big a mouthful for the Italian steward and he called me Mr. Beeton. Soon, they were all calling me that. I must confess that I started what I thought was a mere flirtation with Elaine. It suited me for her not to know my proper name. Then, it grew to something deeper and real, and I couldn't tell her I'd been deceiving her. I've been Martin Beeton to her always."

"Let's go, then. We've a long way to travel, you know."

They returned to *Little Meadow*. Hardcastle's two women treated Littlejohn like a friend of the family and insisted on giving him tea and biscuits. Dad's story was readily accepted. They seemed used to his erratic travels and didn't ask too many questions. It was pathetic to see Mrs. Hardcastle packing his clean things in the familiar suitcase, telling him to take care of himself, to get good food and sleep well on his travels, and to write if he could.

"I know you're home as soon as a letter would be, and you don't write, but I like to remind you that we're thinking of you all the time you're away, dad. Good-bye."

Littlejohn went away with a heavy heart. He was not only thinking of Hardcastle as a bigamist, but as a man who would probably be charged with the attempted murder of Robert Cromwell!

15
THE RETURN OF MARTIN BEETON

All the way back by plane and taxi to the police station at Wiston, Littlejohn and Hardcastle sat side by side. Hardly a word was exchanged between them. There seemed very little to say. Hardcastle nursed his black hat on his knees all the time, lost in thought. Sometimes a strange smile crossed his face as though he remembered something pleasant.

Tandy was there waiting for them. He looked overjoyed to see Littlejohn again.

"Good afternoon, Superintendent!"

"Good afternoon, Tandy."

He almost added *comment-ça-va?*

The three of them entered Tandy's small private office and hung their hats on the hatstand. There was little else in the way of furniture there; a couple of small chairs and Tandy's own bentwood armchair at the plain wooden desk. A filing-cabinet, notices and a picture of Her Majesty on the walls; that was about all.

They sat down. The place was a bit stuffy and Tandy opened a window. Outside, a policeman in his shirt-sleeves was planting some potatoes in the constabulary kitchen-garden at the back.

Another was cutting daffodils for tomorrow's bulb-show, in which the police exhibited as a gesture rather than a hope.

Hardcastle sat down quietly, pulled up his trousers to keep the creases intact, and waited. They had drunk a cup of tea at the airport and he looked better. The return to the neighbourhood of Rushton seemed to be working on him already. He was becoming transformed into Beeton again.

Littlejohn spoke first.

"Mrs. Beeton is older than you?"

"No. We're about the same age. Until she became ill, she looked younger than me. It's being indoors and the pain that have changed her."

"You realize, of course, that we shall charge you with bigamy. You need not talk, therefore, if you don't wish. Whatever you say may be used in evidence. You know that, too?"

"Yes. I've nothing I wish to hide. I want to make a clean breast of everything. I knew this would come sooner or later. I've been prepared for it for a long time."

"Have you anything you wish to say about the shooting of my colleague, Cromwell?"

Tandy was the one to be surprised. He sat upright and gave them both a keen look. Littlejohn cautioned Beeton again. Beeton took it calmly. He must have been ready for that, too.

"Yes. I want to say that I did it. I'm sorry. It was all a mistake. If he'd died and anyone had been accused, I would have come forward and made a confession. I deeply regret it."

"Hadn't you better begin at the beginning?"

Littlejohn passed his cigarette-case to the other two and lit three cigarettes from his lighter. It might have been a tranquil business deal they were all discussing together, instead of a double crime.

"First of all, I want your promise, sir, that Mrs. Beeton won't be involved in this matter. She had nothing to do with it. I don't want her questioning or upsetting. She's a sick woman and couldn't bear it. I'd like to be allowed to speak with her alone before I go to prison; in fact, after we've finished here. It wouldn't be fair of you to bother her with my wrongdoings. May I have your promise and then I'll make a statement?"

He began to look distressed and his eyes pleaded for a favourable answer.

"I can't bargain with you, Mr. Beeton. You are in no position to strike a bargain either, or ask for promises. However, I'll do my best to see that Mrs. Beeton isn't unduly distressed."

"It wouldn't be fair. If I confess and take my medicine, she ought not to be troubled at all. It really doesn't concern her, does it?"

"Suppose you tell me about the shooting and leave the rest to me."

Beeton nodded gravely.

"I don't really know why I did it. It was out of sheer fright. I arrived home the day your friend was shot. Mrs. Beeton was in great distress. She said there'd been a man about the place making inquiries about us. He was a sergeant from Scotland Yard. Mrs. Prentice, who comes to look after Mrs. Beeton, told her all about him. He'd had a long conversation with Turner in the garden and then had returned for more talk. My wife asked me if anything was amiss. Had I been wrong in my books or embezzling funds? I pooh-poohed the idea to her face, but my heart sank. I thought my past had suddenly come to light, my bigamy had been found out, and they were on my track. Mrs. Beeton pointed him out to me in the evening. He was there again, walking past along the road, and he glanced keenly at *Rushton House* as he passed. Then he went in the chemist's shop. I was sure he was still spying on us. It was dark when he came out and I saw him standing in the doorway of the chemist's, looking across at us again. He crossed and paused at our gate and went on."

Beads of sweat appeared on Beeton's forehead and he wiped them away with a clean handkerchief he took from his pocket. On the way home, he had opened his bag, changed into a clean collar, and taken a clean handkerchief. They seemed to mark his return to his higher standards at Rushton.

"I suddenly panicked terribly. I saw the results of my misdeeds and saw no way out of the problem. The police had found me out."

He mopped his forehead again.

"I had a little revolver in a drawer. I used to carry it on some of my travels when I felt things might be a bit rough or unsettled. I took it and went out on the road. The sergeant was standing about some fifty yards away smoking quietly. I thought that at any moment he'd call at the house and accuse me. It was moonlight and I could see him plainly. I walked softly along. There was nobody about. And I pointed the gun at his head and pulled the trigger. He was about five yards away... He fell..."

"And you left him there?"

"What could I do? I was terrified. I ran indoors. My wife was asleep. I hid the gun and went to bed. I couldn't sleep. Early next morning, I went off to Birmingham. I kept an eye on the papers. I could have cried with thankfulness when I read the news that he was improving... That's all. You must think I'm a swine. Well, I deserve what's coming to me. I'll pay my dues. But don't take it out on Mrs. Beeton. She was asleep all the time."

He kept saying Mrs. Beeton, as though unable to use the expression 'my wife'. And funnily enough, Littlejohn could only think of him now as Beeton. Hardcastle seemed to have been left behind at *Little Meadow*.

"You know now, don't you, Beeton, that Cromwell had no idea about you and your affairs? He just wasn't interested. He was here on quite another matter. You simply shot him wantonly because of a guilty conscience and panic. You never gave him a chance..."

"I'm sorry."

Beeton hung his head and said it in a whisper.

The eyes of both detectives were hard. Here was a criminal of the worst type. Littlejohn had kept from his mind any idea of judging Beeton until he'd heard his story. Now, it was an unsavoury account of deception, intrigue, and finally, a cold-blooded attempt at murder to save his own skin. The two women had been betrayed into believing he was the best man in the world. He had used them for his own purposes and then, faced by the discovery of his crime, he had, without thought of anything but a cowardly attempt to avoid the results of his folly, shot Cromwell in cold blood.

Beeton licked his dry lips and looked at Littlejohn from under his heavy lids, a sidelong, appealing glance, almost begging for clemency.

"Why didn't you take to your heels and run?"

Littlejohn's voice cut like a whip. The man sank even farther down in his chair. He almost raised his arm to protect himself as though fearing physical punishment.

"What would have been the use?"

"What do you mean?"

"My world was with the two women."

"You didn't think that somebody else's world was with Cromwell. You deserve all that is coming to you. Had Cromwell died, you would have been charged with murder. As it is, you will be held in custody for attempted murder. Please charge him, Tandy."

The usual formal charge and caution. Beeton gave a little hopeless shrug.

"I admit, I deserve all I'm going to get. But don't forget what you promised about Mrs. Beeton."

There was no reply.

There was a question of finding Beeton accommodation for the night pending a hearing in the summary court.

"Would you like something to eat?"

Littlejohn knew Beeton hadn't properly eaten since breakfast. It seemed years since he'd disturbed him dining with Myra in the kitchen of *Little Meadow,* with his jacket and collar off. Now Beeton or Hardcastle, whichever you cared to call him, looked quite a different man. All the life had gone from him. His body sagged and his eyes were dull and lifeless. He was like a man in the grip of a mortal disease.

"I'd like a drink of tea, please. And perhaps a sandwich. It's a long time since I had any food."

In every circumstance, Beeton seemed to look well after himself. Littlejohn didn't even glance at him.

"Ask one of the constables to get him some tea and sandwiches, please, Tandy."

Tandy turned with blazing eyes.

"Would he like ham, tongue, or smoked salmon?"

The telephone bell in the charge-room rang furiously. The constable could be heard answering it and listening.

"Yes, he's here. I'll get him."

The bobby entered, his eyes popping.

"It's P.C. Bloor, asking to speak to you, Inspector."

"What's he want, Duff? Can't it wait?"

"He says it's urgent, sir."

Tandy hurried out and was soon back.

Beeton turned apprehensive eyes on Tandy.

"Has it something to do with me?"

Tandy took no heed of him, but whispered to Littlejohn.

"You'd better tell him, and then we'd better go along. We'll take Beeton, too."

Tandy's eyes looked harder than ever.

"Mrs. Prentice went in to see to your wife a little while ago. She found her dead. She'd taken an overdose of sleeping-tablets."

Beeton rose to his feet, making little whimpering noises. Then, he sat down at the desk, put his head in his arms, and began to sob. Dry harsh sounds, like those of a wounded animal. Then he stopped, rose, and stood stiffly, like one at attention.

"I'm sorry. She needn't have."

Littlejohn took him up.

"If she hadn't, you would have persisted in taking the blame for the shooting of Cromwell, wouldn't you, Beeton?"

Beeton started and his loose mouth tightened.

"I want to see her. I'm not answering any more questions till I've seen her. My poor Elaine. I want to see her."

It was as if he thought they were trying to trick him by pretending Elaine was dead and getting him to make a fuller statement.

They took him with them in the police-car. *Rushton House* was still surrounded by a mob, although Bloor, whose cap was bobbing here and there as he tried to persuade the morbid and curious crowd to break up, was doing his best to disperse them. Mrs. Prentice was near him, talking to everyone. Telling her tale over and over again. The newspaper men were pestering her and taking photographs of her and the house.

"It happened like this. I went in as usual..."

A photographer touched her on the shoulder.

"Just stand at the front-door again and look as though you were going in for the first time. It'll look good with a heading, *Mrs. Prentice entering the House of Death.* You'll be famous overnight and your picture all over the country."

Bloor almost ran to meet the two officers and the constable as they climbed from their car. Beeton got out between them and the crowd made way for them. There were sympathetic noises at the sight of Beeton, whose distress was so great that he staggered like a drunken man. A photographer took two flashes of him, in one of which he later appeared looking like a man who'd been arrested and was being brought to the scene of the crime.

The constable from Rushton Superior was standing on guard at the bedroom, saluted without a word, and opened the door. Clinton had been and gone.

"He's pronounced life h'extinct," said Bloor solemnly and he handed to Tandy an envelope addressed briefly to *Martin*.

Beeton didn't seem to notice it. He staggered into the room, drew back the sheet from the face of the figure lying in the bed, flung himself upon it, and sobbed harshly again.

The room was the same as when Littlejohn had been there before. Someone had drawn back the curtains which, Mrs. Prentice had already stated a dozen times, were closed when she entered.

"I thought she was asleep till I touched her. She was gettin' cold already. She must 'ave taken the pills hours since and laid there with nobody to take any notice."

The housekeeper had followed the police.

"I'll tell you 'ow it happened."

"Please be quiet, Mrs. Prentice."

Tandy's nerves were on edge and he wanted to hear what Bloor had to say.

"At six-ten p.m., Mrs. Prentice called me up to say Mrs. Beeton was dead. I 'urried here and found the deceased in the bed with an empty glass which seemed to 'ave 'eld milk, on the table there. I sent for Dr. Clinton, who said life was h'extinct. I telephoned Inspector Tandy. I also found an empty bottle which Dr. Clinton stated 'ad been given by 'im to deceased and had contained pehobarbitone..."

"Pheno-barbitone," interjected Tandy impatiently.

"Yes, sir."

"I'd been in about three. She must 'ave taken them soon after I left, poor dear."

Mrs. Prentice was determined to tell her tale.

Littlejohn gently took Beeton by the shoulders, pulled him from the bed, and sat him on a chair, where he continued to sit motionless, his eyes staring ahead.

"It was my fault," he said to himself.

The empty drug-bottle bore the label of the village chemist. Mrs. Prentice hastened to tell them all loudly that Mrs. Beeton needed them to make her sleep when the pains came on.

The face of the dead woman was still uncovered. All the lines of pain had gone and Littlejohn could make out how good-looking she must have been before age and suffering had taken away her beauty.

"It was all my fault."

Beeton kept repeating it.

Tandy handed the letter to Littlejohn as though the Superintendent had the right to open it.

"There's a letter here from Mrs. Beeton, Beeton. I propose to open it."

He suddenly seemed to come to life.

"It's mine. Give it to me. She wrote it for me. You've no right..."

He rose and clawed at the envelope which Littlejohn was opening. The Superintendent gently thrust him away.

"You shall read it as soon as we have finished with it. Now, it is vital evidence."

MY DEAREST MARTIN,

Forgive me. This is the only way I can take to save you from suffering. I saw Mr. Littlejohn following you in his car as you left this morning and know that he has found out. Tell him the truth. That I shot his friend. Tell him all that I told you.

I have known almost from the beginning about Birmingham. You mentioned someone called Myra in your sleep once, and I had to know. I followed you. I could not bear to let you go, so I had to be content by sharing you for the sake of my happiness. I have always been your wife, although it was not legal. Forgive me and be happy with Myra.

Thank you, dearest Martin, for all the years of happiness and love you have given me. Forgive me.

ELAINE

It was written in a firm hand. Beeton clutched at it again and Littlejohn let him take it. He read it, panting as he did so, almost as though he were eating the words and every one of them stabbed him to the heart. Finally, he sagged in the chair again, weeping openly.

"It was all my fault."

They gave him a drink of brandy and it was not long after that he confessed.

Mrs. Beeton had gone to bed early and Beeton had turned in, too. He had slept heavily until he suddenly wakened to find his wife at his bedside. How long she'd been there, he didn't know, but his bedside clock showed ten-past two. She was cold and dazed. In her hand she'd held the small revolver which she'd bought before he knew her, as a kind of comfort when she lived alone. He had laughed at it and called it the pop-gun in days past.

Littlejohn nodded. She had known the report of the gun was not a loud one. It was when she hinted as much that he had begun to suspect her.

Elaine had told him she'd shot the man who was shadowing them and, try as he would, he couldn't get her to say why Cromwell should be doing so.

"She must have known about the bigamy all along and thought he was after me... She wouldn't tell me. I suppose she didn't want me to know in case I went away."

He had gone outside and found no trace of the body, but next morning the police were on the scene even before he got up, and he knew it was true. He had taken the revolver, which had one chamber fired, and dismantled and buried the parts separately in various parts of the garden.

"It's funny how, when you want to hide a thing, every place you think of seems to be the one you imagine the police will go to first. I'll show you where I hid the bits and you can put it together again.

"It was my fault and the reason I said I'd done it was because I ought to have paid for what I'd done. It wasn't fair for Elaine to have to suffer for it. I wish I was dead, too."

Littlejohn stood with his back to the room as Beeton talked and talked. Having known him in his happy days, he couldn't bear to look at the contorted, tragic, bewildered face.

"I do hope Myra won't get to know. I don't want to make her suffer, too. I'd do anything... suffer anything..."

The Superintendent looked from the window at the last of the daylight. Lights on in the *Weatherby*, in the ground floor rooms of which he could see knots of excited people talking. The crowd was still standing round the front gate of *Rushton House*, where Turner was now holding the stage, telling a long tale to the newspaper men.

From his own bedroom, he could see the round, childish face of Mrs. Groves looking across at him, just as, in days past, Mrs. Beeton had done from this very room.

Tandy touched him gently on the arm.

"I'm sorry, sir, but I had a message for you from Scotland Yard. In the bother with Beeton, it quite slipped my mind."

He spoke in a whisper and took a paper from his pocket, a typed version of a note taken down over the telephone.

CASADESSUS AND CO.

Went out of business three years ago. Antique dealers to the trade. Apparently used by a provincial auctioneer for disposing of valuable antiques to London dealers and exporters. Proprietor: F. Wainwright, Wiston.

Enquiries in the trade reveal that Fred'k. Wainwright was known by dealers as Mr. Casadessus.

Casadessus & Co., went out of business after prosecution by Inland Revenue for tax evasion. According to Fraud Squad records, Mr. Casadessus avoided imprisonment by a cash payment of £30,000.

16
BATTLE OF WITS

It was quite dark when Littlejohn and Tandy left *Rushton House*. Beeton himself had gone back to Wiston with Buck, where he would spend a night at an hotel. What the magistrates decided to do with him at the petty sessions next day was their own business. He had certainly nothing to do with Mrs. Beeton's death; Littlejohn had been with him all day and was his perfect alibi.

Outside, the village was busy. Small knots of morbidly curious sightseers still hung round the gate of the house. The *Weatherby* was a blaze of light. Reporters had taken Turner to the *Brown Cow* where, in exchange for pints of ale, he was telling them all he knew, and a lot more besides, about the Beetons, the Twiggs, the Canks, and Cromwell.

"Let's go to the *Bull and Bush*..."

Tandy thought Littlejohn was suggesting a convivial hour together and felt it a bit out of place. He was silent for a minute.

"I don't mean for drinks. I want to pick up Wise and his friends. There are one or two matters which must be settled right away. Let's go ..."

The *Bull and Bush* was agog. News of Mrs. Beeton's suicide had reached every quarter of the neighbourhood and the place was packed with customers eager for firsthand news and a good night of talk and scandal over the beer-pots.

"Who'd have thought Mrs. Beeton would make away with herself? They both seemed so happy. I expect she'd got to the far-end with her illness..."

They couldn't believe any scandal could possibly occur in the austere household at *Rushton House*. They were in for a surprise when the case reached the papers!

Wainwright, Wise, and Temple, the three inseparables, were in the *Kennel* again. They all looked surprised when Littlejohn and Tandy entered.

"We didn't expect you here to-night, Super. I hear there have been some queer goings-on in Inferior to-day. You never know what'll happen next, do you? What will it be? Evenin', Tandy. Not often we see you here."

Wainwright had been drinking hard again and was talkative. He behaved as though there'd never been any harsh words between himself and Wise. Wise looked uneasy, wondering what was afoot.

"Will you all kindly come down to Mrs. Twigg's with us? There are some matters we wish to settle, and you'll all be of great help."

Wainwright rose to go, all eagerness; Wise hesitated.

"Must we go at this late hour? I'm sure Mrs. Twigg won't like it. It'll upset her, breaking in on her at this time."

Wainwright was putting on his hat and coat.

"Come on, Wise. Don't be awkward. Do as the Super asks you, there's a good chap."

Wise could do no other. Temple was ready to follow the rest. There were lights on downstairs at *Ballarat* and the doctor's car stood at the door. Mrs. Cank answered their ring. She hadn't changed at all, in spite of her recent widowhood. She either hadn't realized the situation or she didn't care.

As they stood in the porch there was a flash of lightning followed by a clap of thunder.

"Come in. The doctor's here. He came to see me. I don't know why. I'm not ill. But he said he wanted to be sure I was all right. He's saying good-night to Mrs. Twigg. Looks like bein' a storm, too."

She led them in the hall and went to announce them to Mrs. Twigg. Littlejohn's eye fell on the large brass pestle and mortar he'd noticed on his first visit. The mortar looked recently cleaned and stood out brightly among the rest of the tarnished and neglected brass ornaments.

Wainwright was quite at his ease. The other two were obviously uneasy and wondering what was afoot.

Tandy kept close to Littlejohn. The Superintendent had grown fond of his colleague. He was the best type of police officer; sturdy, dependable, calm, and good-mannered.

"She'll see you."

The same room which Littlejohn now knew so well. The desk which had caused all the trouble for Cromwell, the chintz curtains, now drawn, the elaborate chandelier, full-on and lighting every corner of the room.

Clinton was there, standing by the electric fire, the imitation logs of which were glowing, although, on account of the heat of the night, the elements of the stove were cold. He looked surprised at the intrusion, but, in Littlejohn's presence, he had lost all his asperity. He now seemed to regard him as a friend.

"This is unexpected, Superintendent... All these visitors at once. It must be something important."

Mrs. Twigg spoke without moving to meet or greet them. She was taken off her guard and obviously alarmed.

"Forgive our calling, Mrs. Twigg, and taking you by surprise. I thought it would be better if we all met here instead of at the police-station."

They all jumped. Even Tandy. Wise found tongue first.

"I say, Littlejohn, why didn't you tell us? This is most unfair. I thought it was something connected with Richard's business affairs that made you want us here. I prefer to have my lawyer with me if it's anything to do with his death."

Wainwright looked annoyed.

"Now, don't be silly, Wise. A lawyer, indeed! Anybody'd think *you* killed Twigg. We've always found Littlejohn a reasonable chap. He's not likely to try and catch you out. What's all this about, Littlejohn?"

It was a strange situation. A group of men standing there, all except the doctor still wearing outdoor clothes and holding their hats. Mrs. Twigg didn't seem disposed to ask them either to sit or stay.

Mrs. Twigg was dressed up to kill. She'd either been out or had been expecting someone. She wore a black gown of expensive cut, all her jewels, and was made-up to the eyes. She must have been enjoying her *tête-à-tête* with Clinton, for her eyes had been sparkling when the new arrivals appeared. Now they were apprehensive.

"You'll excuse me if I don't ask you to stay, all of you. I really don't know why you've called. I thought you'd come to express condolences with Mrs. Cank. I take it you want to see me, Superintendent. Isn't it rather presuming a lot to bring along a party of men with you like this? What is it all about?"

"Do you mind if we sit down for a little while? As you know, I'm not quite myself yet."

It was Wise, trying to look frail, but really angry at being treated with so little fuss.

"You can all sit down, if you wish. But please don't be long. I can't stand much more."

Mrs. Twigg passed her hand across her forehead. She remained standing, so the rest did the same. Finally, Wise flopped down willy-nilly. Nobody else moved.

Outside more thunder, and then the sound of heavy rain.

Littlejohn was anxious to get it over. The situation was intolerable.

"Mr. Wise... Did Mrs. Twigg visit you at all during your recent illness?"

Wise looked surprised and Wainwright, whose impertinent eyes hardly left Mrs. Twigg's figure or face for a minute, gave a little twisted smile, almost a grin.

"Yes. Nothing wrong about that, was there?"

"Not at all. You were friends. It was natural. Was it at the time Dr. Cruickshank was away and Flowerdew was locum?"

Mrs. Twigg made a sound like a sigh and sat down in the chair behind her. Her eyes were fixed and staring and she searched Wise's face, as though trying to will a message to him without speaking.

"Yes. Come to think of it, it would be. I remember Flowerdew commented on the roses she'd brought. They were particularly nice ones and old Flowerdew used to be a fancier. Matter of fact, he used to win prizes at shows with his blooms."

He rambled on and on, as though what he was saying was of no importance, just pleasant chit-chat to pass the time away.

"Did she come alone?"

Wise looked again at Mrs. Twigg's appealing eyes and hesitated.

"Well?"

"No. She'd Wainwright with her."

Wainwright didn't let him finish.

"Quite natural, wasn't it? Twigg wasn't well and wanted his wife to call and see old Wise and give him good wishes. When he told me over the phone, I said I'd pick Mrs. Twigg up and take her."

A pause. Everyone wondered what was coming next. There seemed to be two storms raging outside. Thunder echoed thunder.

"Mrs. Twigg... What were the tablets you used to put in your husband's tea?"

The rest looked startled, but Emily Twigg didn't even hesitate.

"Saccharines... He was putting on too much weight and Dr. Clinton ordered a diet and to keep off sugar. That's so, doctor, isn't it?"

"Quite right. What's all this about?"

Littlejohn ignored him and continued to address Mrs. Twigg.

"So, Cank couldn't have been blackmailing you about putting poison in your husband's tea."

There was a gasp.

"Cank *was* blackmailing you, Mrs. Twigg. What was it about?"

Mrs. Twigg jumped to her feet and spread out her arms in an appeal to the rest of the company.

"Will nobody protect me against the police? Ever since Superintendent Littlejohn arrived here, he has harrowed and pursued me, accusing me of killing poor Richard, telling me Cank was blackmailing me, making it so I didn't know whether I was on my head or my heels. There's not a shred of truth in it all..."

Wainwright took up the cudgels for her.

"Look, Littlejohn. Don't you think it's time you stopped all this nonsense? You're simply being rude and ill-mannered, bullying Mrs. Twigg this way."

"That doesn't disturb me at all, Wainwright. I keep thinking of Cromwell, involved in what was going on in this house, going out in the night to investigate, shot in cold blood, and lying in the gutter in the dark, unattended, still alive only by a fluke... I'm going to settle that account, here and now, if it's the last thing I do."

Tandy was alarmed. He'd never seen Littlejohn anything but calm, phlegmatic, good-tempered, courteous and kindly in the extreme. This was a totally different man. Icy in his anger, ruthless in the path he was pursuing, regardless now of the courtesies and conventions. He drew closer to the Superintendent to show he was shoulder to shoulder with him.

"I don't intend to stay here all night and I won't waste any more time on you all. You, Wainwright, under the name of Casadessus, employed Mrs. Twigg as your secretary in an antique business in London. You used to sell in London the good stuff you rescued from local sales in your auction-rooms in Wiston. She was your mistress at the time."

Wainwright jumped to his feet and strode across to Littlejohn full of violence. Littlejohn pushed him in the chest and he staggered and sat down again.

"Stay where you are, Wainwright. You are about to deny your affair with Mrs. Twigg. Quite a few people in the Edgware Road area will prove you're wrong."

"I'll make you pay for this. You can't prove a word of it."

"In your rôle as Wainwright in Rushton, and a friend of Twigg, you found he was a very wealthy man. You were married and your mistress was beginning to be an embarrassment. She was wearying of the Edgware Road. You knew Twigg had an eye for a good-looking woman and I think you suggested a way to her in which she could make a comfortable match and yet be near you and carry on as before. You arranged for her and Twigg to meet on a cruise. You paid for her cruise. Twigg and Miss Waldron were married. Twigg knew nothing of her relations with Wainwright. He never dreamed he and Casadessus were the same man."

"What utter drivel! Not a word of truth in it. I never heard of Casadessus. You're trying to pin it all on me without a shred of proof."

Littlejohn flung the envelope he'd found in Cank's box at Wainwright, who read it in surprise. His face flushed.

"Where did this come from? I've never seen it before."

"Cank had it. He stole it from the post, where he was doing temporary duty. Unfortunately for you, someone in London post-office remembered your re-addressing arrangements and was very conscientious. Take the envelope back, Tandy. It's evidence.

With that envelope, Cank blackmailed Mrs. Twigg. He'd been rooting into her past in her old haunts and he knew all about Mr. Casadessus. Everybody did in Strutt Street. He must have licked his evil lips when he saw that envelope. No wonder he stole it."

Mrs. Twigg never spoke a word. She sat with her mouth half open, staring at Littlejohn and then at Wainwright, unable to think of what to say. The air was unbearably oppressive. Outside rain was falling in torrents and lightning showed through the closed curtains.

"When your wife died, Mrs. Twigg thought of you as successor to her aged husband, Wainwright. I don't think you were quite so serious in that direction. You were mainly concerned with her money. All the same, you had a strange fascination for her. You were her evil genius, or maybe she loved you. One can see how much hold you have over her by the look in her eyes whenever you're about."

All eyes turned on Mrs. Twigg, who covered her face with her hands. Wainwright rose and made for the door, trying to look calm.

"I'm going. I won't listen to your nonsense for a minute longer..."

A look from Littlejohn was enough to move Tandy between Wainwright and the door.

"You'll stay until I've finished."

He didn't get any farther. Wainwright, breathing heavily, tried to take Tandy by the throat, but it didn't last long. The drink-sodden auctioneer was no use in a free-for-all. Tandy simply slapped his hands away, took him by the collar, and sat him on the couch again.

"Now, keep quiet. Any more trouble from you and you'll spend the night in Wiston gaol."

Wainwright's bluff and bounce were gone. He sat there, glaring and snorting, but, with Tandy sitting at his side, he made no more attempts at violence.

"If Wainwright thought that by marrying her off to Twigg, he was going to rid himself altogether of Mrs. Twigg, he was mistaken. She'd taken him at his word and expected things to be as before she'd married. In fact, she started a pretty game to *egg* Wainwright on. She was seen with other men in public. Dr. Clinton, for example. He warded her off, but his name was bandied about, all the same. As for Wise, I don't know what would have happened if he hadn't fallen ill."

It was Wise's turn now to roar to his feet.

"What the hell do you mean by bringing me into this?"

"Sit down, Wise. You'll be having another heart attack. Do you remember the hunt ball at which Mrs. Twigg engineered a love scene with you in front of the biggest chatterbox and scandal-monger in the district? Stubbs. She had charm and knew how to use it. You fell for her wiles. It was all done to remind Wainwright that he wasn't the only pebble on the beach."

Wainwright actually smiled. A slow cynical sneer.

"Well, what of it? You're not telling me anything I don't know. After my wife's death nearly two years ago she never left me alone. Wanted to take-up where we'd left off. It didn't suit me to be carrying-on affairs with my friend's wife. I'd grown to like Twigg. It wouldn't have been fair. She didn't seem to mind that. She tried everything and then, when it failed, she killed Twigg to get him out of the way."

Wise and Temple were as white as a couple of sheets. Their features were drawn and they looked like a pair in a nightmare. As for Mrs. Twigg, she remained staring at Wainwright, rigid in her chair, as though changed to stone by utter stupefaction.

"With Twigg dead, all is well, isn't it, Wainwright? His wife inherits his money unconditionally. You ought to know that. You've told me and your friends at the *Bull and Bush* often enough. You even reminded us that it was a good motive for Mrs. Twigg when she killed her husband."

"I don't need Twigg's money. This is all a put-up job. I'll..."

"You need as much as ever you can get out of Mrs. Twigg. You're broke, aren't you, Wainwright? Casadessus and Company went flop. They didn't confine themselves to antiques, but ran a little sideline in twisting the Income Tax Inspector. You'd about thirty thousand pounds to pay to keep you out of gaol... You're almost a beggar and Twigg's money would come in handy, I'm sure."

"You can't prove a thing and I'm saying nothing till I've seen my lawyer. I'll show you."

"You often talked to Mrs. Twigg about the past. You knew about dicoumarin, or she did, and told you about it. You saw a foolproof way of disposing of your wealthy old friend, and either marrying his wife, or having her in your power after she'd killed him, and you could squeeze her for as much money as you liked. I suppose you've borrowed from her already."

And, from the look Mrs. Twigg gave him and the hot flush on her cheeks, they all knew it was true.

"But Twigg did take you into his confidence, didn't he? He heard of his wife's behaviour. That was the irony of it. She kept within the decencies with Clinton and Wise, and probably Twigg knew it, but he also knew her by now and that if he died, she wouldn't be long in finding another husband. He told you, Wainwright, he was going to make a fresh will."

"He didn't... He never did."

Temple, who had been quiet and taking it all in with an amazed incredulous stare, spoke as though he were doing Wainwright a favour in nudging his memory.

"Twigg told *me*... I was the one he used to confide in. I'd been his banker, you see. In fact, I recommended him to come and live here. Wish I hadn't now."

"And you told Wainwright?"

"Of course. Never suspected. In fact, it all seems wrong to me now. I'm sure you've got it all twisted somehow. Twigg said he thought he'd better make his will again. Divide it among his next-of-kin, nephews and such like, in case Mrs. Twigg re-married. Leave her a few thousands and a life interest in the estate. She'd get all the interest on the capital until she died."

"When was this?"

"About two months ago. He wasn't going to hurry, he said. His lawyer was away in the south of France and he'd see him before the year was out. He was in good health and there was time."

"And when you told Wainwright, he got busy. He took old Flowerdew's dicoumarin."

"I did hell as like. You're making it all up."

"If fate hadn't played into your hands, you'd have found some other way. As it was, you happened to be at Wise's when Flowerdew called. He doled out the usual small supply of tablets to Wise and you took the rest from his case. Either you or Mrs. Twigg did it. She had the same opportunity, the same motive, the same urge to end all the illicit meetings and come into the open. One or the other of you took those tablets."

Mrs. Twigg wasn't heeding the argument. She was looking straight at Wainwright.

"So, it was true, you wanted the money. You didn't want me at all. It was just the money."

"Look, Emily. I won't have you making fool talk like the rest of them. We'll discuss this later. You know it was your happiness with Twigg I wanted."

"No, you didn't. I can tell by the way you look and the way you say it, that you're lying to save your own skin. You're afraid."

"I'm a patient man, Emily, but don't try me too far. I said, we'll discuss that later. Here's Littlejohn accusing me of taking Flowerdew's tablets when we were at Wise's. That shows how much he knows and how far you can rely on him. You know, Wise, that Flowerdew left long before we did. Had I a chance of taking the tablets even if I'd wanted?"

"He's right, Superintendent. What he says is true. He hadn't a chance. Flowerdew took the tablets with him in his portable case."

Littlejohn turned to Clinton.

"You remember the dinner given at the *Weatherby* in honour of Moffatt, the retiring M.O.?"

"Of course. I was there."

"Were any of these three gentlemen there, too?"

"Temple and Wainwright. They're both on the Rural District Council."

Wainwright sneered again.

"What does that prove?"

"Only that Flowerdew isn't quite in his dotage, but he might have left his car unlocked. The tablets were taken from his car whilst he was at that dinner. I suggest you took them, Wainwright."

"Go on suggesting. I don't care. You can't prove it."

Littlejohn turned to Clinton.

"What kind of a container do you carry your dicoumarin tablets in, doctor?"

"For the portable case, in a small tube. I've mine with me, in my raincoat pocket in the hall. I always take it out of the car nowadays. It's easy to open a car and take things."

"May I see it?"

"Of course."

Clinton left the room and returned with a small flat case, which he opened, revealing a little battery of drug-bottles. He selected one containing small white tablets.

"That's dicoumarin…"

A tube about two or two-and-a-half inches high, and perhaps half an inch in diameter, sealed with a plastic screw-cap.

Littlejohn went into the kitchen. He could hear voices as he left the room, particularly Wainwright's blustering about being kept for a lot of nonsense.

Mrs. Cank was sitting in front of her 'telly,' as though Cank hadn't died at all. There was a comedian cracking jokes and pulling his face; a second-rate turn to kill the time. Mrs. Cank was gazing at the screen spellbound, her face expressing no emotion whatever. She seemed merely fascinated by the movement and the light of the set. She turned quietly towards Littlejohn.

"Hello, Mrs. Cank. Enjoying yourself?"

"Yes."

"Do you remember telling me about finding Mrs. Twigg putting tablets in Mr. Twigg's tea?"

"The ones Cank hurt my arms for?"

"Yes."

"Yes, I do."

"What sort of a bottle was she taking them from? Was it from Mr. Twigg's saccharine bottle? You know the one he used to use?"

"Yes, I know the one. It wasn't that."

"What was it like?"

"Cank once had some indigestion tablets in a little case made of aluminium. It was like that only glass... Here, the case is here..."

She went to the cupboard in the corner, which contained bottles and boxes of all sorts of patent medicines. Either she or Cank must have been perpetually under self-treatment. She came back with a metal tube, almost a replica of the one Littlejohn held in his hand. He showed it to her.

"Yes. It was just like that."

"Thank you, Mrs. Cank. Now, will you please come with me in the sitting-room?"

She looked scared.

"Will *she* mind? I don't as a rule unless *she* sends for me."

"That will be all right, Mrs. Cank. By the way, have you been cleaning the mortar in the hall, lately?"

"What's that?"

He pointed.

"No. The brass 'as been neglected with all the goings-on here. I can't think who's cleaned that. I never did, although they all need it."

In the lounge, they were sitting wondering what Littlejohn

was doing. When he arrived with Mrs. Cank, they all looked surprised.

"Tell Mr. Tandy about the tablets you saw Mrs. Twigg putting in Mr. Twigg's tea, Mrs. Cank."

She looked at Mrs. Twigg, who gave no sign that she could or she couldn't.

"Well... I saw Mrs. Twigg put the tablets in the tea, jest as I told this gentleman here. It wasn't sacatine, as Mr. Twigg used to use for sweetening his tea. It was a different sort. It was twice as big as a sacatine."

"What colour?"

"It was white."

"In a bottle like a saccharine bottle?"

"No. In a glass tube with a little screw top."

"Like this?"

"Yes. That's like it."

"Thank you, Mrs. Cank."

They could hear the joker on the television shouting his cracks and Mrs. Cank seemed eager to be back and watching him. She almost ran to get there.

"Well. Where does that get us?"

Wainwright was still truculent.

"You stole the tablets, and Mrs. Twigg administered them to her husband."

"*That's right.*"

Mrs. Twigg said it emphatically, in a voice full of despair,

"He wanted my money. That's all. And because of that, he worked it all out to get rid of Richard. I must have been mad. But he could always make me do what he wanted. I can't go on any longer like this. All my life has been one long struggle and now the one I thought would stand by me, he only wanted the money."

Wainwright was on his feet, standing over her.

"Be quiet, Emily. You don't know what you're saying. It's not true. Can't you see, they're trying to trap you. Don't say any more without a lawyer."

Littlejohn didn't seem to hear.

"And did you both arrange the matter of eliminating Cank, too? Cank, who knew too much about you both, and also mentioned that he knew who'd been administering the dicoumarin?"

Wainwright reeled back. This time, he looked guilty for a second, and then recovered.

"I don't know what you're talking about."

"Cank was told to buy salts of lemon for cleaning purposes. He did so, little thinking they were for his elimination and to make it seem he'd committed suicide. He was a bicarbonate of soda addict. Those salts of lemon were substituted for the bicarbonate."

Clinton intervened.

"Nobody would be foolish enough to mistake one for the other. One is crystals, the other powder."

"The crystals were converted into powder in this mortar."

Littlejohn brought the pestle and mortar from the hall. "These were used and then cleaned. Only one person could have done that. Mrs. Twigg."

Mrs. Twigg didn't even look. She spoke in a dead voice without colour or hope.

"He suggested it. Cank, he said, wanted a thousand pounds, and would ask for more."

"Did Cank ask *him*?"

"Yes."

"Why?"

"He'd found out about us both and was blackmailing us both."

"She's off her head!"

"No. I'm not. I see they can't prove anything about you. You've an answer for everything. You've covered up all your tracks and left all the guilt on me. I'm the one they can prove guilty. Well, here's something that Richard left behind that will convince them."

She crossed to the desk at which Cromwell had once caught Cank with the fatal tablets, opened the top, and thrust her hand in a drawer. Then, she drew back. There was a large blue automatic in her hand.

"Here... Put that down. I... I..."

Before they could reach her, she had fired three shots into Wainwright's body. The first killed him. Then she tried to turn the gun on herself. Too late. She went to gaol for life...

Cromwell returned home a fortnight later and, after a long convalescent holiday in Cornwall, where he had first met his wife, he returned to duty little worse for his escapade. He was flabbergasted when he learned the whole of the train of events his shooting affair had touched off.

"If you hadn't come along to see about me, Uncle's murder would have gone undetected."

"I almost lost the case, old man. I knew who and how about it, but I couldn't bring home the guilt. Interviewed separately, I think the pair of them might have wriggled out. In a crowd, in the overheated sitting-room, with a thunderstorm brewing, they broke down... or rather, she did. He was a devil. He'd have slipped through the net, and she saw it. That's why she shot him."

As for Beeton, whose affair seemed idyllic compared with the Twigg murders, he served a mere month or two, nominal sentence for bigamy.

Mrs. Hardcastle forgave him and met him as he came out of prison. She appeared at his trial, after newspapers had made it a public affair, and was even prepared to say what a good husband and father he'd always been, a man who needed a change now and then, because of his lively intelligence.

Mrs. Beeton left all she had to Hardcastle. He is now having a house built in the country not far from Birmingham airport. He wrote from prison to thank Littlejohn for being a true friend!

ABOUT THE AUTHOR

George Bellairs is the pseudonym under which Harold Blundell (1902–1982) wrote police procedural thrillers in rural British settings. He was born in Lancashire, England, and worked as a bank manager in Manchester. After retiring, Bellairs moved to the Isle of Man, where several of his novels are set, to be with friends and family.

In 1941 Bellairs wrote his first mystery, *Littlejohn on Leave*, during spare moments at his air raid warden's post. The title introduced Thomas Littlejohn, the detective who appears in fifty-seven of his novels. Bellairs was also a regular contributor to the *Manchester Guardian* and worked as a freelance writer for newspapers both local and national.

THE INSPECTOR LITTLEJOHN MYSTERIES

FROM OPEN ROAD MEDIA

OPEN ROAD
INTEGRATED MEDIA

Find a full list of our authors and titles at www.openroadmedia.com

FOLLOW US
@OpenRoadMedia

EARLY BIRD BOOKS
FRESH DEALS, DELIVERED DAILY

Love to read? Love great sales?

Get fantastic deals on bestselling ebooks delivered to your inbox every day!

Sign up today at
earlybirdbooks.com/book